"You still look like a model."

An arrow of anger pierced her. Serena was a cop now, and he needed to acknowledge that. "Looks can deceive. I can have you flat on your back in the sand before you can blink."

His glance was measuring, a hint of a smile playing around his generous mouth. "Might be an interesting experience."

Annoyed with herself for thinking along the same lines, she snapped, "You wouldn't think so if it happened. I'm liable to break something."

"I'll consider myself forewarned." He sounded as if he couldn't wait.

The promise in his tone sent sexual fantasies tumbling through her mind. She had to fight to clear her thoughts. This wasn't the time and place, if ever there were such a thing. Not until she knew where he stood.

She drew herself up. "We're not here to exchange sexual fantasies. I need to know—"

He cut off the question by simply kissing her.

Dear Reader,

What better way to start off a new year than with six terrific new Silhouette Intimate Moments novels? We've got miniseries galore, starting with Karen Templeton's *Staking His Claim*, part of THE MEN OF MAYES COUNTY. These three brothers are destined to find love, and in this story, hero Cal Logan is also destined to be a father—but first he has to convince heroine Dawn Gardner that in his arms is where she wants to stay.

For a taste of royal romance, check out Valerie Parv's *Operation: Monarch*, part of THE CARRAMER TRUST, crossing over from Silhouette Romance. Policemen more your style? Then check out Maggie Price's *Hidden Agenda*, the latest in her LINE OF DUTY miniseries, set in the Oklahoma City Police Department. Prefer military stories? Don't even try to resist *Irresistible Forces,* Candace Irvin's newest SISTERS IN ARMS novel. We've got a couple of great stand-alone books for you, too. Lauren Nichols returns with a single mom and her protective hero, in *Run to Me*. Finally, Australian sensation Melissa James asks *Can You Forget?* Trust me, this undercover marriage of convenience will stick in your memory long after you've turned the final page.

Enjoy them all—and come back next month for more of the best and most exciting romance reading around, only in Silhouette Intimate Moments.

Yours,

Leslie J. Wainger
Executive Editor

Please address questions and book requests to:
Silhouette Reader Service
U.S.: 3010 Walden Ave., P.O. Box 1325, Buffalo, NY 14269
Canadian: P.O. Box 609, Fort Erie, Ont. L2A 5X3

Operation: Monarch
VALERIE PARV

INTIMATE MOMENTS™
Published by Silhouette Books
America's Publisher of Contemporary Romance

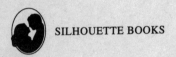 SILHOUETTE BOOKS

ISBN 0-373-27338-X

OPERATION: MONARCH

Visit Silhouette at www.eHarlequin.com

Printed in U.S.A.

VALERIE PARV

With twenty million copies of her books sold, including three Waldenbooks bestsellers, it's no wonder Valerie Parv is known as Australia's queen of romance and is the recognized media spokesperson for all things romantic. Valerie is married to her own romantic hero, Paul, a former crocodile hunter in Australia's tropical north.

These days he's a cartoonist and the two live in the country's capital city of Canberra, where both are volunteer zoo guides, sharing their love of animals with visitors from all over the world. Valerie continues to write her page-turning novels because they affirm her belief in love and happy endings. As she says, "Love gives you wings, romance helps you fly." Keep up with Valerie's latest releases at www.silromanceauthors.com.

For Bat Dame and the Bat Cave denizens.
Every writer should have such a safety valve.

Prologue

Historian's note:

*The events described here take place about
one year after the wedding of Prince Lorne and
Alison Carter depicted in The Monarch's Son*

As a senior member of the Royal Protection Detail, Serena Cordeaux had seen the sovereign ruler of Carramer at times elated, imperious, furious and melancholy, but his emotions were usually so well masked that only those closest to him suspected how he really felt.

Never before had she seen Prince Lorne de Marigny so openly troubled. His dark eyes were clouded with worry and although his pose remained calm, the hands he linked together in front of him were white knuckled.

Seated in a wing-backed leather chair beside the prince's desk, his wife, Princess Alison, looked calm but her eyes were dark with worry. Her fall of nut-brown hair hid much of her expression, but from the way she kept sneaking glances at the package lying open on the desk, Serena wondered if she expected the contents to rear up and strike her husband.

As well they might.

Knowing how devoted Alison was to Lorne and their little son, Nori, Serena wished she could assure them everything was going to be all right, but Serena was far from certain herself.

The prince placed his hands palms down on the leather blotter on either side of the damning evidence. "You did the right thing bringing this directly to me. How did you learn of its existence?"

Wondering if the monarch knew more than he was revealing about the significance of the package, Serena said, "The R.P.D. got a tip-off that Carramer First intended to disrupt the American president's visit, so we've been monitoring the group's activities."

Lorne shifted impatiently. "Naturally."

He knew as well as she did that the antiroyalist group hoped to manipulate international media interest in the first visit of an American president to Carramer to gain publicity for their cause. The majority of Carramer's people supported the monarchy, and dissidents were rare in the peaceful island kingdom, so the group was unlikely to gain sympathy any other way.

Knowing Prince Lorne wouldn't appreciate a history lesson, she straightened a little more. "Two days ago my contact in the group attended a meeting where they were told they'd soon have the means to do more than disrupt the president's visit. They could destabilize the kingdom itself."

Lorne tapped the package. "This."

She nodded. "According to my informant, only the man who took it to the group knew precisely what it contained. He was ordered to deliver it to a prearranged drop-off point so their leader could retrieve it and put it to use."

"Our old friend, the Hand," Lorne said heavily.

Serena heard Princess Alison catch her breath. "The Hand" was the only name by which they knew the leader of Carramer First. The other group members were basically harmless hotheads, but according to R.P.D. intelligence, the Hand was a professional criminal, skilled at covering his tracks. Only a handful of the group's elite were said to know his identity, hampering efforts to pin him down. Through phone calls and taped instructions, he controlled the group's activities with an iron hand, hence his code name. Everything else about him remained a frustrating mystery.

"What will the Hand do when he discovers you've intercepted the package?" Princess Alison asked.

Serena turned to her. "He shouldn't find out for some time. I arranged a special show for him while arresting my contact."

"I hope you've provided protection for your contact," Lorne observed dryly. "From what we know of the Hand, he'll be more interested in getting this back than in rescuing his man."

"Woman. We flew her to a safe location on Isle des Anges this morning," Serena supplied. "I searched her very publicly, making it obvious she didn't have the package on her, so anyone watching us would think she'd passed it to someone else minutes before I got to her. The Hand's people should be kept busy for some time trying to find out where it is now."

The prince's obsidian eyes clouded. "I doubt it will take them long to figure out they've been duped and that we have what they're looking for."

She lifted her hands, palms upward. "With respect, Your Highness, I don't see what harm a fake royal birth certificate can do to the monarchy."

"It isn't a fake."

This time she couldn't control her reaction. If the certificate was genuine…

The prince gestured toward a straight-backed chair in front of the desk. "Sit down, Serena. I take it you examined the contents of the package?"

She perched on the edge of the chair. "Following procedure, I checked everything for explosives and contaminants before bringing them to you."

He stabbed the package with a finger. "Were there any letters or other clues to the origins of the material."

She shook her head. "Nothing we can trace. I found only the birth certificate, a plaster cast of a baby's footprints and the photos you have there, sir."

The prince shuffled through the items, retrieving two black-and-white photos. One showed a superbly fit dark-haired man clad in tight shorts, working out in a gymnasium, plainly oblivious of the camera trained on him. The second showed the same man in a changing room, clad only in a towel. The first time she opened the package and saw the photo, Serena had felt herself go hot and cold by turns. Now she cleared her throat. "Your Highnesses, I think I know that man."

The prince's gaze shone with interest. "Go ahead."

She felt reluctant to admit the truth, but duty demanded it. "I haven't seen him for a long time, but his name is Garth Remy. We went to the same high school."

Her slight hesitation wasn't lost on the prince. She was glad he didn't ask how well she had known Garth.

Princess Alison's sharp look told Serena her feelings toward Garth had been read like a book. The princess's tumultuous romance with Prince Lorne had begun a little over a year ago, when a riptide dumped the Australian tourist at his feet on his private beach. Her affection for Lorne's little boy had won the prince's attention, then the woman himself had claimed his heart. Now it was rumored that Alison might be pregnant. It was well-known that they wanted a brother or sister for Nori. The princess certainly looked blooming. The sudden softening in her expression suggested that she suspected exactly how things had been between Serena and Garth.

Serena held her breath, but the princess shifted her attention to her husband. "I still can't believe the likeness, Lorne."

"At school he was known as Duke because of his resemblance to Prince Lorne," Serena explained. She didn't add that

Garth had hated the nickname. He had come from a poor family, and the name only rubbed it in.

Lorne indicated the photo. "What else do you know about him?"

Her thoughts spun. Even Alison, for all her experience of being swept off her feet by love, couldn't know how attracted Serena had been to Garth when they were teenagers, or how badly he had hurt her when he dismissed her as being no more than a pretty face. He had made no allowance for her parents pushing her into modeling from the time she could walk, primping and pampering her until she had felt like a doll instead of their child. Nor did he care that she hated modeling but hadn't had the courage to give it up because her success meant so much to her parents.

It was hardly her fault that her figure had ripened to model proportions in her early teens, or that the camera had loved her vivid blue eyes and blond coloring. At nineteen to her sixteen, he'd believed her looks were all that mattered to her, when they had meant far more to her parents than to Serena herself.

She had told herself she didn't care what Garth thought of her, yet his censure had rankled for a long time. She told herself he wasn't the reason she had joined the Carramer Police Force, but she knew his comments had planted the seed. She had chosen crime fighting because it was as far away from modeling as she could get, then had found she thrived on the work. When she was invited to join the elite Royal Protection Detail, she had jumped at it. She loved being a royal insider, doing police work at the highest possible level. Not just a pretty face now, she told Garth's photo silently.

He would be thirty-two to her twenty-nine now. The midnight gaze seemed to mock her, although she knew she was imagining that. It was obvious he hadn't known he was being photographed. There was nothing posed about the way he stood with one bare leg on the floor and the other propped on a bench as he dried himself off.

Her throat felt dry as she handed the photo back to the monarch. "Garth and I lost touch after we finished school. Friends told me he'd joined the navy as a diver. Since his parents were in the commercial fishing business, that would seem logical. But I'm afraid I don't know any more. I have no idea why his photo was in the package."

Prince Lorne massaged his chin with one hand as he seemed to weigh how much to tell her. After a long interval he said, "Whoever put this together intended to reveal Garth to the world as the rightful heir to the throne of Carramer."

Princess Alison's hand went to her mouth although she made no sound. Naturally she would already be aware of the possibility.

Serena had no such forewarning, and shock ricocheted through her. "Surely that's impossible, Your Highness?"

The prince looked less perturbed by her outburst than by the possibility he'd just voiced. "I wish it were. Unfortunately, my family history makes it all too possible."

"Since she's already involved, perhaps Serena should know the story," Alison suggested.

A faint glimmer of agreement crossed Lorne's features as he looked at Serena. "The family has always known that my parents had a child before they were married. He was named Louis but was stillborn, or so we believed. I think the certificate, the footprints and the photos are meant to suggest otherwise."

Serena could hardly deal with the thought that Garth's resemblance to Lorne might be because Garth was really Lorne's older brother. Far less that Garth could be the true ruler of Carramer. How was Lorne managing to face the possibility, when he had so much at stake? An entire kingdom, in fact. No wonder his usual composure had been shattered in a way she had never expected to see.

"The footprints could belong to any baby," she said, knowing wishful thinking when she expressed it.

The monarch knew it, too, she saw in his wintry smile. "Except for one small detail."

He picked up the plaster cast and angled it for her inspection. She soon saw what he was indicating, a tiny piece of webbing clearly visible between the small toes of the left foot. "Oh."

"It's a genetic trait common to de Marigny males," Alison contributed.

Serena felt a frown start. "That settles it then. Garth can't be the heir if he doesn't have the trait."

Without comment, Lorne picked up the changing room photo and handed it to her. An enlargement of a section of the first photo, it showed Garth's feet in close-up. At first sight, she hadn't understood its significance. Studying it more closely now, she saw that the two small toes of his left foot were webbed.

She felt the room spin then settle. "Is it possible?"

Lorne's expression told her it was even before he said, "The birth certificate is genuine. I recognize my parents' signatures."

Alison reached for her husband's hand. "The original has been missing from the de Marigny archive for years."

"Even so, it seems unbelievable that Garth could be the heir to the throne. Apart from the resemblance to you, sir, there were no other indications that Garth was more than he seemed. His parents were just everyday people," Serena insisted.

"They could have fostered him without knowing his history," Alison pointed out. "Garth himself may be unaware of his background."

Alice couldn't have felt more unsettled after falling down the rabbit hole to Wonderland, Serena thought. "You're taking this seriously, aren't you?"

Lorne took a slow breath, held it, then let it out. "We have no choice. The certificate, coupled with the cast and the photo, means we must allow for the possibility that my older brother didn't die at birth after all. And that Carramer has the wrong monarch.''

Chapter 1

She would never accept that Garth Remy was the true ruler of Carramer, she thought as she got ready for her assignment. Not by so much as a blink had Garth suggested he was anything other than the child of struggling commercial fishermen. They had lived aboard the boat for most of Garth's childhood, only moving into a proper house after his grandparents died. It was hardly the life of a prince.

Garth may not know who he is, Alison had said. Everything in Serena wanted to reject the possibility, but she knew the princess was right. If Garth had been fostered by the Remys from birth, he would have no reason to suspect he was anything but their biological son.

Commanding her to tell no one what she was doing, Lorne had assigned her to meet Garth in the gymnasium shown in the photograph. She had identified the place from a portion of the name shown behind him on the wall. She was to renew their acquaintance and convince Garth to accompany her to the palace. Lorne would take it from there.

When she had reminded the prince that she was fully oc-

cupied with security preparations for the president's visit in
two weeks' time, Lorne had said he would have her duties
assigned to Jarvis Reid, her rival in the R.P.D.

Although there was nothing she could do about it, Serena
hated the thought of Reid being at the president's side while
she worked on what she still suspected was a hoax. The high
profile of the presidential tour meant when it came to choosing
the new head of the Solano division, a job Serena had been
working hard to earn, Jarvis would have an edge. Once again
it seemed Garth was going to interfere in her life.

He had done it before when she was sixteen and he was
nineteen, she recalled. She had been drawn to the darkly
brooding young man who shone at all kinds of solo sports. If
she closed her eyes she could still see his muscular legs eating
up the running track or his arms carving through the water as
he swam to victory.

She was seized by a sudden, unexpected memory of rising
to her feet in the stands and cheering her lungs out the day he
won the men's medley by half a pool length. He hadn't acknowledged her cheers, looking stonily ahead as he left the
water and headed for the locker room. It was as if he had raced
for himself alone, and winning was enough. She had told herself not to take it personally. He hadn't asked her to cheer for
him. But her fragile teenage ego had ached for a sign that he
appreciated her support, and her heart had bled when none
came.

Instead of getting the message, she had started seeing what
she wanted to see. Every half smile or brusque word they
exchanged had been read as encouragement that she was finally getting through to him. Soon he would ask her for a date
and they would be a couple.

How naive could one person be? The date had never happened. The blossoming romance had been all in her head.
Garth's lone-wolf persona wasn't a cover for shyness or anything else. It was who he was. Who he probably still was.

When she ran a background check on him, parts of his naval
record couldn't be accessed, suggesting he'd been involved in

covert assignments. The discovery seemed appropriate for one who liked being closed off from others, she thought. Not long after making lieutenant, he had been involved in a deep-sea diving mishap resulting in a trainee under his care being injured. Instructor error, the record showed. Defective equipment, Garth had argued. He had lost, and left the service under a cloud.

He hadn't had much luck in his life, she thought. With his navy career in ruins, he had dived on wrecks around the region, living off his salvage efforts. He had also worked part-time in his parents' fishing business, the same one the other students had maligned, she remembered. Even the same boat, as far as she could tell. The aging engine had blown up only a month before, sending the boat to the bottom of Solano Harbor. Both Garth's parents had drowned. A stab of concern welled up inside her. No matter how she felt about him, he didn't deserve so much tragedy.

The record showed no sign of a wife and children. Had he been involved with anyone? She told herself she didn't care. Another woman was welcome to him. But it didn't stop her stomach muscles from clenching at the thought.

As Princess Alison had suspected, Serena's crush on Garth had been deep enough to make her feel hot more than thirteen years afterward. She blushed to recall how her friends had caught her practicing signing her name as Serena Remy and had teased her unmercifully. They had bet her she wouldn't have the courage to kiss him.

Knowing how much she wanted to kiss him, she had accepted the bet, waiting until she found him alone, then throwing herself into his arms and fastening her innocent lips on his. When his strong, youthful arms automatically closed around her, her heart had pounded as if it would leap right out of her chest.

Instead of admitting to overhearing her make the bet, he had kissed her back as if he had been waiting for her all his life. She had felt the stars in her eyes as he held her away from him, and she had been shocked to see how cold he looked. "Looks like you win," he had drawled.

She vividly recalled the sensation of ice water sliding along her veins, his switch from passion to indifference making her light-headed. "What are you saying?"

"You can go back to your high-society friends and collect on your bet. If they want proof, I'll vouch that you kissed me. How much was I worth?"

No money had been involved. Only her pride. "You know about the bet?"

He had leaned indolently against a wall. "I'm not stupid enough to think you'd do it for any other reason. A spoiled society princess doesn't waste her time on the guy from the other side of the tracks unless there's something in it for her."

She had needed something to hold on to, but the only available anchor was him, and if she touched him again she was lost. She had lifted her head, letting a defiance she didn't feel shimmer in her gaze. "I'd hate you to think I wanted to kiss you."

"Oh, you wanted to. You want to do it again," he said. "You might have kissed me for a bet but you enjoyed every minute of it."

How had he known? "You have a high opinion of yourself," she had snapped.

He had straightened. "Yes, I do. Unlike you, I have plans for my life."

"What's that supposed to mean?"

"You're no more than a beautiful doll who lets herself be used to satisfy her family's ego. Before I get involved with a girl, she'll have to do more with her life than trade on her looks."

He had walked away. She had stayed frozen in place until she was sure he was gone, before letting the tears come. All her dreams of togetherness with him lay in pieces at her feet. He not only didn't want her company, he despised what he thought she was.

The worst part was knowing that she *had* let her parents use her to fulfill their ambitions. She had barely noticed when her father gave up his banking job to manage her career. Her mother, once a capable casting agent, had always called herself Serena's stylist. When had that become her sole occupation?

She had known she disappointed them bitterly by walking away from a future as a supermodel. Her mother had been horrified when she chose a career in law enforcement, mainly because of the risk to her perfect features, she assumed. They were happier now she was with the R.P.D., little knowing that the royal security could be as hazardous as any other security work. The modern world was a dangerous place. One day she might have to put her life on the line to protect her royal employers.

She had never expected to have to risk her heart.

The gymnasium overlooked Solano Harbor. She took her own car, and wore a plain teal sweatsuit. Normally she worked out in the luxurious palace gym and wore sweats monogrammed with the royal crest, hardly an option to meet Garth. She had no idea how she was going to convince him to see Lorne and had a feeling that the lower the profile she adopted the better.

He used the gym on Tuesdays and Thursdays, she had learned when she called from the palace. She waited outside the gymnasium in her car until she saw him pull up in a battered pickup, the back cluttered with diving paraphernalia. In contrast to the state of the car, the gear looked pristine.

Garth didn't look so bad himself, she thought, watching him lock the car and securely cover the diving gear. A familiar longing washed over her but she fought it. This time she was no teenager, wishing for the moon. She ducked low but he didn't look around, merely hitched a navy-issue duffel bag over his shoulder and headed for the entrance.

Still as dark and brooding as she remembered, she thought, keeping down as he stalked past. Same sinfully broad shoulders, same narrow hips and grabbable rear, sculpted by the tight jeans he wore slung low like a cowboy's. All he needed was a Stetson to complete the image.

He'd let his hair grow long, she noticed. Dark with lighter streaks from the sun and sea, it touched the collar of his rumpled blue golf shirt. One errant lock still fell across his eyes. She watched him push it back with an impatient gesture that was all too familiar.

Serena knew her scrutiny was hardly professional, but couldn't help noticing how tanned he was from years of outdoor exposure, and the way faint lines radiated from his eyes. His wide mouth was so grimly set that she doubted he smiled any more now than he had when he was younger. Although it was late morning, his chin was dusted with stubble. His rugged appearance should have repelled her but instead she felt a dangerous prickle of excitement.

At the entrance he looked around as if sensing her eyes on him. She felt his jet gaze skim over her, so penetrating that she expected him to wrench her car door open and demand to know why she was watching him. Then he shrugged as if shaking off a phantom touch, pushed the door open and disappeared inside.

Sitting up, she swallowed hard, swimming in more phantoms. Memories of how she had imagined herself as his girl, cheering his sporting prowess from the sidelines, threatened to swamp her. Few others had cheered for him even when he won, she remembered. He had been too self-sufficient, making it clear he didn't need anyone's adulation. She had been the only girl stupid enough to think she was different.

Not anymore. She was here for a purpose, not to revisit yearnings she had grown out of thirteen years ago. She had, hadn't she? The dryness in her throat argued differently. Not sure how honestly, she told herself she wasn't looking forward to this meeting. Only Prince Lorne's assurance that the country's stability depended on resolving Garth's claim to the throne—if he had one—got her out of the car and sauntering across the car park after him as if she hadn't a care in the world.

In truth, she had a handful. This morning at the palace Jarvis Reid had swooped down on her, demanding her files on the presidential visit. He had looked like a cat with his first canary, as well he might. All her hard work preparing for the visit would now give Reid's ambition a boost at the cost of her own. The thought of reporting to him as head of the Solano division made her feel ill. She had counted on it being the other way around.

Garth Remy had *better* be the lost prince, she thought angrily. If this was a clever hoax and he was somehow involved, she'd be kicking his fine-looking rear instead of grabbing it.

At the same time, she had difficulty imagining him being involved in a hoax. He may have been aloof, but he hadn't lied to her. He could easily have taken advantage of her infatuation, but beyond the first kiss, he hadn't. He had told her openly that he knew about the bet and had walked away. A man who lived by his own code of honor, however brutal it had seemed to her younger self.

Taking a deep breath, she pushed open the door of the gymnasium and stepped inside. Garth was nowhere in sight, probably changing in the men's locker room. She signed in and headed for the women's locker room where she peeled off her sweatsuit to reveal a burgundy sports top and black leggings. With her long blond hair caught in a high ponytail, she still looked about eighteen, she thought, grimacing at herself in the full-length mirror. She supposed she should be happy, given the rapid approach of her next milestone birthday. But the image held too many reminders of the girl who had mooned around, waiting for Garth to notice her.

She wasn't about to do any such thing today, she reminded herself. She was a grown woman at the top of her profession. Well nearly at the top. She'd had affairs of varying degrees of satisfaction. Nobody current, through her decision to focus on achieving promotion. The ingenuous girl whose feelings Garth had trampled no longer existed.

So close to lunchtime, the main floor was almost deserted except for an attendant straightening up equipment on the far side of the room. In the background the steady bass beat of rock music signaled a class in progress elsewhere in the building.

Playing the part of a gym regular, she climbed aboard a stationary bike to warm up. Pedaling steadily, she glanced around, finding Garth doing the same at the other end of the row. He didn't see her. He wore a tank top and light-blue gym shorts with a navy stripe down each side and a pair of well-worn cross trainers.

After warming up for ten minutes he got off and went to a bench press where he picked out a pair of dumbbells, then lay on his back on the bench, planting his feet on the floor.

She stopped pedaling to watch as he exhaled and slowly pressed both weights toward the ceiling. With perfect control he inhaled and lowered the weights to the starting position, his muscles gleaming in the artificial light. She counted about four beats on the exhalation and eight on the inhalation phases. Impressive.

In danger of becoming mesmerized by the sight of his self-assured movements, she slid off the bike and chose an opal-colored balance ball suited to her height, nudging the sphere closer to Garth's station. Wedging the ball between her lower back and the wall, she inhaled and lowered herself to a sitting position, bending her hips and knees. The pressure on the ball against her back felt as good as a massage.

Exhaling, she stood, keeping the pressure on the ball with her back. Several repetitions later, she felt muscle fatigue creeping up, but Garth was too intent on his own workout to notice her. Déjà vu, she thought, determined not to let it bother her this time. No wonder he was still unattached.

Deliberately she let the ball escape from under her so it bounced against his bench press. "I'm sorry," she said as she went to retrieve it. Garth had the weights lowered to his shoulders. She injected surprise into her voice. "Garth? Garth Remy?"

Noticing her at last, he swung himself upright. "Serena Cordeaux? It is you, isn't it?"

He didn't exactly sound thrilled to see her, she thought. She forced a grin. "How long has it been?"

He placed the weights on the floor and swabbed his face with a towel, although he had barely raised a sweat. "Years. I heard you left Solano after graduation."

Unwillingly pleased that he'd tracked her progress for a time at least, she nodded. "I went to the police academy."

If she had hoped to impress him, he didn't show it. Merely nodded. "Quite a switch for you, wasn't it?"

"Modeling was my parents' choice for me, not mine. I gave it up as soon as I was of age."

His eyes narrowed slightly. "I hope I didn't have anything to do with that?"

Annoyed because he had, she shook her head, feeling the old attraction resurface. Along with something far less welcome. Desire. Hot, potent, stinging because she didn't want to feel it. She had been talking to him for less than five minutes out of thirteen years, and already she wanted to be in his arms so much she could taste the need. Some people never learned.

"You have a high opinion of yourself," she said, then felt even more annoyed because she had said the same thing to him after they kissed.

He remembered too, she saw in the sudden gleam of interest flaring in his gaze. The flame died as she watched. "Always did," he said easily, but the trace of pain in his voice wasn't lost on her.

She touched his arm. "I'm sorry about your parents' accident."

He half closed his eyes, then opened them, his expression impassive. Too impassive, she thought, as if he was suffering but didn't want anyone to know it. Same old Garth Remy, she thought. Never let anyone get too close.

"I meant to get in touch and thank you for the wreath," he said.

She'd ordered it after seeing the news on television, telling herself it was the decent thing to do, not because she expected a response from him. "That's okay. It can't have been an easy time for you.'' She hadn't meant her tone to soften in concern for him, but it happened anyway.

''I'm fine.''

He moved to a mat on the far side of the bench press, snaring a length of resistance tubing as he went. Dropping to the floor, he stretched his legs out in front of him and anchored the tubing around his feet, then exhaled as he pulled the tubing in to his abdomen. The rowing movement was harder than it looked, she knew, and would help to account for his washboard-flat stomach.

Picking up another length of tubing, she joined him on a neighboring mat. She preferred the cable-row machines but they were on the other side of the room, hardly conducive to continuing a conversation. Not that he seemed to welcome her company. His body language told her he considered the reunion over.

She didn't.

She looped the tubing around her feet. ''What have you been doing with yourself?''

His slow exhalation as he pulled the cable taut was the only sound between them. She had decided he wasn't going to answer when he said, ''I worked my way through college. You might recall I had some catching up to do.''

The defensive tone reminded her that he had been the oldest boy in their high school. His parents had pulled him out of class to help in the family business so often that he had fallen behind academically, although his IQ was the equal of hers. Being older than their classmates, he'd endured considerable teasing, not all of it good-natured. ''Good for you,'' she said sincerely. ''What did you do then?''

''Joined the navy.''

Her arm muscles protested as she paused with the cable at full stretch. ''I joined the police, you joined the navy. Interesting.''

''Not particularly. It was the only way I could make a career out of diving.''

''You didn't want to work with your folks on their boat?''

Seeing his mouth tighten, she cursed herself for mentioning the boat. Its shabby condition had always been a sore point with him. Now it also reminded him of his loss. "Not enough money in it for three people," he said. From what she remembered, the boat had barely supported the family all along.

Too many questions would make him suspicious. She decided to try another angle. "A few years ago, I moved from the police to the R.P.D., the Royal Protection Detail," she explained.

"I know what the R.P.D. is. I've seen you on TV, shadowing Prince Lorne. Being beautiful must be an asset in royal protection."

Torn because he thought her beautiful, but obviously still believed she traded on her looks, she let her anger surface. "I was hired for my skills, not my appearance."

"Such as a black belt in shopping?"

Goaded beyond her limits, she vaulted to her feet and lassoed his broad shoulders with her resistance band, hog-tying him before he had time to react. Leaning back to tighten the band, she let it bite into his flesh just enough to get his attention.

He didn't move but his gaze held a new glimmer of respect. "Old habit. And you are beautiful."

"And you're the same old pain in the—"

Before she could finish, he flexed his muscles, loosening the band enough to throw it off. Yanking on it, he toppled her against him, making her think she was going to find herself in his arms for the second time in her life. The prospect caused her heart rate to rocket, hammering at her shield of professionalism.

For a heartbeat she was back in school, her teenage body pressed against him as her mouth shaped hungrily to his. The memory of his indifference rolled over her anew, giving her the strength to straighten away from him. She could swear he knew what she'd been thinking and had provoked her to see how she'd react.

When she moved back he tossed the apparatus to her, almost

but not quite dissipating the unwanted feelings. "You made your point. Both points," he said, sounding world-weary. Surely he hadn't wanted her in his arms?

It wasn't exactly an apology but it would have to serve. Unnerved by the easy way he'd demonstrated his greater physical strength, she dropped to the mat and continued her workout. After a few repetitions she reminded herself she had a job to do. Her own feelings couldn't be allowed to get in the way.

"Are you on leave from the navy?" she asked.

His powerful movements made the resistance band stretch and contract like breathing. "I left the service after a disagreement with the brass."

She wanted to say, "I know, and I don't believe you were at fault," but couldn't without betraying how much she knew about him. Instead, she said, "You never did like authority much."

"I don't have a problem with authority provided it isn't wielded by fools," he growled.

"Such as the man who got you fired from the navy?"

The cord snapped to his feet as he swung his gaze on her. "I didn't say I was fired. I said we parted company."

"My mistake," she said mildly, although her heart was pounding.

He retrieved the cable and resumed his methodical rowing movements. "As it happens, you're right. Not that it matters who's at fault when a trainee under my care comes close to getting killed."

It mattered to him, she saw, impressed that his concern was all for the injured diver. There wasn't a trace of self-pity or justification in his tone. "You don't believe you were at fault, do you?"

The mask lifted for a moment. "I know I wasn't." Then the shutters came back down. "For all the good it will do me."

"Couldn't you get a lawyer to defend you?"

He unhooked the cable from his feet and looped it around his hand. "What's the point? Admirals are always right. Besides, I'm happy as I am now."

She was genuinely curious now. "Doing what?"

"Salvage diving. Provided they don't mind diving with a black sheep, I take adventurous tourists down at exorbitant fees."

It was out before she knew it was what she wanted. "Would you take me sometime?"

He shrugged. "Your money is as good as anyone's."

Annoyed with herself for feeling hurt, she said, "I was thinking more for old time's sake."

He drew his legs up and hooked his arms around them. "I wasn't aware we had any old times."

"Not because I didn't want to have them," she said softly.

"Is that why you made a bet with your friends that you wouldn't have the nerve to kiss me?"

She felt her face flame. "The bet was their idea, not mine."

"You took them up on it."

"Yes I did, and I've regretted it ever since."

He tossed the cable aside and rolled over onto his stomach, levering himself up on his arms and exhaling slowly as he pushed himself away from the mat.

Inhaling, he lowered himself down to the point where his chest was a few inches from the floor. His control left her breathless. Resignedly she rolled over and began a set of push-ups as demanding as his own. Showing off? She wondered.

By the time she finished her repetitions she was breathing hard. Garth had already finished and his chest was hardly moving, she noted. And she had thought she was fit.

"You shouldn't have regrets, especially about me," he said unexpectedly.

She sat up and blotted her face with a towel. "Don't flatter yourself. I haven't exactly been pining."

A water bottle lay within arm's reach. Picking it up, he drank then offered it to her. She swallowed some water, trying not to think of his lips on the bottle before hers. Too intimate by far.

"I shouldn't think you'd be left to pine for long."

Her head came up. "Because I'm a doll who trades on her looks?"

A shadow darkened his rugged features. "That was cruel. I was out of line."

Better late than never, she thought. "Thanks, but you were right. I let my parents manage my life for too long. Modeling was never what I wanted to do, but they came to depend on the glamour and the excitement. Whenever I go home I hear about what could have been."

"They managed without you."

She laughed hollowly. "I didn't give them much choice." When she finally convinced them she was serious, her mother had started a business advising other would-be models and her father had gone back into banking.

"Asserting yourself must have taken courage."

Finally she had demonstrated a quality he could admire. She fought to stop her spirits from leaping. After he found out why she was here, he wouldn't waste time admiring her. He would think she was being just as dishonest with him as she had been before. He would be right, too. She decided enough was enough.

She dragged in a steadying breath. "This meeting isn't exactly an accident."

"Surprise, surprise."

She felt her eyes widen with astonishment. "How did you work it out?"

"I saw a program on TV about the facilities you people have available at the palace gym. You wouldn't be here without good reason. Obviously your reason involves me."

"I'm sorry," she began.

His gesture sliced across her apology. "Never mind that, Serena. What do you want from me?"

Chapter 2

She looked around. The thumping music had stopped and people were streaming in from the other room, scattering themselves around the equipment. "Not here," she said. "Can we go somewhere more private?"

He draped the towel around his neck. "I'll meet you out front in ten minutes."

She was ready in nine but he was already waiting for her, his dark hair glistening from the shower and his shirt damp as if he hadn't taken the time to completely dry off. She knew better than to think he had been anxious to meet her. More likely he wanted to get the meeting over with as quickly as possible.

He gestured toward the battered pickup. "We can talk in my truck."

She had been thinking along the lines of coffee and a baguette in a café by the waterfront. She saw him read her body language and frowned in disapproval. For the latte set he thought she still belonged to, or for her company?

Probably both, she thought on an inward sigh. One day she would learn that he simply didn't want her around. "Lead on."

He threw his duffel bag into the pickup and opened the passenger door for her from the inside. Before she could climb in, he reached down and pushed an assortment of fast-food wrappers under the seat. If not for the immaculate state of his diving equipment, she would have believed he was a complete boor.

"Now you can get in," he said, sounding as if he didn't care either way.

He slammed the door and she inhaled a mix of chlorine and southern-fried chicken. When he joined her, she asked, "Do you live in this thing?"

"Not usually."

Only since his parents were killed, she interpreted, feeling a surge of compassion for him. She knew he didn't have any other family, and losing them must have hit him hard. Her background check showed that he normally lived aboard his dive boat which was presently in dry dock. He would have inherited his parents' house, but maybe he couldn't bring himself to move in there yet and was living out of his car until his boat was repaired.

He could also be the rightful heir to the Carramer throne, she reminded herself, although without much conviction. If he ever assumed the crown, the country was in for a shock. The members of the royal family she had met were fairly down-to-earth, but none could match a long-haired, fried-chicken-eating bad boy like Garth. That he could be a de Marigny by birth seemed fantastic beyond belief.

Luckily she didn't have to make the decision, only bring Garth to the palace so Prince Lorne could investigate his relationship to the throne. She choked back a smile as she pictured them together, alike enough in looks to be brothers, but as different in temperament as night from day.

"What's so funny?"

"Nothing, really. I'm here because Prince Lorne asked me to renew our acquaintance."

"How did you know where to find me?"

This was the tricky part. A man as private as Garth wouldn't take kindly to learning she'd been asking about him. "The castle has its resources."

"Resources like having me watched?"

"Only so I could bring you to meet Prince Lorne."

He slammed his palms against the steering wheel, making her jump. "The hell with that. Carramer is supposed to be a free country."

In many countries he would probably have disappeared before he could destabilize the monarchy, she thought. "It's precisely because it's a free country that the prince asked to see you, instead of having you arrested and brought before him."

He looked as if he didn't particularly appreciate the courtesy. "Don't tell me the navy has seen the error of its ways and the monarch wants to apologize and restore my commission personally."

His cynical tone made her want to squirm. She didn't tell him that the prince had already started a discreet investigation into Garth's experience with the navy. No sense getting his hopes up in case nothing new was uncovered. "I wouldn't know about that. He has something more personal to discuss with you."

"You aren't going to tell me, are you?"

"I can't. It's a matter of national security."

"Is it, Serena? Or are you enjoying keeping me in the dark to punish me for hurting your pride all those years ago?"

She half turned, wishing the space weren't so confined. Garth was so big that their knees were touching, only the gear shift keeping their bodies apart. If she pressed against him, would he feel as hard and lean as he looked? In the gym she had seen how toned he was, wanting to touch him then. She wanted it more now. Evidently she was the only one. Anger drove away the urge, leaving only bitterness. He hadn't changed. "I'm not that petty."

"No you're not."

The admission sounded so genuine so that she felt her eyes

mist and she blinked hard. "To what do I owe the concession?"

He massaged his eyes, digging his fingers into the temples as if his head hurt. "You always managed to bring out the worst in me. I thought I'd grown past it, but evidently not."

So he was far from indifferent to her! Struggling to keep her seesawing emotions under control, she said, "My father says the same thing about his brother. Even in their fifties, they still fight over little things. It's called sibling rivalry." Maybe she could manage her runaway responses by thinking of him in those terms.

He gave a humorless laugh. "Believe me, whatever I thought of you, it wasn't brotherly."

Hurt speared her in spite of her attempt to remain unruffled. "Because we came from such different backgrounds?" Was he holding that against her even today?

"Because we come from such different genders."

It took a moment for his meaning to penetrate. "Oh."

"They must have taught you about the birds and the bees in security school?"

Thinking of the ways she had been taught to disable a man who even looked as if he had birds and bees on his mind, she felt a smile start. "Yes, but not in the way you're thinking."

"You have no idea what I'm thinking. If you did, you'd be out of this truck like a shot."

If she had any sense, she would leave anyway. But when had she ever had any sense around Garth Remy? And she still had her job to do. She tried for a light tone. "Let me guess. You're wondering if you made a mistake letting me slip through your fingers the first time."

He stilled so completely that she wondered if she was on the right track. Surely not? After graduation he had made no attempt to contact her, although he had admitted knowing where she was. And his reaction to seeing her again today couldn't have been less welcoming. "You were never in my fingers to slip through," he said after a long time. "All we did was kiss once so you could win a bet. Hardly the love affair of the century.''

How had they strayed onto this track? She felt weary of her body's betraying response to him, and the one-sided nature of the game. "You're right. We had nothing then and we have nothing now. At least we agree on something.''

He didn't look as pleased as she thought he should. "There's still the reason you're here.''

"I told you, to arrange a meeting between you and Prince Lorne.''

Garth's eyebrow lifted. "The ruler of the whole country doesn't own a telephone?''

"This is too important to discuss by phone. Can't you just come with me and be done with it?''

A glint of challenge lit his dark gaze. "Maybe I enjoy giving you a hard time.''

"Nothing new in that.''

"When does the prince want to see me?''

"As soon as you're available.''

"What's wrong with right now?''

She knew her quick glance at his clothes gave her away as soon as she saw him bristle. "My dress suit is at the cleaner's. Now or never, your choice.''

"Let me make a phone call.''

He waited with obvious impatience as she called the castle, using Prince Lorne's private number as instructed. If the monarch was taken aback at Garth's insistence on an immediate meeting, she didn't hear it in his voice. "Give me an hour,'' was all he said. From experience she knew how much juggling it would take for the prince to free his time. If she wasn't already aware of it, Lorne's readiness to do so signaled the gravity of the situation.

She flipped the phone closed. "The prince can see you in an hour.''

He looked satisfied. "The castle is ten minutes away. That gives us some time to kill. I don't know about you, but I could use some coffee.''

The last thing she wanted was to spend more time than she had to with him, but neither could she let him out of her sight. "Okay. We can take my car."

"What's wrong with this one? Oh, I forgot, this meeting is black tie. It's probably treason to roll up at the castle in a car you haven't cleaned in under forty-eight hours."

Forty-eight days looked more like it. "I doubt if the prince will care what you're driving," she said heavily. She could have one of her security team retrieve her car from the gymnasium later.

"But you do."

"Stop it," she insisted. "I'm only doing my job."

"What made you give up the glamorous life for a gritty job like policing?"

She had to get out of the confined space before she did something really silly, like run the back of her hand down his stubbled cheek to see how it felt. "Can we swap life stories over coffee?"

"Sure."

She jumped as he reached across her, his hand brushing her breast by accident or design. Either way, her pulse rate shot up. But it was only to lift a black, zippered case from a shelf near her knees. He opened it and took out a portable razor, turning it on and filling the compartment with the sound of angry bees.

Fascination gripped her as she watched him steer the razor across the faint hint of a cleft in his chin. Up and down and across without once looking in a mirror. When he flicked the razor off, the silence was deafening. He lifted her hand to his cheek. "Better?"

His freshly shaved skin felt taut and vital. She was alarmingly aware of his hand guiding hers but couldn't bring herself to pull away, not even when he made her index finger skim along his lower lip. She felt a little hollow there she hadn't noticed before. Her breathing shallowed. Half an inch higher and he could close his lips around her finger.

He let her go and she masked her disappointment. It was

for the best, she reminded herself unsuccessfully. "Much better."

Ten minutes ago she had wanted caffe latte by the waterfront. The place he took her to hardly qualified as a café although it was in the open air. More like a kiosk with an awning that folded down when the place was closed, it boasted a few plastic tables and chairs scattered on the grass in front. At least it was waterfront, if she counted the commercial fishing fleet as a view.

He surprised her by pulling out a chair for her. "I eat breakfast here most mornings. Alice's food is the best."

So was her coffee, Serena had to admit when the woman brought it for them with a warm smile of welcome. Latte for her, espresso for Garth. Appearances could be deceptive. "This is really great coffee," she said after the first sip.

Garth looked at the waitress. "Your place is Solano's best-kept secret, isn't it, Alice?"

The woman pretended offence. "The number of people you bring here, we'll always be a secret."

"I don't want to share you with just anyone," he confided.

He wanted to reassure his friend, not make Serena feel special, but he had that effect, she found to her dismay. This would have to stop. As soon as she delivered him to Prince Lorne she would be finished with this. Finished with him.

What would she do if he turned out to be the heir to the throne? Request a transfer back to active policing, she thought. She couldn't imagine working with him, guarding him, even if he would allow it. He was used to fending for himself, keeping his private life private.

Who would get the greater shock? Garth because his life would be an open book as soon as his heritage was established, or the Carramer people who would have to deal with having a lone wolf as their monarch?

While Serena was lost in thought Alice had moved away to serve another customer, a fisherman, judging by his appearance. The practical setup of the place began to make sense. You could come straight from your boat to a table without worrying about sea-soaked clothes or muddy boots. Serena leaned back. "This is nice." The salt tang of the air, smelling faintly of fish, was refreshing. Gulls wheeled over the boats, diving on scraps as fishermen cleaned their catches. In its own way, the scene was as beautiful as if the commercial boats had been millionaires' yachts.

He nodded. "Alice is like a mother to half the fleet. Alice and my mother used to go to the Marine Benevolent Society together to visit the old sailors. She was a good friend to my folks."

And to him, she heard. "Where do you keep your dive boat?"

As soon as his accusing gaze flayed her, she knew she'd made a mistake. "When it's not in dry dock, it's moored around the point, but you know that already. Is there anything your inquiries haven't told you about me?"

She couldn't stop herself. "Two things—why you have such a colossal chip on your shoulder, and what you've got against me personally."

He cupped his hands around his coffee mug. Large, practical hands designed for hard work. But not callused or workworn. He might forget to shave in the morning, but his hands looked cared for. She remembered the well-maintained diving gear in the back of his truck. He cared for what was important to him.

"My chip is my business."

He'd deliberately answered only part of her question, she noted. "You said we could exchange life stories over coffee."

"You first."

She wasn't going to get anything out of him that he didn't want to share, she understood. She was surprised how much she wanted to share. Maybe if she set an example. "As I told you, I went to the police academy. Graduated third in my class. Worked in uniform for a couple of years then in plain clothes undercover. Then got an invitation to join the R.P.D." One of only a select few.

He nodded. "Nothing there I couldn't find out on the public record. What about marriage, children?"

Don't read anything into the question, she ordered herself. He was probably trying to even the score. "They'd be on public record, too, if I had any."

"So presumably you don't. What happened? Afraid of spoiling your model figure?"

She refused to give him the satisfaction of baiting her. "You never know when you'll need something to fall back on." She knew she'd said the right thing when she saw respect spark in his gaze. She crossed her forearms on the table. "Your turn."

"Joined the navy. Thrown out of the navy. Not much more to tell."

She tossed his own words back at him. "What about marriage, children?"

"Didn't want to spoil my model figure," he said, grinning.

Despite herself, she returned his smile. It felt good to laugh with him. She may not have learned much but the ice felt well and truly broken. She was surprised when he said, "I had my share of relationships, one even looked as if it would last. Remember Julia Francis?"

Quick flare of jealousy, just as quickly squashed. "The redhead star of the track team?"

"The same. We lost touch for a few years until she joined the navy, so we had that in common, among other things."

She didn't like imagining the other things. "What happened?"

"When I was kicked out of the service, she thought associating with me might tarnish her career. She didn't mince words. Told me bluntly why it had to be over."

Underneath that gruff exterior he had feelings and they had been hurt, Serena concluded. Her hand was halfway across the table before she pulled back, sure he wouldn't welcome her touch, however well-meaning. "I gather it was a long relationship until then."

"On and off for a few years, depending on what we were doing. Luckily Julia hadn't wanted children, so the ending was painless."

He hadn't said whether he wanted children. And she

doubted whether the break had been as painless as he made it sound. She looked at her watch, wishing they could talk for longer.

He caught the gesture. "I know this is boring stuff."

This time she did touch his hand. "I'm not bored. I don't want to keep the prince waiting."

She reached for her purse, but he had already dropped money on the table. "I'll buy the next round," she said, wondering what had happened to delivering him to Lorne and moving on.

There wouldn't be a next round if he had anything to do with it, Garth thought. He had brought Serena to Alice's kiosk to remind himself that she didn't fit into his world, then had been surprised by how comfortable she had looked.

Thirteen years ago she would have recoiled in disgust at the stained plastic furniture and the thick stoneware mugs Alice served her coffee in. She wouldn't have breathed in the fish-tainted air as if it were perfume.

Could Serena have changed so much? Her grooming still screamed class. Even glistening with perspiration in the gym, she had looked like a million dollars. And she still had the longest legs he'd ever seen. She'd always had a great body, and her work had honed her shape to a new level of perfection.

When he had pulled her against him in the gym, his hormones had gone into orbit. He'd wanted to take her in his arms more than he'd wanted anything in a long time.

He hadn't exactly been honest with her. The thing with Julia Francis had been more off than on, and she had ended it about twenty-four hours before Garth could suggest it himself. They had been good in bed together, but out of it, had disagreed about almost everything.

Pride had driven him to let Serena think he had a string of relationships behind him. And stopped him from telling her why he hadn't. What would she think if he told her she had been his yardstick for the perfect woman all these years, and he had yet to find anyone who measured up?

Time and again he'd cursed his foolishness in letting her haunt him. As he'd told her, one kiss hardly amounted to the romance of the century. It hadn't stopped him from looking for her in the background whenever there was a story about the monarch on TV or in the papers. After she sent the wreath, he hadn't responded because he'd feared the effect she might have on him. With good reason, he now saw.

Now she was here, he hated feeling so stupidly glad about it. He couldn't let it lead to anything. Her pedigree hadn't changed and neither had his. As a navy lieutenant he might have had something to offer her, but not anymore, thanks to Admiral McRafe. He had presided over the inquiry that had ended Garth's career, supposedly because his error led to a trainee almost dying during Advanced Nitrox Training.

The admiral hadn't wanted to hear about Garth's suspicions of the stage bottle that carried the nitrox mix, probably because the admiral's brother-in-law's company had supplied the equipment, something Garth hadn't found out until too late. He had gone to the admiral with the truth, mainly to stop anybody else from getting hurt. To Garth's disgust, the admiral had denied everything and had him escorted off the base. Later, he had heard from a friend still in the service that the defective stage bottles had been quietly replaced and a new supplier found. It was something, he supposed.

He had no idea why Serena had come looking for him or why Prince Lorne wanted to see him, unless he wanted private diving lessons. But he would go along because he respected the monarch. Although born to his role, the prince worked hard for the country. From what Garth had read, he had gone through hell with his first marriage, but stuck it out to set a good example rather than change the law that made divorce illegal in Carramer. Fate had intervened when his wife was killed driving too fast along a cliff road, then Lorne had married Alison Carter, the Australian tourist who had turned out to be the love of his life.

Jealousy gripped Garth. He wanted what the prince had, but had only met one woman he considered worth a lifetime commitment. She was so far out of his reach he'd need decompression time if he stayed around her for very long.

Not that he was going to, he assured himself. He would meet the prince, be whatever use the monarch thought he could be to his country, then get back to his own life before Serena worked her way any further under his skin.

Finding out that he'd been under surveillance by the palace had made him feel like the boy from the wrong side of the tracks all over again. He hadn't felt this inadequate for a long time, and his instinctive response had been to bite back, Serena being the handiest target. He wouldn't blame her if she wrote him off as a world-class jerk for the second time in their lives, he thought, watching her glide back to his truck. Her hips swayed sensuously and her long blond ponytail kept time. Police training hadn't stopped her moving like a model, he noticed. He wondered if she still kissed like a dream.

Chapter 3

Although Garth had lived in Solano most of his life, he hadn't set foot inside the castle grounds for years. Located on a promontory, the distinctive European- and Pacific-influenced building could be seen from every part of the city. Today the blue-and-jade Carramer flag flew above the battlements, indicating that the monarch was in residence.

Garth could have taken a tour of the public rooms anytime he wanted, but he considered the royals irrelevant to him and his day-to-day concerns. He couldn't imagine what Prince Lorne could want with him. By rights Garth's treatment by the navy should have soured him on serving his country. Maybe because he knew he had been wronged by one man rather than the whole service, it hadn't. He was curious in spite of himself, although he wasn't about to let Serena know it.

She broke into his thoughts. "Turn left here and pull up beside the sentry box."

They were at a private entrance, he saw. Recognizing Serena, the soldier on duty came to attention and saluted but also took careful note of the ID she handed to him. When she introduced Garth, the soldier checked his details against a computer screen, then signaled to another sentry. In front of them a boom gate rose slowly, allowing them to pass.

As soon as Garth drove through, the gate lowered behind them. Ahead loomed the main castle surrounded by a cluster of smaller buildings in similar architectural style. More like a walled city than a single building. Below them, the capital was strung out jewel-like along a series of bays. The view from the upper levels of the palace must be really something.

He glanced at Serena. "Your soldier friend wasn't keen to let me pass without you vouching for me. He probably thinks I'm a suspect you're bringing in."

She smiled. "Your fault for not wearing your black tie."

It was probably the truck, he thought. The soldier looked as if he was more accustomed to waving limousines through than dusty pickups.

"You're enjoying yourself, aren't you?" she asked.

Her comment startled him. He hadn't meant to let it show. "Maybe a little."

"Admit it, you like thumbing your nose at convention."

He wasn't ready to admit anything. "What makes you think so?"

"The diving gear you're carrying around is worth a fortune, so you can obviously afford a better vehicle. My guess is, you like shocking people into accepting you as you are."

"It's as good a way as any to find out who your real friends are."

Had she passed muster by agreeing to ride with him to the palace in his truck, she wondered? A glimmer of satisfaction greeted the thought. Maybe now he would stop regarding her as a hothouse flower. Not that she was going to let his opinion affect her. But like him, she disliked being judged on superficialities.

The staff had obviously been alerted to expect them. As soon as they reached the executive wing, they were shown to the prince's office with none of the usual formalities, then left alone with him, also as apparently instructed.

Approaching the monarch's desk, she was surprised when Garth came to attention and bent his head in deference. She was sure he didn't bend his stiff neck to many people, so he obviously respected Prince Lorne.

She made a similar gesture. "Sir, may I present Garth Remy."

The prince stood and offered his hand. "Thank you for agreeing to this meeting at such short notice, Garth."

Garth shook the prince's hand with a confidence that suggested he met reigning monarchs every day. "My pleasure, Your Highness. I don't know what I can do, but I'm at your service."

Lorne inclined his head in acceptance. "Greatly appreciated." To Serena, he said, "The resemblance is indeed remarkable."

Seeing the two men together, she had to agree. Garth was almost exactly the prince's height. With their dark coloring and athletic build, they could be mistaken for brothers. Or be brothers. She caught her breath. Was it possible?

Garth looked as if he was absorbing the fact, as well. "You aren't looking for a double, are you, sir?"

"You would certainly qualify, but no. Please sit down, both of you. I gather Serena hasn't told you what this is about?"

"I'm assuming you don't want me to take the American president diving while he's in town, sir."

As she seated herself beside Garth on a leather-covered couch, Serena hoped she didn't look as stunned as she felt. Had Garth forgotten he was addressing the country's ruler? Or had he specifically chosen not to use "Your Highness"? Lorne only chuckled. "Golf is more his game, but I might run the suggestion past his Secret Service."

He moved to a chair set at right angles to the sofa and sat down, crossing one long leg over the other. "How much do you know about your family background, Garth?"

She felt rather than saw Garth tense as the line of questioning caught him off guard. "The usual. One mother, one father, both from Carramer, both recently deceased. No siblings.'' He shot a sharp glance at Serena. ''Should I know any more?''

''Perhaps.'' Lorne reached across and lifted a package off his desk. Recognizing it, she braced herself as the prince offered it to Garth. ''Serena intercepted this during her preparations for the president's visit. Go ahead, take a look.''

Garth took the package and opened it. The cast of baby footprints and the birth certificate caused no reaction, until he came to the photos. Anger vibrated off him like an electrical charge. ''How were these taken without my knowledge?''

''Not by anyone in royal service and not on my authority,'' Lorne assured him. ''More importantly, the photos and the other items clearly suggest that you could be the rightful heir to the Carramer throne.''

Not by so much as a muscle did Garth's expression betray his shock, although his bearing became more rigid as he absorbed the monarch's words. He looked like a man turned to stone, she thought, wishing she had been able to prepare him for this. Perhaps nothing could have done.

He exhaled heavily. ''With respect, sir, that's garbage and we both know it.''

At this Lorne's mouth twitched, as if he understood that in any other company, Garth would have expressed himself in far more earthy terms. ''I thought so, too, when Serena brought me the package. The source of the material forces me to consider the possibility.''

Hands tightening on the plaster cast as if he would like to crush it to dust, Garth said, ''First I'd have to be a member of your family, your…''

''…older brother,'' Lorne finished for him. ''Also a possibility.''

''How?''

The prince stood up. ''Come with me.''

Motioning for his guards to remain where they were, he led the way along a corridor, coming to a halt in front of an oil painting of a woman in her late twenties. Flawless of complexion, as dark of coloring as Lorne himself, her sashed gown

and diamond-encrusted crown proclaimed her rank before
Lorne said, "My mother, Princess Aimee." He turned to
Garth. "It seems she may have been your mother as well."

Unable to deny the resemblance they could all see, Garth's
fists clenched. He was fighting himself, she saw. Being related
to this lovely, aristocratic woman would make a mockery of
the pigheaded reverse snobbery that had ruled his life.

Her pulse jumped. If Lorne was right, Garth had no reason
to hold her background against her. Assuming that was really
why he had rejected her all those years ago. She felt giddy
with possibilities and slightly afraid.

His snarled denial brought her back to earth with a rush.
"No way. I know who my mother was."

"Can you be sure of your facts?" Lorne asked.

"Can you be sure of yours—sir?"

So this was what happened when two alpha males met head-
on. They'd squared off in mirror positions of anger and challenge. As if he could no longer tolerate the portrait's gaze upon
him, Garth suddenly spun around and shouldered his way
through a set of etched glass doors leading to a walled garden.

When she and Lorne caught up with him he was pacing the
length of an ornamental pool. Pebbles crunched under his feet
and the glasslike surface of the water reflected his set expression. "This whole notion is crazy, Your Highness," he
snapped.

Lorne's dark brows lifted. "So you do remember who I
am?"

Garth looked unfazed by the implied rebuke. He didn't seem
to care that he had walked out on the monarch, but he sounded
more respectful as he said, "Your parentage isn't in question,
sir."

Lorne nodded in recognition of Garth's turmoil. "However,
yours is." He clasped a hand to the other man's shoulder.
"Will you at least hear me out?"

At the prince's touch Garth flinched, but then inclined his
head stiffly in agreement. When he lifted it, his gaze settled
on Serena as if she was an anchor in a raging sea. She sent

him a silent message of support and was gratified when she saw his expression thaw. "I guess anything else would be high treason."

"First I require your promise of discretion. What I'm about to tell you is known only within the royal family."

Garth's response was immediate. "You have it."

Lorne dragged in a deep breath. "Princess Aimee—then Lady Aimee Sewell—was my grandmother's principal lady-in-waiting. She was being courted by Roy Keer, a nobleman's son and former commando who loved her passionately. Unfortunately he possessed a cruel streak that made her afraid of him. She ended their relationship but he refused to accept that it was over between them. Then Crown Prince Eduard came home from the navy, and she had eyes for no other man."

Garth frowned. "Bet that went down well with Keer."

Lorne's expression lightened. "As you say, he took it badly. He walked out on his job in palace security, vowing that no man would have her if he couldn't."

Experience made Serena say, "Such a threat could be grounds for arrest."

"If Aimee had pressed charges. She was so in love with Eduard that she didn't want their happiness marred by unpleasantness."

Garth stirred restively. "This is fascinating, but…"

"You don't see how it concerns you? Does it help to know that her son, Louis, was accidentally conceived during that emotionally charged time?"

Lorne had Garth's attention now, Serena saw. Pieces were starting to fall into place. All but the most crucial one. "Why didn't Eduard marry Aimee as soon as they learned she was pregnant?"

"My grandfather, Prince Guillaume, was out of the country and they needed his blessing. When he returned he was angry because he thought they were too young, but he gave his consent because of her condition. They were planning their marriage when Aimee received more threats from Keer. Prince

Guillaume had the couple spirited to a royal hideaway until Keer could be apprehended.''

Garth picked up a pebble and skimmed it across the pond's pristine surface in a smooth action that made her lick annoyingly dry lips at the fluidity of his movements. Where the pebble touched, ripples spread out like the consequences of Lorne's mother's actions, Serena fancied.

''A commando-trained security man wouldn't be stopped that easily,'' Garth predicted.

Lorne watched the ripples subside. ''Indeed. He eluded the authorities, tracked the young couple down and broke into the royal compound, attacking Aimee before he was apprehended. The shock drove her into early labor, and Louis was born several weeks prematurely. Stillborn, or so she believed. Yet no one from the family saw the child after the birth. Aimee was so distraught that public news of the birth was suppressed to protect her. Her need for seclusion was explained as a consequence of the attack.''

Bad enough to be attacked. Devastating to lose her child as a result, Serena thought. No wonder none of this had been made public. ''What happened to Keer?''

''He served a long prison term, earning a further term for killing another prisoner.''

Where was Keer now, she wondered? Still in prison if his track record was any guide. ''Surely there was a funeral service, a memorial or something for the baby?'' she asked.

Lorne nodded. ''There was a private service and a cremation. A rose garden was planted at the estate as a memorial.''

''There's no conclusive proof that the baby died,'' Garth observed. ''If the child was stolen, the perpetrators could have arranged for an empty coffin to be cremated.''

He sounded as if he was starting to believe in a living heir, she noticed. He wasn't the only one. ''The baby could have been farmed out to foster parents who may not have known whose child they had adopted,'' she surmised, mentally compiling a list of suspects starting with the medical attendants and the staff at the hideaway when the baby was born. If any of them had been connected with Keer, it could make for an interesting trail.

"What makes you think this involves me?" Garth demanded. "My parents didn't talk much about the past and I have no relatives I can ask, but surely I'd have picked up some hint that something wasn't right?"

"Your lack of siblings could be a clue in itself."

She voiced what she guessed Lorne was thinking. "If the Remys desperately wanted a baby and couldn't have children of their own, they'd have been the ideal couple to approach about an illegal adoption." She gave Garth an apologetic smile before going on. "I doubt they could have afforded to go through regular channels."

Garth's expression hardened. "Unfortunately, you're right." His relentless gaze thanked her for pointing it out. She felt his pain but silently begged him to understand that she had to do her job. At the same time she wished she could tell him how much she admired how he was handling this. If she'd had everything she'd ever believed about herself turned upside down, she doubted she could discuss it as dispassionately as Garth was doing.

He'd mastered the art of guarding his feelings at an early age, she recalled. Whether he was taunted about being the oldest boy in school, or didn't have an answer in class because he'd been working on his parents' boat when the subject was studied, he'd acted as if he didn't care. She saw it carved on his face now. Sticks and stones, it proclaimed. Or a core of certainty about who and what he was that no external force could touch.

Lorne projected the same air, she realized. Was it an alpha quality they shared, or something more?

Garth folded his arms across his chest. "Being illegally adopted doesn't make me royalty."

"As well as the strong family resemblance, you carry a genetic trait unique to the de Marignys."

"Coincidence."

"Or a scheme to keep you hidden until your existence could

be revealed when it would do the most harm to Carramer,'' Lorne suggested. "If you consent to it, DNA testing will establish beyond doubt whether you could be my parents' child.''

"Of course I consent.'' Garth's tone said the sooner the better.

"Assuming the test is conclusive, under Carramer law, as the eldest son you would be the heir presumptive.''

"Hell's teeth.''

Lorne's mouth twitched. "Precisely.''

Her mind whirled. "Carramer First must be planning to announce Garth's existence on the eve of the American president's visit.''

Garth shot her a sharp look. "What would that achieve?''

She suspected the reason but looked to Lorne, who answered. "The president wants to establish an American base on one of the outer islands in exchange for long-term trade and defense benefits to both our countries. Any uncertainty about my right to finalize the agreement could derail the talks.''

Garth's breath whistled out. "Sounds like someone doesn't want that base built.''

She chewed her lower lip. "Carramer First has a republican agenda, but they've never gone beyond noisy demonstrations and minor acts of sabotage. Their antics are mainly aimed at gaining publicity and supporters. Stealing the heir to the throne and announcing his existence years later is beyond their scope.''

"It isn't beyond somebody's scope,'' Garth said. "If not Carramer First themselves, then who and why?''

"Someone could be using the group to push an agenda of their own,'' Lorne suggested.

She had been thinking the same thing. "The members may not know they're being used.''

"Also a presumption.'' Lorne thrust his hands into his pockets. "Unfortunately, DNA testing takes at least two weeks to obtain a result, more time than we have before the president's arrival."

"Someone evidently took that into account," Serena said. "They're obviously not stupid, which means they won't be easy to pin down."

Lorne became all business. "That's why I'm assigning you to find who's behind this and stop them before the president's visit. You'll have to work quietly. If word gets out about a possible claimant to the throne, it could not only derail the summit, it could throw the whole kingdom into turmoil."

She drew herself up. "Understood, Your Highness. However, I could be recognized by some of the Carramer First members. I've broken a few of their heads during demonstrations outside the palace."

"You may have to break a few more before this is over," Lorne said wryly. "They must know by now that the package is missing. They'll expect us to learn of its existence. If you're seen with Garth they'll think you've been assigned to protect him until we get to the bottom of this."

Protect Garth? She almost laughed out loud, unable to think of any man less in need of her protection.

His body language also rejected the notion outright even before he said, "Respectfully, Your Highness, if I'm going to help I'd prefer a more active assignment."

"And if you are the true heir?"

Something knotted inside her as she thought of him putting himself at risk, not because of who he might be, but because…well because he was Garth. "In any case you don't have a security background," she said.

"I have my navy experience. It covers a lot of ground." He faced Lorne. "Unless the circumstances of my discharge means you're not willing to trust me."

Lorne's expression betrayed nothing. "I know only what the record shows."

Garth's mouth firmed. "The record is wrong."

"Not according to Admiral McRafe."

''Admiral McRafe is an ass—admiral, sir. He isn't a diver. Defective equipment caused the trainee's injury.''

She saw Lorne suppress a smile at Garth's blunt description of the admiral, censored barely in time. She had met the admiral at a palace briefing once, and the dislike had been mutual. But would he destroy a man's career before admitting he was wrong?

''The question of the succession is our priority right now,'' Lorne said. ''The court physician is out of the country, but I'll have his deputy arrange the DNA test under the strictest secrecy. I'm told she needs to test as many members of the royal family as possible, so I've announced that I wish to establish a DNA data bank for historical reasons.''

''I recommend setting up a command post at the summer palace at Allora where it would be easier to keep the investigation under wraps,'' Serena proposed.

Lorne inclined his head. ''I concur. The two of you will go there as soon as the testing is completed.''

The two of you.

Instant heat coiled through her, disturbing in its intensity. Basing the investigation at Allora was logical and Garth had to be involved, but she hadn't counted on Lorne sending Garth to the summer palace with her. Already her awareness of him put her senses on overdrive. Tough to function efficiently when unsettling currents ripped through her every time he looked at her.

She debated whether to claim emotional involvement as a way out, but could she honestly? Sexual awareness wasn't the same thing, and that's all she was prepared to acknowledge. ''Isn't Garth safer here, Your Highness?'' she suggested anyway.

Before Lorne could answer, Garth snarled, ''To the devil with safe. I should have some say in this. If I am the heir, I outrank both of you.''

Unperturbed, Lorne smiled. ''When and if the crown is yours, you can do as you wish. Until then, I rule here. I want you out of harm's way until we know the truth.''

Even Garth couldn't argue with a man whose word was quite literally law. His bent head conceded the reality, although the rest of his stiff pose telegraphed defiance. "As Your Highness wishes."

For now, she heard, although he didn't say it. In the stubbornness stakes the two were evenly matched. Another indication of their relationship? Carramer was in for a shock if it got Garth as a monarch, but not as much as Lorne himself, she thought. He'd been born to rule. Garth ruled no one but himself, and he didn't take kindly to following another man's orders. How had he survived so long in the navy?

Lorne narrowed his eyes. "Serena?"

She resisted the urge to sigh. "As soon as the test is done, we'll leave for Allora—together, sir."

"Good. I'm putting you in charge."

Garth looked as if he would like to strangle someone with his bare hands. If she had a problem dealing with him, he obviously had a bigger one with answering to her. Good. It might distract him from making her job harder than it already was.

Chapter 4

Serena thought of Garth's solitary bag in the back seat of the unmarked car she had commandeered from the R.P.D. fleet. Only by arguing that it was a security risk had she dissuaded him from taking his pickup. It was now locked away at Solano with her car. For now the less attention they attracted the better. For that reason she had decided they would remain in contact with the castle, but without an escort of police or R.P.D. She hoped she wasn't being overconfident.

"Are you sure you brought everything you're going to need? I can have someone swing by your boat."

His dark brow arched upward. "Curious about how the other half lives, Serena?"

She concentrated on driving. "No. But we'll be at Allora until the results of the test are known. You haven't brought much with you."

Out of the corner of her eye she saw him shrug. "I'll get by. Lorne invited me to help myself to anything I need at the summer palace."

The resemblance between Garth and the monarch extended

to their size, she'd noticed. "You two got along well, didn't you?"

"Considering the circumstances."

"This must be a lot to take in. If you want to talk about it…"

"I don't," he said shortly.

She decided against heeding the warning in his voice. "Finding out that the people who raised you might not be your parents after all—I can't imagine how that must feel."

"Then don't try. Once we have more facts about my background will be soon enough for you to start arranging counseling for me."

His message was clear. He had decided to treat this as a hoax until proven otherwise. Professionally, she knew he was correct. Personally was another story. "Some men would take advantage of the situation," she commented.

"In what way?"

"Expecting to be treated like royalty."

He snorted his reaction. "Try calling me Prince Garth and see where it gets you."

"I wouldn't dream of it." To her Garth was still the school bad boy, the kind her parents had warned her against. Although *boy* didn't begin to describe the man he had turned into, nor her infuriatingly female response to him. Sharing a car with him, about to spend a couple of weeks in relative seclusion in an emotion-charged situation was even more disturbing. No wonder her nerves felt as if they were on fire.

"What will you do if this isn't a hoax?" she asked him, curious in spite of herself.

He began ticking off points on his fingers. "First, bring in a two-day working week. Then decree free candy for every kid. Deep-sea-diving lessons for all the adults."

She slammed her hands against the steering wheel, making the car slew until she wrestled it back under control. Her reaction shocked her. They were on the coast road that linked the capital with Allora, and the sea foamed against rocks sixty feet below them with only a narrow shoulder between them and the drop. "Do you have to make a joke of everything?"

"The joke is me as the ruler of Carramer," he said, unruffled.

"Is it so hard to contemplate?"

"Try impossible."

"You can't conceive of yourself as the prince?"

"I'm surprised you have to ask."

She slanted a look at him. "Because I'm from what you call 'the other half'?"

"Aren't you?"

"You made it clear you thought so. I never saw myself that way."

His silence told her he still considered her a spoiled princess. Did he think her dedication to fighting crime, to protecting the royal family who ensured Carramer's stability were the choices of someone who only cared about her own pleasure? Couldn't he see the truth right in front of his nose, that she couldn't help being who and what she was, but had turned her life around because she wanted to make a difference?

Why should she care what he thought anyway?

"In any event, if I turn out to be Lorne's older brother I won't live long enough to wear his crown," he said as mildly as if he was commenting on the weather.

She tightened her hold on the wheel. The thought had occurred to her but she had kept it to herself. "What makes you think so?"

"It suits someone in Carramer First to have me identified as the heir to the throne. For reasons we still have to determine, they want to create enough chaos to stop the Americans building a base here. They're not likely to want to exchange one monarch for another."

"So you think you'll be targeted for assassination as soon as you've served your purpose?"

"You think so, too. Lorne, as well. Isn't that why he wants me at Allora?"

It was her turn to lapse into silence. She had reached the

alarming conclusion while he was at the palace infirmary, taking the DNA test. "You realize that means Lorne and his family are also in danger?"

"Go back to them. I don't need a baby-sitter."

"The prince wants me here."

"What do you want, Serena?"

I want you to stop treating me like the enemy, she thought but didn't say. *I want you to look at me as me, not as a poor little rich girl you labeled a long time ago.* None of it was appropriate to the present situation. "I want you to shut the hell up and let me do my job," she snapped, provoked as much by her reaction to him as by his behavior.

"Is that any way to talk to the future monarch of Carramer?"

"Oh, so now you're the heir? Can I expect you to pull rank whenever things don't go your way?"

"They've never gone my way without a fight. I don't need a title to get what I want."

"What do you want, Garth?"

Throwing his question back at him was supposed to buy her some peace. She didn't expect the answer he gave.

"You."

Feeling anything but peaceful, she kept her gaze on the road ahead. "I'm so glad that's out in the open."

Her sarcasm washed off him. "You asked. I answered."

"Well you can't have me."

"I never could, could I? You want me to think you've changed, but one thing is still the same. There's a gulf a mile wide between us. Even if I'm crowned king of the world, in your eyes I'll never be good enough for you."

"You said it, I didn't."

"But you believe it."

It wasn't a question. Nothing she could say was going to convince him otherwise, so she didn't try. "What does it matter anyway? We're here because of a political situation. It's not personal."

"Everything is personal sooner or later. It's the only reason anybody gives a damn about anything."

Sudden understanding flooded her. "It is personal, isn't it? I wondered why you agreed to everything so readily. The Garth Remy I used to know would have told Prince Lorne what he could do with his DNA test and would never have agreed to being stashed away at Allora. I'm right, aren't I?"

Accustomed to reading body language as part of her job, she glanced at him and saw his tension in every line. His careless shrug didn't negate the conclusion. "You're the one with all the answers. You tell me."

So she did. "This is your revenge for all the hurts you endured growing up. Being behind everybody else at school through no fault of your own. Always scraping to get by. Then being thrown out of the navy for something you didn't do. If you are the heir to the throne, you'll have the last laugh."

"Some laugh if it gets me killed."

Hearing the raw note in his voice, she let her eyes narrow. "I don't think you care as long as you can rub everybody's noses in your true heritage first."

"You're supposing I care what anybody else thinks of me in the first place."

"Oh, you care. You want us to think you don't, but you care."

"Sounds as if you've made a thorough study of *Homo Remyans,*" he said. "Well let me tell you, you're wrong. You're the one who cares who I am and where I come from. For me, people can label me whatever they like as long as they stay out of my face."

He might think he was telling the truth but she didn't believe him. Nor did she feel as if there was a gulf between them, certainly not a social one. If he only knew, she could have done with a few more barriers between them to take the edge off the aching desire that consumed her whenever she was around him. It wasn't making a tough job any easier.

The feeling had taken hold from the moment she recognized his photo in the package. It had grown stronger when they'd returned to the palace together. Garth had agreed to Lorne's wish to have the DNA test done immediately, but had tried to argue against leaving for Allora right away. Lorne had won that argument, too. In her job Serena had to be packed and ready to travel at a moment's notice, so the logistics hadn't bothered her as much as her troubling response to her traveling companion.

"Let's leave it, shall we?" she asked tautly, not sure for whose benefit.

"The typical answer of a female on the losing end of an argument," he said.

Her sigh of exasperation hissed between them. If the Carramer First rebels didn't get to him first, she just might. "It's nothing of the sort. We've arrived."

Although known as the summer palace, the royal residence was actually a rambling granite villa, the horseshoe-shaped building a local landmark atop a cliff a couple of miles along winding cliff roads from the seaside town of Allora and its famous Saphir Beach. The walled complex had its own private beach and a vast swimming pool overlooking the ocean. Separated from the main building by a man-made lake was an art studio used by Princess Alison, a talented artist, when the family resided here during the summer.

An ideal place for a honeymoon, Serena thought, then frowned. What was it about Garth that put such thoughts in her head? For the last few months she'd been so focused on becoming head of the Solano R.P.D. that she'd had no room in her life for a love life, far less anything permanent. Now suddenly she was thinking honeymoon?

Serena was too damned perceptive by half, Garth thought angrily. When Prince Lorne had told him he might be the true heir to the throne, Garth's thought, right after dismissing it as impossible, had been that he would finally show everybody.

Who did he want to show? He'd long ago come to terms with who and what he was. He mourned his parents and regretted that they'd never had the time or money to enjoy life, but he wasn't bereft. His father had been a closed book who never showed affection to anyone, and his mother had been too worried about keeping up with the bills to notice that her son's boyhood was being eaten up with adult concerns.

At some level he'd envied Serena. Everything came so easily to her. Her beauty and success as a model meant she never lacked for male attention. She was wealthy. She was smart. Not for her the frustration of being yanked out of school to help in the family business, thus ensuring he was always ten steps behind his peers.

He wondered if he would have felt so frustrated if she'd directed her dazzling smile his way, although even as a teenager, he'd known it was a fantasy. Then she'd amazed him by turning up in the stands to watch him compete in the pool and on the track. She'd cheered his victories so enthusiastically that he'd wondered who might have gotten her attention. When he'd realized she was cheering him, he'd felt ten feet tall, spurring himself to greater performances to impress her. He'd actually started to hope something could happen between them.

It had taken him weeks to find the courage to invite her to go to the beach with him. Then on the way he'd overheard her accept her friends' bet that she wouldn't have the nerve to kiss him and had felt as if the ground had been torn from under his feet. So he was nothing more than a joke to her. Anger and disappointment had prompted him to accuse her of being nothing more than a pretty face, not because he believed it, but because of the need to hurt her as badly as she'd hurt him.

He hadn't meant to change the course of her life.

He glanced sideways at her. She was showing her ID to the sentry guarding the main entrance of the royal complex. It struck him as unbelievably arrogant to think he'd had anything to do with what she'd become. What next? Thinking of himself as the true monarch?

No, he refused to take any credit for her achievements. Her parents may have steered her life when she was too young to argue, but she would eventually have made changes with or without his influence. He'd seen a sample of her potential when she wiped the floor with her opponents on the debating team in school. Through relentlessly reasoned argument, she'd demonstrated her belief that right should prevail. A career in law enforcement was logical for her. He wouldn't be surprised if she ended up running the R.P.D. one day.

The sentry returned to his post. Seconds later the ornate wrought-iron gates bearing the royal crest swung inward, and Serena drove through. The gates closed silently behind them and she started down a wide drive lined with century-old Tallow wood trees.

"Everything okay?" he asked.

"The villa staff were briefed to expect us and security is at maximum," she stated. "If the Hand or any of his people show up here, we'll be ready for them."

He let his brow arch. "The Hand?"

"The code name for the head of Carramer First. We haven't been able to identify him beyond that."

Her tone said she found the situation intolerable. She wouldn't like not knowing, he thought. "Then the Hand could also be a woman," he pointed out.

"Possible but unlikely."

"Don't you think a woman capable of plotting to bring down the royal house?"

"I've no doubt they could, but my instinct and the intelligence we've been able to gather tells me the Hand is male." She tossed him a challenging glare. "It could even be you."

At the castle she'd made no secret of not wanting him to accompany her to Allora until Prince Lorne had insisted. Garth hadn't considered that she might suspect him of being involved in this. So much for the notion that her reluctance had been fueled by an attraction she didn't want to feel. *More arrogance, Prince Garth?* he asked himself, feeling chilled. What next? Deluding himself that she cared about him?

"If you think I'm behind this, why didn't you have me arrested and thrown into jail?" he demanded.

"Prince Lorne thinks you could be part of his family."

"But you don't."

It wasn't a question. He saw the answer in the cold gaze she turned on him. "You don't think I'm the lost Prince Louis, either, do you?" he persisted.

"In law enforcement I learned not to make assumptions. I'll keep an open mind until I have enough evidence one way or another."

"Enough to hang me," he said quietly.

"That isn't what I want."

"It's what you've always wanted," he insisted. "I'm the proverbial thorn in your side, the man you hate yourself for hankering after but don't know how to stop."

Paydirt, he thought as her knuckles whitened around the wheel. So he wasn't deluding himself after all. "It would suit you just fine to prove that I'm the Hand or somehow in cahoots with him," he went on relentlessly. "Then you'd have all your problems solved in one neat package."

Her head swung from side to side. "I told you, this isn't personal."

She hadn't denied the part about wanting him, he noticed with grim satisfaction. If that wasn't personal he didn't know what was, and before this was over she was going to acknowledge it, he resolved. He would let her decide what she wanted to do about it, but he wasn't going to let her pretend it didn't exist. In the meantime they needed to get something else straight. "You'll have to trust me if we're going to work together."

Her head shot around. "Who said anything about working together?"

"Lorne wanted me here."

"For your protection in case you're the true heir to the throne. This is *my* case. Solving it doesn't concern you."

He clamped a hand on her arm. "The hell it doesn't. You've just admitted you suspect me of some involvement. You owe me the right to prove you wrong."

She took a deep breath then said in a low, vibrant voice, "I suggest you remove your hand from my arm while you still can. The only thing I owe you is gratitude for spurring me to choose my present line of work.''

He took his time retrieving his hand. ''I thought you said this isn't personal.''

''I work better solo.''

She was dodging the question again. He had more pressing concerns for the moment. ''As it happens so do I, especially when my life is the one being tampered with. So we'll do it your way. You run your investigation and I'll run mine.''

She steered the car to a stop beneath an arched portico supported by a row of handsome white columns. ''That isn't what I meant and you know it.''

He shrugged. ''You can't have it both ways.''

''Do you have to be so stubborn?''

''I've never been any different.''

He saw her lovely gaze cloud. ''No, you haven't. I remember when you twisted your ankle during a race. Anybody else would have limped off, but you stuck it out right to the finish line. You came in third but you finished.''

Hearing her voice soften, he wished he could touch his hand to her cheek, to turn her head and taste her mouth. It pleased him to know she remembered. ''It was fifth place, actually.''

''You still finished, although everybody could see you were in agony.''

''It wasn't so smart. That stunt put me out of action for a month.''

She gave a low chuckle that sent shivers sparkling down his spine. ''And you still haven't learned.''

A uniformed footman emerged from the villa and approached the car. Before he reached them, Garth said, ''We'll talk about this again after we settle in, Serena.''

Her look said it was already settled as far as she was concerned, but she gave a reluctant nod. ''Talking can't hurt, I guess.''

Garth was right, this was personal and there was no way she could make it otherwise. If she had any sense she would ask Prince Lorne to assign someone else to this case, someone who didn't risk losing every shred of objectivity whenever Garth cast one of those long, lazy looks her way.

There was no one else. She knew that, too. The fewer people who knew about a possible rival claimant to the throne, the better for the country. So she would just have to harden herself against those looks and avoid being alone with Garth as much as she could. Lorne had arranged for the villa to be staffed by a handful of trusted people. She should be able to have someone else around whenever she needed to be with Garth.

She hefted a bag onto an upholstered bench at the foot of a bed big enough to throw a party on. The housekeeper had offered to have someone unpack for her but Serena preferred doing it herself. Being waited on reminded her too much of her modeling days, when people used to follow her around, primping and fussing with her hair and makeup whenever she stopped to draw breath.

Despite what Garth thought, she had never enjoyed modeling. The best thing about it had been her parents' obvious pride in her. Occasionally she wished they took as much pleasure in her present activities, then chided herself for needing their approval at this late stage. It should be enough that she was happy with her life.

She had finished unpacking one bag and had started on the second when a knock came on the outer door. Expecting one of the staff, she was startled to find Garth standing there.

"Settled in already?" she asked, unhappy with the little jump her heart gave at the sight of him propped in the doorway.

"How long does it take to open a closet door and throw a bag inside?"

She felt a rueful grin start. "I must try that sometime."

"Why not now? This place is begging to be explored. Come with me."

Apart from the suspicions she still hadn't shared with him, there was the problem of her reaction to Garth himself. Until she had that under control she didn't want to go anywhere with him without full body armor.

Why she felt the need for it, she didn't want to think.

"I'll take a rain check, thanks. This isn't a vacation. I didn't come here to experience the delights of the summer palace."

"Part of your job is to protect me. I don't see why you can't do it while experiencing delight at the same time."

She folded her arms across her chest, lowering her head a little against a barrage of unwanted sensations. "That's not what I said."

"Close enough." His mouth hovered over hers.

Her own lips parted instinctively until she pressed them together. When she could speak without doing a breathless Marilyn Monroe impression that would betray his effect on her, she said, "You may be able to treat this lightly, but I can't. There's too much at stake."

"For the crown or for you?"

"Both." She hadn't intended to say that but it was too late.

He combed his hair with his fingers. "You really hate me for dragging you away from the presidential task force, don't you?"

"Prince Lorne has to take some of the credit."

"I'd change it if I could."

It helped a little. "Maybe you're right," she conceded, "the unpacking can wait." So could the soul-searching that she knew would follow if she stayed in the suite much longer. Standing beside him, with his gaze warm on her, she could feel herself falling all over again, not as a teenager this time, but as a grown woman who knew what she was doing—and couldn't find a way to stop.

Somehow she had to. Until she knew where Garth stood, not simply in relation to the crown but whether he was on the side of good or evil, she couldn't afford to let her personal feelings matter.

She stepped past him into the corridor. "I could use a walk after being cooped up in the car."

He fell into step beside her, not touching her. "Why do I have the feeling that there's something you're not telling me?"

She let a heartbeat pass. "Probably because there is."

Chapter 5

She said no more, and he didn't ask her to elaborate until they were outside in the sparkling, orchid-scented air. By unspoken agreement they followed a path between stands of ironwood trees to the crescent of white sand that was the villa's private beach.

Automatically she scanned it from end to end looking for anything that might represent a security risk. The beach was guarded by sentinel cliffs extending into the water at both ends. She quartered the ocean looking for vessels but there was nothing to disturb the tranquility.

"The water looks inviting," she murmured, surveying the gentle waves that rolled almost to her feet.

"You haven't been here before?"

She shook her head. "When Prince Lorne and his family come here in the summer I usually take my own vacation." She didn't add that she found it too disturbing watching the prince and princess, so obviously in love, sharing their enjoyment with the delightful crown prince. They reminded her too strongly of what she had so far foregone in her own life.

Garth picked up a shell and skimmed it over the waves. He was good at that, she thought, remembering when he'd done the same thing at the palace in Solano. "The ocean around here is a lot more treacherous than it looks. You must have heard of the serpent?"

She might not have visited the villa but she had done her homework before coming here. "It's the local name for a dangerous current."

He nodded. "One that has claimed more than its share of lives."

She shuddered. "I prefer to do my laps in a swimming pool."

"You've never dived?" He said it as if she'd just admitted to never having tried breathing.

"I took a course after I joined the R.P.D. It was a kind of aversion therapy."

His interest sharpened. "Aversion therapy?"

"To get over a morbid fear of sharks."

He was decent enough not to make fun of her. "They can be intimidating if you don't understand them."

"They eat people. What else is there to understand?"

"Is there any point in reminding you that more people eat sharks than the other way around?"

"I don't have a problem with that."

"Practically every recorded shark attack has been on surfers, swimmers or people snorkeling and splashing around on the surface. To a shark, that spells food. They almost never bother scuba divers. If you let me take you diving one day, I'll prove it to you."

She rubbed her hands over her arms, not liking the way a tremor slipped through her. Was she afraid of him or the sharks? Both made her more uneasy than she cared for. She hated feeling so vulnerable. "One day."

He read her expression. "As long as it isn't soon."

"I'd rather tackle the sharks on land. Those I know I can handle."

"Spoken like a cop."

"It's what I've been for most of my adult life."

He turned to her, lifting a hand to push a strand of wind-blown hair away from her face. His touch was light but when he took the hand away her breathing was ragged.

"You still look like a model."

An arrow of anger pierced her. She'd left that side of her behind a long time ago. She wanted him to acknowledge that, again wondering why his approval mattered. "Looks can deceive. I can have you flat on your back on the sand before you can blink."

His glance was measuring, a hint of a smile playing around his generous mouth. "Might be an interesting experience."

Annoyed with herself for thinking along the same lines, she snapped, "You wouldn't think so if it happened. I'm liable to break something." She couldn't even be sure it wouldn't be in her.

"I'll consider myself forewarned." He didn't sound troubled. He sounded as if he couldn't wait.

The promise in his tone sent fantasies tumbling through her mind. She had to fight to clear her thoughts. This wasn't the time and place, if there ever was such a thing for them. Not until she knew where he stood.

She drew herself up. "We're not here to exchange sexual fantasies." Not even when hers made her want to lick her dry lips. "I need to know…"

He cut off the question by simply kissing her. She wasn't prepared, and the touch of heat against her mouth ignited wild-fires all through her. Memories of being sixteen and dreaming of his kiss rushed back. But she wasn't sixteen anymore. She'd been kissed, only not like this.

As his mouth claimed hers, sensation gripped her, starting as a gentle flutter that fast became full-blown, thrilling pleasure. Untamed thoughts of where the kiss might lead danced in her mind. She'd said they weren't exploring sexual fantasies, but he'd triggered hers like lighting a fuse.

By the time he lifted his head she was trembling.

She turned blazing eyes on him. "Do that again and you won't have to ask what a cop can do."

"You just gave me a fair idea."

The kiss had awakened too many memories. She'd thought, hoped, she was immune to him by now, but all it took was the lightest touch of his mouth to hers to prove her wrong. She tried to tell herself it was better if they got it out of the way now, but couldn't make herself believe it.

Far from getting him out of her system, the kiss had fired a dangerous longing for more. "You're trying to distract me," she said weakly.

He gave a devil-may-care grin. "It worked."

She didn't need to ask how he knew. The carelessness was in his smile but not in his eyes. They were dark with a desire she knew only too well because its counterpart throbbed through her. Diving with sharks would be tame by comparison with the promise she read in his gaze. Not only of desire satisfied beyond her wildest dreams, but of a deeper, more meaningful involvement.

The kind that terrified her because it stood between her and what she wanted to do with her life.

She couldn't, *wouldn't* allow that he wanted that kind of involvement with her when he had always maintained that he didn't want it with anyone.

He was Garth, remember? He was good at sending messages she didn't want to receive.

He was doing it now. She stood for several heartbeats, feeling herself drown in his gaze, until she shook her head. "No."

He didn't ask what she was refusing, probably because he already knew. "You started to ask me something."

It took an effort to get her thoughts back on track. Much more of this and she'd be useless to Prince Lorne and to Garth. She felt useless to herself, her training no help against this. Her question came out more accusing than she had intended. "When were you planning to tell me you were a member of Carramer First?"

She'd caught him off balance, she saw. Good. It was his

turn. Asking the question had acted like a cold shower for her, too, stemming some of the desire running rampant through her, and not before time.

"How long have you known?"

"You may not think so to look at me, but I take my job seriously. I can tell you what you eat for breakfast and what size and style briefs you prefer."

This time he didn't take advantage of the opening to taunt her. Instead he used an old Carramer oath that sounded almost poetic in the musical language. It was a fallacy that the Carramer language had no swear words. Only tourists believed it.

"Anatomically impossible," she stated. "And it doesn't answer the question."

"I'm not a member now."

"You were once."

He ran a hand through his hair. "A long time ago, just after I got out of school and well before I joined the navy."

"Why?"

"You have to ask why I had antiroyalist leanings?"

She scuffed the sand with the toe of her shoe. "I'd be surprised if you hadn't." For a family as struggling as his, Carramer First's message that royalty sucked the country dry would ring true even though it wasn't. The promise of equality and liberty for all was an old one, but still seductive.

"You didn't really believe their propaganda, did you?"

"I had some crazy idea of working from within, making them into a political force to be reckoned with."

If anyone could he probably could, she thought. "What happened?"

"They turned out to be a bunch of placard-waving, slogan-chanting fools, social misfits who thought exchanging a president for a prince would wave a magic wand and solve all their problems."

"You didn't agree?"

"After I joined, I started researching what the royals actually do. To my amazement, it's a lot more than take salutes and open fetes."

As a castle employee she'd known it for a long time, but was pleasantly surprised to hear him say it. "They're the glue that holds Carramer together."

He nodded. "I found out that they don't rest on any inherited laurels. Most of them work their butts off for this country, and if one of them doesn't, the others soon pull them into line." He gave a harsh laugh. "I expected to find the royals raking in money from their oppressed citizens. Instead I found that many of their activities are funded by their private fortunes."

She felt her spirits lift. "Is that why you got out of Carramer First?"

He shook his head. "I was disillusioned but I still believed anyone with the potential should have the chance to lead the country, whether or not they're born into the right family."

Ironic, considering the situation he found himself in now. "We do have a government," she observed.

"Headed by a prince who inherits his right to rule. If not for an accident of history he'd be a king."

Every Carramer child learned from infancy about the ancient king who had so cruelly oppressed his people that when his son inherited the crown, he swore to remain a prince as a sign that he would never follow his father's evil example. The island kingdom had been ruled by a prince ever since.

"Doesn't that tell you something?" she asked.

"If you mean does the fact that Lorne chooses to remain a prince make a difference? Whatever he calls himself he's still a de Marigny, the only one entitled to wear the crown."

"Maybe not the only one," she reminded him. "If you're the heir, how will that fit with your republican beliefs?"

"I didn't say I still believe them," he countered. "I was there when Lorne's parents were killed helping their people during a cyclone. Despite the weather warnings a group of Carramer First members insisted on demonstrating outside the castle. When the cyclone struck, the prince and princess didn't discriminate. The castle gates were opened and the placard-wavers were taken in along with anyone else who needed shelter.''

His tone turned harsh and he paused, the memory obviously still painful. ''We were heading for the main building when a gust of wind ripped a chunk of roof the size of a football field off a building a couple of miles away then dropped it right on top of us. A second before it hit, someone dragged me clear. I didn't know till later that it was Prince Eduard. But for him I'd be dead.''

A knot of tension pulsed at her temples as she dragged out the rest of the memory. ''Seconds later a piece of debris hit the prince in the chest, crushing his heart.''

''Prince Eduard didn't know me from a bar of soap. Nor did he care that I opposed everything he stood for. He saved my life at the cost of his own.''

Silence fell between them. She let it stretch, wondering at the strange forces that had moved the prince possibly to save his own son without ever knowing it. She saw the recognition on Garth's drawn features. ''His wife also died that day trying to help others. No wonder you changed politics,'' she said softly.

''How could I not? I'll never be a flag-waving monarchist, but I'll also never forget what a prince of royal blood did for me. Your research can't be as good as you think if it didn't tell you any of this.''

''After the cyclone things were chaotic. Many records were lost or destroyed, and the death of the monarch and his wife caused a power vacuum until Prince Lorne assumed the throne.'' He was only twenty at the time, she recalled.

''Carramer First lost a lot of members, not only those who died in the cyclone, but folk like me who saw another side of the monarchy,'' he told her.

''Around the same time the Hand saw his opportunity and took over, filling another power vacuum. Pity you didn't stay around a little longer or you might be able to help us identify him.''

He slanted her a grin. "Does that mean you've stopped thinking I could be the Hand?"

"If what you've told me checks out, it would be unlikely. We know he has some heavy-duty connections in the underworld, probably a criminal past of his own. And he's proved he's willing to kill." She couldn't bring herself to believe that of Garth.

"Guaranteeing his followers will be too frightened to talk."

She nodded. "If they know anything. Our friend operates on a strict need-to-know basis. According to my informant in the group, only one man reports directly to him."

Garth massaged his chin with one hand. "Have you considered this man may *be* the Hand, creating a phantom leader to keep the others in line?"

"I thought of it but it didn't check out. It's my belief that the only way the Hand can remain so elusive is if he doesn't live in Carramer permanently." She scanned the horizon. "On a boat at sea perhaps."

"Interesting concept. It limits your chances of pinning anything on him."

"Why do you think he's still walking free?"

Garth was not good at feeling helpless. Allora might be safe, but he didn't want safe right now. He wanted action. He hated the idea of staying cooped up in this luxurious cocoon for the next two weeks while a nerd in a laboratory determined his fate based on a genetic code you couldn't even see with the naked eye.

The two days he'd wasted since they got here were already making him chafe. When he'd demanded something useful to do, Serena had parked him at a computer with a list of questions they would need answered.

He could make a computer sit up and beg, a talent he'd unexpectedly discovered at night school and later honed through specialist courses in the navy. But he took no satisfaction in the skill. He'd already finished sifting through Serena's list, although he suspected it was meant to keep him busy for longer.

He now knew that both the doctor and nurse who'd assisted at Louis de Marigny's birth were dead. The doctor of a stroke brought on by years of alcohol abuse. The nurse in a hit-and-run car accident. The ex-commando who'd attacked Princess Aimee, triggering her baby's premature birth, had been released from prison ten years before and had drowned on a fishing trip after a storm blew up, capsizing his small boat. The sharks were welcome to him, Garth thought.

All he was getting were dead ends, dead being the operative word. The growing body count made him uneasy, but all the deaths had been investigated. No loose ends. Even the hit-and-run driver who'd killed the nurse had eventually been brought to trial.

He swung his gaze to Serena seated at a desk at the other end of the reception room she was using as a command center. Tilting her chair back, she'd swung her legs onto the desk. Someone should tell her not to do that wearing minuscule denim shorts and a hot-pink T-shirt that left her midriff bare. It gave a man all sorts of ideas.

He dismissed them and concentrated on the conversation taking place between her and someone at police headquarters in Solano. The acoustics in the room were impressive. She kept her voice low but he could follow the conversation without really trying.

"Matt, Alain Pascale is the royal physician, for goodness' sake. He wouldn't just drop out of sight. What if Lorne got sick and needed him? Yeah, I know he's known for being crusty and difficult, but he's also the prince's closest friend." There was a pause while she listened, then said, "I'll take anything you can dig up. I owe you." She chuckled. "Not *that* much. Well okay, but only for one night, and the information had better be worth it."

Still smiling she flipped the phone closed, then jumped as Garth loomed beside the desk. She swung her feet down. "Don't do that."

"Matt?" he queried.

Her gaze narrowed. "What's it to you?"

He dropped a bundle of printouts and computer disks on the desk in front of her. "Now you owe me, too. Do I qualify for the same reward Matt was angling for?"

"Don't tell me you're jealous?"

For that he would have to care, and he didn't. His reaction to hearing her talk to the anonymous Matt had caught him off guard, that was all. The low, throaty pitch of her voice had needled Garth. She didn't sound anything like that when she spoke to him.

Matt wasn't even here. He didn't have to put up with doing some lousy make-work job designed to keep him out of Serena's hair. When it came to payoffs, justice demanded equal treatment. "I'm not jealous, but fair's fair," he insisted.

"In that case you'd better scare up a couple of kids under the age of seven."

"What?"

"Matt Hayes was my partner when I was in uniform," she said with exaggerated patience. "He's married to my best friend, Melanie, and they have two kids, four and six. Their anniversary is coming up and Matt was trying to coerce me into baby-sitting for them in exchange for getting me some information."

Garth pasted on his best poker face "I knew that."

"You did not. You *were* jealous."

He refused to let her bait him, knowing he was nothing of the sort. "Baby-sitting, huh? What do you do, cuff them and read them their rights instead of a bedtime story?"

"Not that it's any of your business, but I'm a very good baby-sitter. Carla and Ben are great kids."

Garth had no trouble imagining her surrounded by children. She would treat them as equals and they would love her for it, he thought. He had already seen that she treated everyone in the royal household the same way. Within half a day of their arrival, she'd even had Anselme, the stuffy Jeeves look-alike senior footman, calling her Serena and acting as if they were old friends.

"How come you don't have any of your own?" he asked.

"Again it's none of your business, but I have other priorities," she said.

He perched one hip on a corner of her desk. This was far more interesting than chasing dead ends on a computer. "Since I'm in over my head already, what are your priorities?"

"Number one, getting your butt off my desk. Number two, finding Alain Pascale."

Garth took his time straightening up, thinking of the conversation he'd overheard. "He's the crusty, difficult one who's currently missing."

She gave him a sour look. "Next time why don't I put my calls on the speaker to make it easier for you? Yes, he's the royal physician. He's also like a father to Prince Lorne."

"So he's not likely to go off without telling Lorne where he can be contacted?"

"He and his wife, Helen, were booked on an island cruise, but they never showed up, and the ship sailed without them."

"Could they have changed their minds?"

"If they had, they'd have notified the palace. Matt is going to look into it and get back to me."

"You think this has something to do with Operation Monarch?"

Her eyebrows tilted. "Operation Monarch?"

"Don't you security types give your assignments catchy names?"

"You've been watching too much television. Well, okay, I think there may be a connection to Operation Monarch." Her mouth twisted as if the name left a sour taste. She tapped the file Garth had just delivered. "Of all the people connected with the birth of the lost royal baby, Alain Pascale is the only one who hasn't turned up dead."

He thought about his own research findings. "I had noticed the escalating body count, although every death has a perfectly reasonable explanation."

"Still too coincidental for my liking."

He could see why she'd been headhunted from the police to work for the R.P.D. She took nothing at face value. Time he followed her example. "You think my parents' death wasn't an accident, as well, don't you?"

"It made sure they couldn't answer questions about your birth, strengthening the idea that you're the heir to the throne."

He'd slowly arrived at the same conclusion and had to work at controlling his rage now. "If it's true, there'll be another accidental death before this is over."

"I'll pretend you didn't say that. Whoever's responsible will answer to the law, not to you, understood?"

He felt a muscle work in his jaw. All very well for her to say. She didn't have to deal with his loss, or worse, the chance that it might not have been an accident. Then he saw anger sparking in her gaze and knew it was on his account. He took a deep breath. "Understood."

"We will catch whoever's responsible," she vowed.

It had to be enough for now.

Tempted to reclaim his corner of her desk, he settled for spinning a gilt-framed chair around beside it, straddling the velvet-covered seat and resting his arms along the back. "What's Alain Pascale's connection with the birth?"

She tilted her chair back but kept her feet on the floor. "Only an indirect one. When the baby was born he was one of two nominees for the job of royal physician. He was supposed to attend Princess Aimee, but was in the middle of a life-and-death operation when the baby came prematurely. The baby was delivered by Pascale's rival."

After chasing phantoms on the computer all morning, Garth knew the name. "Dr. Armand Junot, the alcoholic who all but drank himself to death a year ago." Nothing accidental about that.

She snagged a paper clip and began straightening it out with great concentration. "In those days he was more of a problem drinker. He didn't become a full-blown alcoholic until after Alain Pascale had him dismissed for incompetence."

"In the process, getting the job Junot wanted," Garth concluded. "Didn't it strike anyone that Pascale may have been biased?"

"You don't know Alain Pascale. He'd turn himself in if he had good reason."

"You're saying he couldn't be involved in stealing a royal child and pretending it had died?"

"His disappearance might look suspicious, but it's so out of character as to be virtually impossible. He's delivered almost every royal baby including Lorne, and appointed himself as their conscience into the bargain. The prince wouldn't let him dictate to him unless he had unshakable faith in his morality. Right now I'm more worried that the doctor is the only lead to what really happened when Louis was born."

Garth stood up. "Then we'd better find Pascale and his wife before they become the next accident statistic."

Chapter 6

"We?" Serena echoed. She let her look play over him, not wanting to admit even to herself that it wasn't exactly a hardship. He'd taken Lorne's invitation literally, outfitting himself from the supply of clothes the prince kept at the summer palace. Also the prince's subtle and very expensive private blend of aftershave lotion, if her keen sense of smell wasn't mistaken.

The transformation was astonishing. From one-step-up-from-the-streets scruffy, Garth now looked...*regal* was the only word springing to her mind.

In place of his low-slung, faded denims, his legs looked longer than usual in tailored black pants. He'd teamed them with a deceptively plain open-necked white shirt. Judging from the way the fine material hugged his wide shoulders and skimmed his body everywhere else it touched, the shirt alone was worth the equivalent of a week or more of her salary.

She would bet he'd never worn so much money on his back in his entire life, yet he did it with as much ease and style as any of the de Marigny princes. Except that she had never seen them wearing designer stubble or scuffed boots. The combination was lethally attractive.

"There's no 'we' involved," she stated. She coughed to clear her throat. "I'll find the Pascales through the proper channels. You're staying right here."

"Driving a computer and hunting for more useless information?"

"It's hardly useless. If you hadn't stuck with the research, we wouldn't have found out so quickly that everyone connected with the birth of the royal baby has died one way or another."

"A good research assistant could have given you the same information."

"Be glad you're a good research assistant. 'They also serve' etcetera, etcetera."

"If you think I'm going to stand and wait while you go after the Hand, you're in for a rude awakening," he stated.

She'd had one the day she set eyes on him as a grown man, but she didn't tell him so. The royal villa was a big place but he managed to reduce it to a cottage for two. Every time she turned around he was there, crowding her personal space. Heaven help her if he knew he turned her on without even trying.

"This isn't between you and the Hand," she insisted.

"You said yourself there's a good chance he had my folks killed for his own ends."

"I also said the law will take care of him."

He planted his hands on his hips, his confronting stance challenging not just her authority, but her femaleness with his maleness. "You have to catch him first."

She swallowed hard. "How will having you underfoot make that easier? I'd have to watch your back as well as my own."

"I can watch my own back."

She didn't doubt he could, but shook her head. "My orders from Prince Lorne don't include putting you in harm's way."

"Or yourself."

"It's my job. I've been doing it for a long time."

Garth found he didn't like the idea one bit. "All the same, your choices are between taking me with you or handcuffing me to my bed here."

"Now that's an idea."

She would do it, too, Garth thought as he saw her jaw firm. With effort he steered his imagination away from the provocative fantasy of him cuffed to the bed and her leaning across him. "What do you have in mind?"

"Matt Hayes is checking the Pascales' movements on the off chance the doctor went against character and changed his plans. If not—"

She broke off as her phone beeped. "Cordeaux. Oh, hi, Matt, that was fast. What did you get?"

Garth forced himself not to shift impatiently as she talked to her former partner. She didn't know it yet, but he was sticking to her like glue from now on. He no longer cared whether or not he was the heir to the throne. Plenty of time to deal with that when they got the test results back. He had a more immediate agenda. Ever since this started she'd been telling him it wasn't personal. If the Hand was behind his parents' death, it couldn't be anything else.

Frank and Sylvia Remy might not have been ideal parents. They hadn't known how to be. Frank hadn't even known who his own family was. He'd been left on a church doorstep when he was two weeks old. His mother had never been traced.

Sylvia had endured a succession of stepfathers and euphemistic uncles until her mother died when Sylvia was seventeen. Sylvia and Frank had made their own family together, sharing a love of the sea and diving. They'd loved Garth, in their own imperfect way. He'd thought it fitting that they'd died in the ocean together. Now that he knew it probably wasn't an accident, he was filled with violent fury and a determination to get answers.

Serena ended the call and looked pointedly at his clenched fists. "Ease up. I have some news. The Pascales' driver took them to the harbor and put their bags onto the cruise ship. They said they were going for a walk around the waterfront before boarding and told him not to wait. They haven't been seen since.''

''How long ago?''

''Three days. I know, the captain should have told someone they hadn't boarded, but apparently it happens, especially with VIPs. Something comes up and they write off the tickets. Nice if you can afford it.'' She lifted her shoulders. ''Matt said Dr. Pascale drew the driver's attention to a yacht in the harbor, flying a flag he'd never seen before.''

''He noticed one yacht and one flag?''

''Pascale is renowned for noticing details. The driver remembered the name, *Cradle Rock*. Odd name for a boat.''

Garth thought for a minute. ''There's a Cradle Rock on the northern coast of Nuee. It's a well-known diving site. The owners could come from there, or they're keen divers. People name their boats all sorts of things. My folks called theirs *Onalos*.''

''Meaning?''

''It's their home port, Solano, spelled backward. They thought it was hugely clever and original.''

''It is to me. I didn't think of that, but I was never good at word puzzles or cryptic crosswords.'' She touched his arm. Under her fingers his muscles felt rock hard. ''Trust me, Garth. Whoever killed them will be brought to justice.''

He nodded tautly. ''I may have seen the *Cradle Rock* near my folks' boat a short time before the explosion. There were a lot of yachts in the area, and I would have assumed it was taking part in a race.''

''Maybe it was.''

''And maybe it wasn't.'' He balled his hands into fists again, his arms like steel rods at his sides. ''I was working on my boat in dry dock when I heard the explosion. I had to borrow a friend's dinghy to get out to the *Onalos*. I'm certain the *Cradle Rock* was one of the yachts in the area.''

''You saw nothing to tie them to the destruction?''

''I was too worried about my parents to think of looking. By the time I reached them, their boat had sunk without trace.

I dived after them but it was too late.'' His voice wavered. ''They didn't stand a chance.''

''The police would have interviewed everyone in the vicinity.''

He nodded. ''They must have covered their tracks well. Did your friend Matt tell you where the *Cradle Rock* is now?''

She shook her head. ''No, but if there is a connection, I think I know where to start looking.''

Allora Harbor was better known for its beautiful Saphir Beach than as a boating paradise. The harbor itself was too hazardous and the currents too unpredictable for shipping, although a safe channel had been dredged to provide smaller vessels with access to moorings close to shore. A private marina occupied one of the deeper inlets a few miles past the beach but it was badly managed and struggling to survive. When Serena and Garth arrived, only a handful of boats were berthed beside the rickety boardwalks, like the last beads on a broken string.

She'd given up trying to convince Garth to remain at the villa. Short of carrying out her threat and handcuffing him to the bed, there wasn't much more she could do. He wasn't under house arrest, and the only thing he was suspected of was being the country's monarch.

He didn't look like one now, she thought. Aware that his resemblance to Prince Lorne would make him conspicuous, he'd borrowed her eye liner and filled in the stubble on his chin so it looked like a short beard, adding black-rimmed glasses borrowed from one of the footmen. From the villa's storerooms, he'd unearthed a black suit and a priest's white collar from among a collection of costumes left over from a masquerade party.

During police training, she'd learned that the simplest disguises were the most effective. The small changes made Garth look like a different person. A biker who'd taken holy orders, say.

Her floral dress and vinyl purse also came from the costume

collection. She'd added a scarf over her hair and hidden her eyes behind red-framed sunglasses shaped like cats' eyes. Again, simple but effective. They could be a priest and a member of his flock taking a stroll around the marina.

Unfortunately the dress was a little too roomy for her compact frame, and the bodice revealed an expanse of décolleté that was at odds with the matronly style. Stopping to scan the moored boats, she saw Garth fixate on her cleavage. "Much as I appreciate the attention, you're blowing your cover," she murmured.

He gave a toothy smile, the whiteness of his teeth emphasized by the piratical beard. "Not if I'm an Anglican priest and you're my doting wife."

She resisted the urge to slam the purse into his ribs. "I've never doted in my life."

He tucked her arm through his. "I'll happily give you pointers."

"In your dreams." As he pulled her against him, heat washed through her. She couldn't free herself without drawing attention to them. "Do Anglican priests wear dog collars?"

He was unfazed. "I'm from the Church of New Ecumenism."

With her arm through his, their bodies were uncomfortably close. Her nerves jangled. "More like New Eroticism?"

"How do you think my doting wife and I came by our ten children?"

"I knew I should have gone with the handcuffs."

She knew she'd made a mistake when his eyes gleamed. "It might be a novel way to try for eleven."

She tossed her head, the effect somewhat negated by the unflattering scarf. "Some man of the cloth you'd make."

He patted her hand. "Charity, my dear, charity."

She was about to tell him what he could do with his charity when she stilled. "There, at the end of the last boardwalk, it's the *Cradle Rock*."

His arm muscles were corded with tension. He'd spotted it at the same moment. "No wonder Dr. Pascale questioned the flag. It belongs to Mingrelia, a principality in Georgia that was annexed by Russia two hundred years ago.''

She wondered if she looked as stunned as she felt. ''You must come in handy at trivia nights.''

''Flags were a hobby of mine when I was a kid. Every time I came across a new one, I drew it into a scrapbook.''

And remembered them all this time. ''So it's a flag of convenience in the literal sense.''

''Looks like it. I'll find out if anyone's onboard. Wait here.''

Before she could argue that it was her job to check out the boat and he could be walking into danger, he'd left her standing.

He made it look good, she had to admit. By altering his walk and stooping his shoulders a touch, he managed to look like a goofy theologian who was fascinated by the boats. Following him slowly as if sightseeing herself, she saw him reach their target.

The yacht was old but kept in better trim than it looked from a distance, she saw when she got closer. The little she could see of the wheelhouse looked state-of-the-art. But to a casual observer, other than the bizarre flag, there was nothing remarkable. It could have been the plaything of any reasonably well-to-do vintage-yacht enthusiast.

A fit-looking Polynesian man appeared on the deck and she ducked into the shadow of another boat. She judged the man to be about six-two, weighing two hundred pounds of solid muscle.

As if he wasn't outweighed by forty pounds, Garth continued his bumbling way forward then touched a finger to a nonexistent hat. ''Good morning. Lovely day, isn't it?''

''This is a private marina…ah, father.''

''So I see. I'm a big fan of vintage yachts. General Douglas MacArthur used one just like this on his tours of the South Pacific war zone. It couldn't be the same vessel, could it?''

''No chance.'' She suspected the answer would have been the same no matter what Garth had asked.

''Looks the same,'' he went on as if talking to himself.

"Sixty-six feet overall. Copper-sheathed New Zealand Kauri over spotted gum ribs. Built about 1938. You don't mind if I take a closer look?"

Before the nonplussed brute could open his mouth to object, Garth had swung himself onto the deck. She braced herself for an almighty splash as the brute threw him overboard. But he was buying it. He was fuming with frustration, but he was letting the daffy priest putter around the deck admiring bollards and davits, or whatever the shiny bits on yachts were called.

She had to admire Garth's chutzpah. She would have crept around noting whatever was to be noted, but wouldn't have gone onboard without a warrant. There was something to be said for bad-boy tendencies. And even dressed in priestly garb, Garth still looked like a bad boy.

The brute had positioned himself in front of the wheelhouse, confining Garth to the open deck aft. When Garth tried to move past him, the man reacted in a blur of movement. She heard a sound of something falling and a grunt of pain.

Heart racing, she peered out, expecting to find Garth flat on his back. Braced to spring to his rescue, she heard him say, "I asked you a question. Where's the captain of this vessel?"

"You're no priest," the brute said, sounding winded. She could only see his upturned feet sticking out of the wheelhouse.

Garth's back was to her as he loomed over his victim. "I can give you proof, such as the last rites."

"Who the devil are you?"

"Right now, your worst nightmare."

She winced. He really had been watching too much television. She got ready to intervene before he broke any more laws but froze, ice slithering down her spine, as he said, "If you want that American base stopped, you'll tell me where to find your skipper."

Whose side was he on?

"I don't know what you're talking about."

There was another grunt as of boot connecting with kidneys. She really had to stop this. She began to move, then checked herself. She was legally bound to identify herself and if the brute was armed, her arrival might give him an opportunity to shoot.

A phantom ache in her right shoulder had her massaging it. She'd been shot just once as a cop, and the bullet had only grazed the fleshy part. But it was enough to remind her that it wasn't an experience she was anxious to repeat. Nor was she prepared to risk Garth. She stayed where she was and listened.

"Okay, have it your way," the brute capitulated. "Just tell me who you are first. It's more than my life's worth."

"I'm a member of Carramer First. My code name is First Prime," Garth said in a low voice. "I report directly to the Hand."

"You're lying. Nobody does that except—" Catching himself, the brute struggled warily to his feet as if expecting Garth to knock him down again. When he didn't, the man straightened slowly, a hand clamped against his side, his breathing shallow. "If you're really First Prime, why didn't you say so instead of barging on board as if you were the law?"

"Belonging to Carramer First isn't illegal," Garth said. "Why would you be scared of the law?"

"I'm not," the man blustered. A lie if ever Serena heard one. "Since they announced the American president is coming, the cops have been harassing the group every chance they get."

"Then it's time we gave them good reason. When is the skipper due back?"

"Not until tonight. How did you find out about this boat?"

Garth took a step toward the brute who backed up before he could stop himself. "Tell the skipper I'll be here at ten."

She fought against anger. For the sake of Dr. Pascale and his wife, Garth was arranging to walk into what could be a deadly trap. He'd be great at playing good-cop, bad-cop, as long as he got to play the bad cop, she thought. Too bad she wasn't about to let him go through with it.

He almost walked past her hiding place, swearing as she grabbed his arm and yanked him into the shadows. His hard body collided with hers. She was glad he couldn't see the flush that leaped to her skin. "What the hell do you think you're playing at?" she hissed, as angry with herself as with him.

He glanced over his shoulder but the brute had retreated to the safety of the wheelhouse. "Getting information," he said calmly.

"We have proper procedures for that, not to mention a law against inflicting grievous bodily harm," she snapped, strongly tempted to inflict some of her own.

He clamped his wrists together and held them out. "Cuff me, Officer. And yourself as an accessory, since you didn't stop me."

"I didn't want to distract you, and give Tiny Tim the chance to pull a weapon."

He gave a wolfish smile, his teeth gleaming in the shadows. "Worried about me, Serena?"

She batted his hands down. "Only about the Pascales, and my job if I let anything happen to you."

"Does sexual frustration count?"

"Yours or mine?"

She hadn't meant to blurt it out, regretting it when his interest sharpened. "We'll talk about this later, strictly in the interests of keeping your job," he said, his voice rich with a promise she didn't even want to think about. "Right now we'd better get out of here."

They wouldn't talk about it ever, if she had anything to say about it. She had only mentioned her job as a distraction. Her main concerns were protecting Garth and finding the Pascales. The doctor and his wife had been guests at a police benefit and had charmed everyone there. She didn't like to think what might be happening to them now. Or to Garth if he insisted on investigating on his own.

Using the boats for cover they started back. Serena's shoulder blades prickled, as if anticipating the slam of a bullet between them at any minute. But when she checked on *Cradle Rock,* she saw no one on deck, and the boardwalk between them was clear.

As soon as they were safely in her car, Garth peeled off the white clerical collar and thrust it into his pocket. Clad all in black, he looked like a riverboat gambler from the Old West. Tall, dark and dangerous.

Which reminded her.

"You told Tiny Tim your Carramer First code name was First Prime."

He watched her steadily. "So?"

"First Prime means you were more than a rank-and-file member."

"I was."

She sucked in a breath. "You made it sound to me as if your membership was a youthful indiscretion."

"I didn't say I wasn't good at it."

"How high did you climb in the group hierarchy?"

He hesitated. She hoped he wouldn't insult her with a lie. "If the Hand hadn't appeared on the scene, I'd probably be running the show," he admitted.

Her breath rushed out in a whoosh. "Some youthful indiscretion."

He stretched his arm along the back of the seat, making the small hairs stand up on her nape even though he didn't touch her. "I don't make commitments lightly, Serena. I was dedicated to ending the de Marigny hold on Carramer. If Prince Eduard hadn't saved my life, I might still be working toward that goal."

"How do I know you aren't?"

She'd hurt him, she saw when his gaze clouded. "I could have told Tiny Tim you were there."

But he hadn't. She wanted to believe it was because they were in this together, but she couldn't be sure. Because of his parents, he had a personal matter to settle with the captain of the yacht, and having to explain Serena's involvement would only complicate his mission.

She couldn't hide her doubts. "I want to find the Pascales alive as much as you do," he said softly. "I know how it looks, but I'm not a traitor to the crown. If I turn out to be the true ruler of Carramer, I'll swear fealty to the people of this country and mean it with everything in me.''

''And if the DNA test proves you're not?''

''Prince Lorne will have my total loyalty. I made that commitment after his father saved my life, and I haven't reneged on it.''

''I believe you.'' She was probably crazy but she did.

He slumped a little, enough to tell her that her faith in him mattered. She knew how he felt. Hearing him talk to the brute aboard the yacht as if they were kindred spirits had shaken her. She wanted to believe in him. She only hoped she wasn't letting her personal feelings get in the way of her professional judgment.

It had never been an issue before. The men she'd dated had either been cops or in related professions like the assistant district attorney, and they'd all understood there were parts of herself she couldn't share. Garth was different. She had a feeling he wouldn't permit any barriers between him and the woman in his life. All or nothing could be his motto.

Serena felt frightened suddenly. She'd had that kind of closeness once before, when her parents had molded her into an extension of themselves. For a long time she hadn't known where she ended and they began. Garth had goaded her to set boundaries, and she'd guarded them jealously ever since. Now he was the one chipping away at them and he didn't even know it. Or care.

''I'm coming with you tonight,'' she stated.

''This is between me and the skipper of that boat.''

''We've already discussed this. It's between the captain and the law.''

He pivoted to face her. ''This isn't only about revenge for my parents' deaths. You saw Tiny Tim's reaction when I mentioned the American base. There's more going on here than rocking the monarchy's foundations. The Pascales were taken away aboard that yacht as part of a more sinister plan. I'd stake my life on it.''

"It may come to that. Garth, you're not doing this by your-self."

"I'm the only one who can. I may not be active in Carramer First anymore but they still think I'm loyal to them. You did."

"Low blow. The way you talked onboard the yacht—"

"Is the way I'll keep on talking until we find out where they're holding the Pascales before they become the next sta-tistic. You said you believe me, well trust me. Letting the skipper of that boat think I'm still one of them is the only way we'll find out what the Hand plans to do in time to stop him."

"I can't let you."

"Because it's your job." He sounded savage.

"No," she said, finally abandoning all pretense of imparti-ality.

He looked thunderstruck, and she couldn't tell if it was good or bad. "You do care about me," he said.

Chapter 7

"I didn't say that."

"You don't have to. I can see it in your eyes." He shifted uncomfortably. "Don't you know by now that I'm the last person you should get involved with?"

What had he said to Tiny Tim? I'm your worst nightmare? Suddenly it struck her as more than a line of tacky dialogue. "It doesn't change anything," she said.

"Well it should."

She met him glare for glare. "Are you saying you don't feel anything for me?"

He let the silence lengthen. She'd decided he wasn't going to answer when his arm dropped around her shoulder and he pulled her against him.

It had been too long.

The thought spun through her mind, as terrifying as it was exhilarating. She hated feeling like a teenager again in his arms, but she didn't stiffen or pull away. Either would have told him he was right about her. And she was getting infernally tired of him being right.

His hand was warm on the side of her face, his fingers tangling in her hair. Goose bumps shivered down her nape.

She had some crazy notion of getting this out of her system, but the moment his lips skimmed hers she knew it couldn't be that simple. Nothing to do with Garth was simple. Especially not a kiss.

He took his time, shaping his mouth to hers until she felt light-headed. As his tongue danced with hers, heat swirled through her, fiery as desire, sweet as revenge. Shooting stars ignited in her brain. She kissed him back with thirteen years' worth of stored-up need.

There had never been anyone like Garth, she thought in the fragment of her mind that remained clear. He was everything she shouldn't want in a man, and everything she did. She freed a hand to slide it around his back. The compact car didn't let them get nearly close enough, and if they went back to the villa they'd be surrounded by people. Now was all they had.

What was she thinking? She didn't want to be alone with Garth. All she wanted was to kiss him and assure herself she'd long outgrown whatever she'd felt for him once.

It wasn't working.

Needs and fears tore at her, and she put them all into the crush of mouth to mouth. His stubble rasped against her skin, the alien texture exciting. She breathed in the mingled scents of costly French aftershave lotion and Garth's seductive brand of masculinity.

There was more here than desire. His hold on her delivered something novel—a feeling of security, of having someone on her side against the world. More than passion, it spoke of giving and taking. She'd been giving for so long, her whole life. First to her family, then to the people she'd sworn to protect and now to the royal family. She'd almost forgotten what it felt like to take something she wanted for herself.

She took it now, opening to him in a way she distantly recognized as dangerous, but unwilling—unable?—to stop.

The gearshift stabbed into his thigh and he swore softly.

"We have to find somewhere. I want you, Serena, in every sense."

The part of her that was still sane planted both palms against his chest and pushed. "We can't think of ourselves. Lives are at stake." She tried for a level tone, but her voice shook.

"There's nothing more we can do until we talk to the skipper." He gave her room but the rapid rise and fall of his chest was a dead giveaway. "What did you think would happen if we kissed? I'd turn into a frog?"

She turned her head away, glad they were parked in shadow. "If there was any justice, you would."

"You like justice, don't you? Everything neat and tidy in a package with a bow on top."

She kept her gaze averted. "It's what I do. What I am."

"Look at me, Serena. Damn it, don't turn away from me. I can't stand it."

Slowly she turned, welcoming the fury that blazed through her, although she knew it was directed as much at herself as him. Still she couldn't hold the words back. "You can't stand it? This is all about you, isn't it? It was the last time we kissed, and nothing's changed."

He passed a hand across his chin. "Everything has changed except how you make me feel. I'm not the hormone-driven teenager I was then. To a boy that age, the woman's feelings barely exist. All you think about is how far you can go before she stops you. How wondrous her skin feels to your inexpert touch, how much softer and silkier it is than your own. How her breasts mold themselves to your hands."

"Stop it," she snapped, because she could feel it all as he talked. "You were right the first time. This isn't going to work."

He used a tissue to dab at the makeup the kiss had transferred to her chin, the touch intimate enough to make her catch her breath anew.

"It was working brilliantly until you started thinking," he said.

"I should never have stopped."

"Thinking or kissing?"

She swatted him on the shoulder. "You puzzle it out. We have to get back to the villa. We have a lot to do before tonight."

Work was also on Garth's mind, but it didn't alter the effect of Serena's kiss. He'd meant it when he said she shouldn't get involved with him. She had her life and career all mapped out and the talent to achieve whatever goal she set for herself.

She didn't need a known black sheep like him holding her back.

It didn't take a genius to work out that she'd put marriage and family on hold to roar up the ranks of the R.P.D. According to talk around the royal villa, she was being considered to head up the Solano division, a plum appointment. Handling security for the visit of the American president would probably have clinched it for her.

Now Prince Lorne had assigned the high-profile job to someone else while Serena baby-sat Garth. Until they had the results of the DNA test there wasn't much he could do to make it up to her, but he didn't have to add to her problems.

He wasn't being entirely truthful when he said he'd stopped thinking with his hormones when he left his teens. It would take the priest he was disguised as to claim that with any sincerity. The difference was he could control them now, and he would, for Serena's sake.

He leaned across her and tucked the gaping bodice of the borrowed dress a little tighter into place, reducing the amount of cleavage on show. Controlling himself was easier when she didn't tantalize him quite so much.

She couldn't help it, he thought. She must have looked sensational in uniform.

It was nearly midnight and the moon was lost in cloud. "Being First Prime of the group has its uses," Garth said as he slid into the car seat beside Serena moments after he finished speaking with the skipper. All she could see of him was the white gleam of teeth and clerical collar.

She'd shadowed him as he kept his appointment with the skipper of the yacht, waiting gun in hand for something to go wrong. Now it hadn't, she could start breathing again. "Didn't they check your current status?"

"As far as they would be able to find out, that is my current status. I let them think the First Prime has been lying low on the orders of the Hand. And before you ask if I have, you already know the answer."

"What did you learn about the Pascales?" she asked instead.

"I acted as if I already knew where they were and wanted transportation to get there. As I hoped he would, the skipper argued that his job was to snatch them from the cruise and take them to Black Cat Cay, not to run a ferry service for them."

"Black Cat Cay?"

"It's a small coral island in the Carramer Strait between Celeste and Isle des Anges. I've dived on a couple of wrecks not far from it. The only habitation is a ranger's hut used by bird-watchers."

"And the Pascales."

She started to drive off but Garth stopped her. "You should keep that yacht under surveillance."

She'd already called it in to Matt. "Any particular reason?"

"The Hand uses it when he needs to come to Carramer."

"Do you think the skipper is the Hand?" She couldn't believe it was the crewman she'd dubbed Tiny Tim.

Garth shook his head violently. "When I mention the Hand, the skipper's manner reminds me of the chauffeurs at Solano Castle."

"If the yacht is the Hand's limo, it makes sense. I've always believed he lives offshore somewhere. He'd need a way to get to Carramer to do his dirty work."

"What better than a yacht with an untraceable registration?"

She gave him a look of reluctant admiration. "You know, you wouldn't make a half-bad cop."

He yanked the clerical collar off and took a tissue from her supply to scrub at his beard. "It's an improvement on Father Remy."

Imagining him as a cop was hard enough. He was too much of a rule breaker. But a priest was beyond her, especially the celibacy part.

"If it makes you feel better, I already asked Matt to put the yacht under surveillance. As soon as I tell him about Black Cat Cay…"

Garth's hand closed around her wrist. "From the way the skipper and Tiny Tim were talking, the Pascales will be dead long before the cops can get to them."

"You have a better idea?"

"We borrow a helicopter from the villa and fly down to Valmont tomorrow. A friend of mine keeps a boat moored at Perla. If we go to the island under cover of darkness, we can snatch the Pascales and get out before anyone knows we're there."

She regarded him suspiciously. In Carramer there wasn't much demand for covert operations, but as a navy diver he could have undertaken the necessary training. Suddenly the parts of his navy record she hadn't been able to access made sense. "You were a DARE, weren't you?"

The letters stood for Dive and Retrieval Expert, one of the most highly skilled operatives in the Carramer Royal Navy. His grin gleamed whitely in the darkness. "I could tell you, but then I'd have to kill you."

So the answer was yes. Knowing he would have risked his life in situations he couldn't even discuss made her blood run cold, but their work was not hugely different. His element was the sea, hers the land. The only reason she felt fearful had to be on his account.

He was right, she was starting to care and she couldn't afford to. "I'll have to clear it with the castle first," she said.

He looked as if he was about to object, then clamped his

mouth shut. More than anything else, that told her he hadn't entirely abandoned the discipline of the service. Everything was starting to fall into place: his skill at disguising himself, his eagerness to go aboard the yacht and the easy way he'd won the confrontation with Tiny Tim. "How long were you part of the DAREs?" There was another long pause, and she sighed into it. "I know, you could tell me…"

"…but I'd have to kill you, and that would be a crying shame," he finished.

Heat zinged through her. She resisted it. "Who writes your lines? You can't possibly talk like that, even in the DAREs."

"We don't waste time talking. We prefer action."

She didn't ask what kind. The promise was in his tone. When this was over, she thought, then drove that thought away, as well. When this was over he would either be the monarch of Carramer, or she'd be back at Solano protecting the present one. Neither option allowed room for a personal relationship.

The only reason she was so attracted to Garth was that they shared some ancient history, not because of anything current.

Nothing she would allow, anyway.

When she contacted Prince Lorne by phone he was uncomfortable with her proposal to stage a rescue attempt. But he was also furious that the man he thought of as a father substitute had been kidnapped, despite the palace's security measures.

Worry fringed the prince's voice. "Maybe after this he'll let me assign him a bodyguard."

"Dr. Pascale's driver is R.P.D. trained, sir."

"And what does the fool man do? Dismiss the driver so he can take a walk. If I did anything like that, Alain Pascale would have my head."

The rapport between the monarch and the doctor who'd delivered him was legendary. She heard traces of it in the prince's tone now. The doctor was also known for speaking his mind regardless of titles or status. She could easily imagine

Pascale lecturing the prince on security, while disregarding his own. "I don't think he or his wife have been harmed yet," she said, hoping it was true.

"What the devil could Carramer First want with the royal physician?"

"They may think he knows the whereabouts of the package, sir."

"He can't tell them about something he doesn't know exists."

"I'm counting on him not revealing that, Your Highness." She didn't have to add that it would keep the Pascales alive a lot longer.

The prince heard it, anyway. "I still don't like the idea of risking Garth."

"You do know he was with the navy DAREs?" The information wasn't on the public record but Prince Lorne would have his own resources. She tried not to feel affronted that he hadn't seen fit to share the information with her.

"He told you that?"

She couldn't restrain a smile at the prince's obvious surprise. "Hardly, sir. Let's say he demonstrated it."

"I don't think you'd better tell me in what way."

"The main thing is, he knows what he's doing." She took a deep breath. "Frankly sir, I don't think I have a prayer of persuading him to remain behind."

The prince chuckled cynically. "From what I'm told, he isn't known for his blind obedience."

Her heart leaped. "You've learned something about his navy record?"

"Enough to seriously doubt that his dismissal was justified."

She'd suspected it all along, telling herself it was because of her own attraction to Garth. "That's good news, sir."

He didn't ask why it should be so to her, and she wondered if Lorne suspected there was more between her and Garth than duty.

"Indeed," he said. "However I'd prefer you to keep my observation to yourself until I receive a full report."

She kept the disappointment out of her voice. "Of course, Your Highness."

She looked up as Garth came into the reception room. Instead of going to his own desk, he perched on the corner of hers in what was becoming an annoying habit.

He'd changed out of the black clerical suit into a chocolate-colored silk robe. He looked so sinfully attractive that her concentration wavered.

She pulled it back with an effort. "Do we have your authority to go to Black Cat Cay?" she asked Prince Lorne.

"You're sure there isn't time for the police to set something up?"

"I'll notify them as backup, but I don't think we should wait."

She could practically hear the wheels turning in the monarch's brain, as he evaluated the risk to Dr. Pascale and his wife and reached the same conclusion she had. "Do it," he said, his tone banishing any hint of indecisiveness. Another pause, then, "Get Alain and Helen out of there in one piece. Keep me informed."

"I will, sir," she said and replaced the receiver.

Garth folded his arms. "I take it we're good to go?"

She couldn't resist it. "I'm good to go."

Muttering an oath, he reached for the phone, but she put her hand on top of his. The heat radiating from him almost made her pull away. "No need to call the palace. Lorne's instructions include you."

He slid off the desk, impatience in every line of his body. "This may come as a surprise to you, but it wouldn't make any difference."

"That's what I told Prince Lorne."

Garth looked annoyed at being read so accurately, then eased into a relaxed pose that didn't fool her for a minute. "His response?"

"He wants his friends back in one piece."

"Then we agree on our objective."

She caught his arm. "Why do you care enough to risk your neck? It's my job, but the navy kicked you out. By all rights you should be Carramer First's biggest fan."

He looked at her hand on his arm. "The doctor and his wife are innocent victims. I don't like injustice in any form."

She wished she could tell him what Prince Lorne had told her about the investigation into Garth's dismissal from the navy, then realized it also wouldn't make any difference. As long as Garth knew he wasn't at fault, it would be enough for him. He didn't need her validation any more than he needed Prince Lorne's. Slowly she let her hand slide to her side.

"Then we'd better get some rest. We won't be able to approach Black Cat Cay until after dark, so we can finalize our plans tomorrow."

She disliked inactivity almost as much as Garth hated injustice, but she saw the sense in being well-rested before setting off on their mission. Whatever they had to deal with on Black Cat Cay would be easier if they were fresh and alert.

Rest didn't come easily, and she wondered if Garth had fared much better by the time they met for breakfast. Six hours of sleep, most of it fitful, had left her feeling worse than when she went to bed.

"One thing I'll say for royalty, the coffee is excellent," Garth observed when she joined him. His new-minted appearance banished any suggestion of a bad night. In front of him was a plate piled with sausages, eggs and at least three pieces of toast.

She poured herself a cup of coffee from a silver carafe, breathing in the fragrant steam before taking her first sip. "Wonderful," she murmured, feeling the liquid spread warm tentacles through her. She looked around. She must be getting used to having servants wait on her, when she noticed them only in their absence. "Where is everybody?"

"I told them we'd serve ourselves. I'm getting tired of being fussed over."

Delicious aromas were coming from silver covers ranged along a buffet. She lifted the first one to reveal fluffy omelets laced with herbs. Replacing the cover, she worked her way along the row until she came to grilled tomatoes and field mushrooms glistening with butter. She began to fill a plate.

She topped the food with a croissant and sat down opposite him. "If the DNA test comes back positive, you won't have a choice," she pointed out.

"There's always a choice. I could abolish the monarchy."

"You wouldn't."

"No, I wouldn't. Like it or not, the institution has served the country well. I just don't plan on living in an institution."

She lowered her fork. "If you turn out to be the true heir, you're going to step aside in favor of Prince Lorne."

He nodded. "So fast your head will spin."

She wondered if Lorne had guessed. "Carramer First isn't going to like that."

He steered toast around his plate, mopping up egg yolk. When he looked up, she saw the flash of anger in his gaze before he blanked it. "Their agenda isn't going to dictate how I live my life."

"You hate this, don't you?"

He glanced around the morning room. Sunlight streamed through the leadlight windows, gleaming off the antique furnishings, oil paintings and crested silverware. "As a luxury vacation it has its moments, but I won't have any regrets about returning to my own life."

"It's your life I'm talking about. How do you deal with finding out that everything you believed about yourself could be a lie?"

"The same way you deal with anything, one day at a time. Not that I expect you to understand. You've always been a planner, a goal setter."

His matter-of-fact tone did little to soften the criticism she heard. "Is there something wrong with that?"

He shrugged. "It works for a time. Then something like this happens and plans go right out the window."

"If you don't have goals, what do you work toward? What do you hope for?"

"To stay alive and healthy." He pushed his plate away. "What do you want me to say? That I dream of a house with a picket fence, an adoring wife and one point five kids?"

"You don't dream of those things any more than I do." To her ears, the words didn't carry as much conviction as they should have.

"It helps if you have the right role models."

It was the first time he'd come close to admitting that his family life had left a lot to be desired. "Mine weren't much better," she said. The best she could say about her parents was that they had stayed together through thick and thin. Her mother often joked that they were the only two people who'd put up with them.

"They loved you."

She stared at him in amazement. "They exploited me, you said it yourself."

"They didn't see it that way."

"How the devil can you know that?"

"I saw you together when they came to the school. They could hardly take their eyes off you. They wanted the whole world to appreciate your beauty and your talents."

Choked because she didn't want to think of them in that light, she turned away. "We should talk about the mission."

"We did that last night. Oh, I get it. It's okay to analyze me, but you don't like the tables being turned. No wonder there's no one close in your life."

"My career keeps me too busy," she stated, annoyed at the defensiveness she couldn't keep out of her voice. She'd had her share of affairs. So what, if none of them had lasted? She liked her life the way it was. She didn't want the picket fences and children any more than Garth did. Too much risk of turning into a clone of her mother, depending on her children to fulfill her fantasies. He might think her parents had pushed her into modeling out of love for her, but she knew differently.

"No biological clock ticking away?"

She shifted uncomfortably. Whenever she baby-sat for her former partner and his wife, she felt *something,* but she wasn't about to admit it to him. "When this is over I might get a puppy."

He rolled his eyes. "I suppose you want a fluffy white thing small enough so you can carry it around?"

"It's more than you're prepared to let into your life."

"I had a dog once," he said unexpectedly.

"Let me guess, a Rottweiler."

"Close. A mixed breed big enough to plant both paws on my shoulders when he stood up."

"What happened to him?"

"When I joined the navy, I gave him to the friend who's lending us the boat."

"Do you visit?"

He shook his head. "What would be the point? I'd only confuse his loyalties."

And he talked about *her* dodging commitment. Maybe they *should* get something going. At least they wouldn't expect it to last till death did them part.

The forced closeness must be affecting her thinking, she decided, aware of a warmth rampaging through her that had nothing to do with the coffee. If she hadn't been thrust into this situation with Garth, he would be the last man she'd imagine having any kind of relationship with.

She wasn't that much of a masochist.

The reality check didn't stop her imagination from running riot. She already knew his kiss tasted of pure seduction. It wasn't a big leap to imagine what would come after. Pure arousal ripped through her, soul deep and powerful, hammering at the boundaries she'd constructed so carefully around herself. She wasn't sure if she wanted to laugh, scream or wrap her arms around him so tightly he'd never let her go.

She'd never felt this way about any man and didn't want to now. The problem was, she had no idea what to do about it.

It was going to be a long day. And that was before taking the mission ahead of them into account.

Chapter 8

As Garth pushed the door of his friend's house open, a blur of movement had Serena dropping into a defensive crouch until her brain caught up with her reflexes. "Good grief, is that a dog?"

The creature standing on its back legs with both massive front paws planted on Garth's chest looked more like a jet-propelled carpet than an animal. Its coat was the shaggy gray of an Irish wolfhound with a body that was part setter and part lion, and quite possibly larger than either.

Garth ruffled the thick fur around the ears, and the animal growled in delight. At least she hoped it was delight. Then he set the animal back on its haunches. "Serena, meet Gusto." A shaggy paw was extended. "Go ahead, shake hands."

"You're sure he won't take it off at the wrist?" The dog looked more than capable.

"I'm sure."

She let the dog sniff her hand first, then took the huge paw and shook it. "Hi, Gusto. Pleased to meet you, I think."

"His name is really Cousteau, after the marine biologist

who invented scuba gear, but Brett started calling him Gusto and he seems to like it.''

"Judging by the welcome, it suits him better. Is this Brett's house?"

Garth nodded. "His dog, too."

So he was the friend who had taken custody of Gusto when Garth joined the navy. Seeing the dog glued to Garth's side, she wasn't sure that Gusto had entirely transferred his allegiance, no matter how many years had passed. The sight of such devotion made her uneasy. She had always been too busy to have an animal in her life. Why did it feel like a lack suddenly?

"Where is his nominal master?" she asked.

"Checking on the boat. He told me to use my key."

"You two must be close."

"We did DARE training together."

This was the first time he'd volunteered any information about his friend since they set off from Allora. During the helicopter flight he'd assured her that Brett Curtin was loyal to the crown and would help them in any way he could. None of this was news to her since she'd had Matt run a background check before letting Garth contact his friend. Garth's revelation of his true role in Carramer First had made her wary. She didn't want any more unpleasant surprises.

So she knew that Brett had been invalided out of the navy after an accident, the nature of which wasn't specified. But if they had served together, why had Garth given his friend the dog? Brett would have had the same problem taking care of an animal as Garth himself.

Her first sight of Brett solved the mystery. He was a big man, as tall as Garth but more solid around the chest, with muscular arms that felt as if they could break her in two when he wrapped them around her in greeting. He was obviously no shrinking violet. And he had just as obviously lost one leg below the knee.

Her questioning look swung to Garth but he was playing tug-of-war with the dog. Then it dawned on her. He hadn't wanted to part with Gusto, who had been living happily with his parents. He had wanted to give his injured friend a companion. A lump the size of an orange jumped into her throat. How many more facets of Garth was she going to uncover before this was over?

Garth embraced Brett, almost knocking the crutches out from under his friend. "You should feed your dog better. When we walked in here he tried to eat Serena."

Brett looked at her in concern. "Did he hurt you?"

"Not unless you count being licked to death." The dog's banner tail was liable to do more damage as it battered her. She pushed it aside, and the dog parked himself at her feet, leaning heavily against her side. "Thanks for letting us use your boat. Did Garth tell you what we need it for?"

The test question won her a black look from Garth, but Brett shook his head. "I didn't ask."

Thank goodness for DARE training, she thought, happy to avoid further explanations or worse, lie to Garth's friend about their mission. She had taken a liking to Brett Curtin at first sight, but the fewer people who knew what was going on the better. They had left the helicopter and royal pilot at Perla's private airport. He had no more idea of what his passengers were up to than Brett did.

"Lunch?"

Hearing the magic word, Gusto's tail thumped furiously. She followed Brett into a vast country-style kitchen, seating herself at a wooden table beside Garth while their host pottered around. From the easy way he used the crutches, she assumed his injury had happened some time ago.

As Gusto settled himself on her foot, she looked around with interest. In contrast to the almost sterile neatness of the living room, the kitchen was painted a sunny yellow and cheerfully cluttered with maritime memorabilia and boating magazines. Not hard to discern Brett's passion, she thought.

The rich patina of old timber suggested generations of family use. A set of open French doors led down a ramp to an overgrown garden. Beyond it she could see a jetty jutting out into an arm of the harbor, presumably where Brett's boat was anchored.

He put a plate of doorstep-size sandwiches and a jug of ice water on the table then sat down, propping the crutches beside him. He gave her a long, assessing look. "Your taste is improving, Garth."

To her annoyance she felt color flood her neck and face. She never blushed. But there was something oddly appealing about Brett's backhanded compliment. As if she liked being mistaken for Garth's latest. And considered an improvement.

Refusing to let herself wonder about the women in his life that she might be an improvement on, she bit into a roast beef sandwich. English mustard seared her throat. Seeing her eyes tear, Garth offered her water. "I should have warned you. Brett likes a little meat with his mustard."

As she took the glass, her fingers brushed his. Tension powered through her, the effect of the mustard tame by comparison. Someone should have warned her, she thought. She gulped water. "I'm okay, I like hot things, too." Her look dared Garth to read a single, solitary thing into her statement.

He did, she saw by the flames leaping into his gaze, but to his credit he kept quiet. He had possibilities, she decided. She took a more cautious bite of sandwich and decided the mustard added something. But she kept the ice water handy. When the thick crusts proved too much of a challenge, she slipped them under the table. Gusto didn't seem to mind the mustard.

By the time the sun was an orange ball balancing on the horizon, she and Gusto were best friends. Brett wasn't far behind. She could see why Garth was so fond of the man. He answered her questions without asking any of his own, although he must have been curious.

They were relaxing—or trying to—on a wide planked deck behind his house. Screened by a thick growth of trees, it was totally private except for the section looking toward the harbor. "What else can you tell us about Black Cat Cay?" she asked. They had spent the afternoon going over charts and maps, but that wasn't the same as local knowledge. Garth had dived in the vicinity but without landing on the island.

"It's a long, thin island with two small peaks to the north and a thin spit of land to the east. If you have a good imagination they represent the cat's ears and tail. The black part comes from the thick stands of trees fringing the leeward side."

"And the cay part?"

"Most islands are originally the tops of mountains once attached to the mainland. In prehistory, the land sinks and the sea floods the low parts, cutting off the islands from the new coast. A true coral cay is made from the skeletons of coral polyps built up on the sea bed over millennia," Garth explained. "As time passes, waves, tide and wind break up the coral turning it into boulders, then shingle and finally sand that's piled up by waves and wind until an island forms."

She nodded. "Then the sea birds move in, deposit their droppings and make soil, so wind- and waterborne seed can take root."

Garth's lazy grin acknowledged the accuracy of her conclusion. "Here endeth the lesson."

Brett levered himself to his feet and reached for his crutches. "Is this the part where I go make coffee?"

"Sounds good." As Brett had guessed, she needed to talk to Garth privately, and the caffeine would provide fuel for the job ahead.

"I'll help you bring it out when it's ready," Garth said.

She waited until Brett was inside. "I like your friend."

"He likes you."

He made it sound as if she was one of a select few. "How did he lose the leg?"

"Somebody else's war."

When he didn't elaborate, she let it rest. Carramer had been at peace for a thousand years, but they occasionally lent their military expertise to other countries when the cause was just. Like America's Navy SEALs, the DAREs were highly trained and equipped for peacetime rescue or operational duty.

Garth had been one of them. A shudder gripped her as she imagined him in Brett's place. Brett could even have been injured on the same mission. Slowly she let the air out of her lungs. She needed to concentrate on the here and now. Rescuing Dr. Pascale and his wife was her priority. She would keep Garth well out of it because of who he was or might be. Not because she needed to keep him safe for herself.

She had to believe it.

By the time Brett yelled that the coffee was ready, she had quelled Garth's protests and outlined exactly how she wanted to proceed. If he didn't think that was enough action for him, too bad. This was her show.

He went into the kitchen. Their voices reached her as a low murmur, and she heard laughter. Was Garth talking about her to Brett? What was he saying?

When the two men came out bearing steaming cups and a plate of mango muffins, she had almost convinced herself she didn't care. Almost.

Garth didn't like her plan. If he was truly the heir to the throne, protecting him made sense but he didn't have to like it. Technically she was running this, and he'd been taught to respect the chain of command. Not always follow it, but respect it.

Still, the idea of her going in to get the Pascales while he created a diversion didn't appeal one bit. So he had edited the plan slightly without telling Serena. She was going to be mad as all get-out, but he'd worry about that later.

For now he dressed in silence, putting on Brett's fishing vest, with its tangle of gear, over the bottom half of a wet suit. A floppy hat concealed his features. Serena had changed into a sleek one-piece bathing suit that fitted her like a second skin. He watched her tuck her lovely hair under a swimming cap and felt his throat go dry. She had a shape like a professional swimmer, wide-shouldered and narrow-hipped with legs so long they seemed to go on forever. The navy suit skimmed the outlines of her breasts as if she was naked.

She looked up and caught him watching her. "Never seen a woman in a bathing suit before, Remy?"

"Not this woman."

His husky tone alerted her. "Don't get any ideas."

Too late. He quelled the desire running through him like a flood tide. After this was over—he quelled that thought, too. "I thought you were afraid of sharks."

She gave him a withering look. "You had to bring that up."

So she had thought about them but was determined to see this through, anyway. Who was it said courage was doing what you were afraid to do? She had it in spades. He picked up the fishing gear they'd agreed he would use as his cover. "I'm ready if you are."

"Ready." Her voice was rock steady.

Brett accompanied them down to his private jetty, showing Garth how to use the inboard motor on the old clinker-built lifeboat moored there. Serena eyed the boat dubiously, then Garth saw her run her hand over one of the rust patches staining the hull. Amazing how easily he could read her expression, he thought, watching her note the smoothness and lack of corrosion.

He waited for her to ask why a perfectly good boat was disguised as an ancient hulk, but she simply climbed in and settled low between the seats as they'd agreed, pulling a worn blanket over herself.

To an observer it would look as if Garth was a lone fisherman. When they neared the island, she would slip over the side and swim to shore, while Garth motored to within sight of the ranger's cabin before pretending to fish close to shore, hopefully diverting the attention of whoever was holding the Pascales inside.

Serena wished she felt as calm as her name suggested. Garth hadn't needed to mention the sharks. She already jerked every time the boat bumped against a wave, imagining a torpedo-shaped form passing under the thin aluminum skin, the dorsal fin sandpapering against the hull.

It had reassured her to note that the boat wasn't as rustic as it appeared. Nor did she fear that Brett was involved in anything illegal. Apart from Matt's clean background check, everything about Brett inspired her confidence. The boat was more likely to be a relic from his days as a navy DARE, or maybe he was still active in some way, in spite of his disability. He hadn't asked about her mission. The least she could do was return the favor.

After over an hour of bumping over waves that increased in size as the sun set, she heard Garth say quietly, "Black Cat Cay is in sight. I'm going to approach from the seaward side so you can slip into the water without being seen from the cabin. As we go over the reef it will get rough so hang on."

Rough was an understatement. The imaginary sharks she felt grazing the hull grew into whales. Nausea clogged her throat but she fought it. Now was no time to get sea sick. She slid a waterproof pack onto her back and braced herself to go over the side, knowing it would take every ounce of courage she possessed.

"There are no sharks. There are no sharks," she repeated to herself.

Garth slowed the motor. "Now."

She didn't give herself time for second thoughts. A quick glance oriented her to the direction of the island, then she slipped into the water.

He had taken her in as close as he dared, putting her over the gray beach rock that was neither purely mineral like granite, nor purely animal like coral. It was spiky and treacherously slippery, making her appreciate the rubber-soled shoes she'd donned with her suit. Being in only waist-deep water was also a bonus, and she wondered if he'd taken her fear of sharks into account, saving her the horror of being dropped into deeper water.

The ranger's cabin was on the sheltered side of the cay. She had landed on the windy south side, where the trees were stunted and distorted into fantastic shapes by the prevailing winds. Her heart jerked as a diamond-shaped ray lifted from the rocky bottom, its long tail grazing her leg.

She made an effort to steady her breathing. Garth was doing his part, taking the boat around the island to where a rickety jetty jutted into the sea, making his lone-fisherman act look good. Soon she could see him only in silhouette against the blood orange of the setting sun as he let the boat drift close to the jetty. Anyone watching was bound to get antsy about seeing him there, but that was the idea.

She slogged through the water feeling the level reef rocks gradually give way to sloping sandy beach. Sea cucumbers lay like thick, dark sausages on the bottom. She dodged them and tried not to twist an ankle in the craters in the sand among the dugong grass that provided homes for the crabs that were just starting their nocturnal activities.

More worrying were the stone fish camouflaging themselves by lying completely flat on the sand or in the rubble on the reef flat. There was no way to beware of them, and their poisonous spines could spear through shoes. They did not use their spines to attack, but waited to snap up small fish as they swam past the deceptive "stone." Antivenom was available on the mainland but the painful effects of an encounter were well enough known to make her wary.

She released a breath as she emerged onto dry land, having avoided the ocean's numerous traps. How could Garth take such risks and call it fun? She glanced to where she could see his silhouette as he cast his line close to shore. He would keep up his act until she'd had time to get the Pascales out of the cabin and down to the rendezvous point, she knew.

She saw him reel in a soggy mass of seaweed. As he untangled it, the variety and ingenuity of his curses carrying on the still air made her smile. He was navy all right.

By the time she reached the white sand—not ground-up rock as on the mainland, but composed of minute morsels of pulverized coral, she knew by now—the sun had almost completely set, leaving an orange glow as if a bushfire burned just beyond the horizon.

Her pack contained a waterproof torch, but the glow and her night vision enabled her to pick her way through the casuarina forest fringing the beach. Compared with the sheltered northern side, there was little undergrowth to impede her progress. She soon reached the clearing where the ranger's hut was located.

Male voices and bobbing torches around the front near the jetty suggested their ruse was working. Two guards, if such they were, were discussing what to do about the fisherman who had drifted so close to the island. Was it better to get rid of him, or lie low and hope he left by himself. "If he's stupid enough to land, we can deal with him then," one of them said, freezing Serena's blood. She had a fair idea what they meant by getting rid of him. Their plan hadn't included him setting foot on Black Cat Cay, so she could only hope he stuck to it.

She stole closer to the cabin and peered through the single window. A sack had been draped across the glass but the occupants had evidently pushed it aside to look out, leaving her a clear view inside. There were two rooms linked by an open door. She was looking into the inner room. Through the open door, the light of an oil lamp showed her a table with hands of cards lying facedown on it, and two wooden chairs pushed back.

The inner room was lit only by a sliver of light from the lamp in the other room, revealing two single beds pushed up against the wall at right angles to one another. On one, a woman lay fully clothed with an arm thrown across her eyes. On the other, a man sat with his back against the wall and his arms resting on his knees.

When she tapped on the glass, the man's head came up, and she recognized Dr. Alain Pascale. He came to the window. Through sign language she gestured for him to cover the glass fully with the sacking and stand to one side. As if he did this sort of thing all the time, he complied instantly.

She delved into her pack and retrieved a length of plastic kitchen wrap. She pressed it against the glass and tapped firmly with a rock. The glass, already cracked with age, broke into lethal shards. Most of them came away when she removed the wrap, leaving only a few shards to be picked out and tossed aside until the opening was big enough for the captives to crawl through.

Dr. Pascale had remained silent during the process and, without prompting, tore the sacking loose and draped it over the hole as protection against any remaining slivers. Serena nodded approval and gestured toward the sleeping woman.

The doctor padded to the bed and pressed his hand across his wife's mouth as he shook her awake. She struggled for only a second before realizing they were being rescued. She sat up and seeing Serena framed in the window, gave her a tired smile. Helen Pascale was an Australian nurse who'd met and married Alain when they'd worked at the same hospital forty years before, Serena recalled from their file. A resilient pair, she decided.

"Serena Cordeaux, R.P.D.," she whispered as soon as the doctor and his wife stood beside her outside the cabin.

The doctor gave her a look of recognition. "Thought I'd seen you around the palace. About time you got here."

She ignored the taunt. In royal circles Dr. Pascale was well-known for his sharp tongue. Even the monarch was not immune. "Come with me, we're getting you out of here," she said.

Needing no further urging, the doctor took his wife's hand and plunged into the forest after Serena. The scents of beach hibiscus and wild ginger rose to meet them. It was darker now but their night vision had adjusted, so Serena again decided against using the torch. She was anxious to get her charges to the rendezvous point before their captives missed them.

They had reached the outcropping of rock that supposedly represented the black cat's front paw, when all hell broke loose at the cabin. Shouts of rage told Serena there was no longer any need for stealth.

"Are there only the two guards?" she asked the doctor.

"Yes. Only one is armed. From the look of them they're barely out of their teens. They think this is all a big joke."

"Some joke," she muttered. "Are you both all right?"

"Helen's a little weak from rejecting their atrocious food, but I'm fine," he growled.

"Weak?" the older woman objected. "Who tried to clobber one of them with a chair leg?"

Serena restrained a smile. "Sounds as if you didn't really need me."

"We needed a gun and a boat," Pascale said. "Tell me you brought both."

"Boat yes, and a knife in case things get awkward." It had been up to her to ensure they didn't.

Pascale didn't look impressed. "It'll have to do."

As if on cue, the black shape of a boat loomed closer, and she discerned the outline of a man on board. Garth. Heart pumping, she led the older couple across the sand and onto the beach rock. Water lapped at their feet.

"There they are!" a voice shouted.

The cries and running steps told her they'd been located. She gave Pascale and his wife a shove toward the boat. "Get in. I'll lead them away."

Before anyone could argue she zig-zagged across the beach, ducking low as sand sputtered around her feet from shots fired out of the trees. Semiautomatic, she concluded from the rapid fire. Too late now to wish she had brought a gun, after all.

As she crashed into the forest, bark splintered off a casuarina close to her head. The captors were following, although she wasn't sure anymore if that was good or bad. Right now her main concern was to let the Pascales get safely away, if possible while keeping herself alive into the bargain.

She had reached the hut when a plan formed in her mind. Dashing through the open front door, she grabbed the oil lamp and threw it as hard as she could into the other room, aiming for one of the beds. It shattered against the bedstead and almost instantly, flames licked at the bedding. The room was ablaze in minutes.

She was outside again when she heard a scream of rage. "Bloody hell, our money's in there."

Oblivious to the warning cries from his companion, one of the guards rushed into the burning hut. For a moment she thought he was going to succeed in retrieving their ill-gotten gains, then an almighty crash heralded the hut's inward collapse. The searing heat told her no rescue was possible. She took no pleasure whatever in knowing that she had one less pursuer to worry about.

Enraged by the loss of his companion, the remaining guard charged at her through the forest. She barely had time to register that Garth had brought the boat around to the leeward side, as far out of range as he could, and was calling to her to swim out, when she saw the remaining guard taking aim.

She had no time to think. She took a running dive off the jetty into the water as bullets rained around her, puffing up jets of spray close enough to spatter her face. With terrible timing, the moon had silvered the water, making her an easy target. A chill swept through her. She wasn't going to make it out to the boat.

A fresh fusillade of shots peppered the water around her, and she braced to feel a bullet tearing through her, when suddenly something grabbed her ankle and she was jerked completely under.

Shark.

She couldn't scream without filling her aching lungs with water. Nor could she make out more than a sinister black shape beneath her in the churning maelstrom. She kicked savagely but couldn't shake off the monster holding her under. Terror swept through her, then anger. At least if she'd been shot in the line of duty, she would have died a hero instead of finishing up ingloriously as shark bait.

Crazily, it also came to her that she would never have the chance to find out what Garth would be like as a lover.

Chapter 9

It took Serena a moment to realize that the monster holding her under had an all-too-human shape. Then it released her and kicked upward until they were face-to-face. Through the glass of a mask she recognized Garth's grinning features. He removed his breathing regulator and held it out to her. Thinking of all the painful things she would do to him later, she took the regulator and breathed slowly and steadily, recalling the scuba diving classes she'd forced herself to take.

When her lungs stopped feeling as if they were bursting, she passed the regulator back to him. Taking turns breathing from it, he hooked an arm around her waist, swimming underwater with her until the shape of the boat loomed above them.

He signaled for her to surface on the seaward side, out of sight of the island. The Pascales were huddled together on a bench near the stern, and Brett was steering with the tiller under one arm. "How did you get here?" she sputtered as he hauled her onboard with the other.

"Later. We need to get out of here," he said. As soon as

Garth piled in on top of her, Brett gunned the motor and aimed the boat back in the direction of Perla.

"Won't the gunman follow us?" she asked when she had her breath back. Although she was mad enough to do him serious injury, finding Garth on top of her wasn't entirely unpleasant, she discovered.

"Not after Garth disabled their only boat," Brett assured her.

She aimed a scathing look at both men. "Seems like Garth's been a busy boy."

"You're welcome," he said mildly.

"Okay, you saved my life. But did you have to scare me half to death in the process?"

He shrugged out of his scuba tank then helped her to sit up, keeping an arm around her shoulders. Reaction was fast setting in, and she needed the body heat, she told herself. She could hurt him later. "And as for your friend here…"

Brett gestured to a tarpaulin covering what she'd assumed was fishing equipment. Instead it had concealed the scuba gear and presumably Brett himself. He must have placed the diving gear aboard when he was supposedly checking out the boat earlier, then climbed aboard as soon as she pulled the blanket over herself. Not bad for a man with a disability, she thought. He saw her working it out. "Clever, don't you think?" he asked.

She refused to agree. "You could have gotten yourself killed."

Garth looked unrepentant. "We saved your life instead."

"If you two have finished with the mutual admiration society, maybe somebody can explain what the devil is going on," Dr. Pascale asked, annoyed.

Helen Pascale patted her husband's hand. "It's all right, dear, they're young and in love."

"None of the above," Serena insisted. "It's a long story, but believe me, it has nothing whatever to do with love."

Helen looked unconvinced. "I guess this isn't the time to go into it. I feel rather drained myself."

For a woman Serena knew to be in her sixties, it was the understatement of the year. "You're certainly entitled. Do you have any idea who your two captors were?"

"One called the other Henri, and the other immediately told him to shut up," Helen explained.

"We never learned the second man's name," Dr. Pascale added. "They knew who I was, and made sure we knew they were mixed up with Carramer First, although I have no idea what that group of republican hotheads has to do with us. I only work at the palace."

"I think I can explain as soon as we all get back to Perla and dry off." She glanced at Brett. "Can we impose on your hospitality a little longer?"

"My place is yours," he said with a crooked smile. "I'll even throw in a pot of hot coffee."

"Make mine a decent scotch, preferably a double," the doctor growled. He jerked a thumb at Garth. "While you're at it, you might explain why Sir Galahad here could double for Prince Lorne. For a minute I thought the monarch himself had come to rescue us."

She had wondered how the doctor would react when he recovered enough to note the resemblance. He knew Prince Lorne better than anyone else in the kingdom. At the same time she felt a stab of disappointment. It seemed Pascale wasn't going to provide them with the easy answers she'd unconsciously hoped for.

For two people who'd been through what Dr. Pascale and his wife had, they recovered remarkably quickly. By the time she had reported the success of the mission to Prince Lorne and arranged for the police in Perla to pick up the kidnapper on Black Cat Cay and launch a full investigation, the Pascales had showered and changed into dry clothes borrowed from Brett.

When she joined them in the living room they were cradling glasses of the promised scotch. Since her bathing suit had dried anyway, Serena had settled for wrapping herself in a terry cloth robe she had found in the bathroom. It was also too large and she'd had to roll the sleeves almost to the elbows to free her hands. She saw Garth give her a startled, then warm, look of approval.

Brett was performing barman duty. "There's pizza on the coffee table. Help yourself."

She followed her nose to the open boxes, scenting pepperoni, her favorite. She took a generous slice and bit into it standing at the table. She hadn't realized how hungry she was. Judging by the empty boxes, she wasn't the only one. She took another slice with her to the couch.

Gusto heaved himself up and came over to her, tail thumping. She stroked his massive head, and he settled across her feet as soon as she sat down. She had a suspicion that the pizza crust was the bigger attraction, confirmed when she offered him some. Feeding him was like posting a letter, she thought as a chunk of crust disappeared.

"Drink?" Brett asked.

"No thanks, but I'd kill for a cup of coffee."

Such a trite phrase, she thought, the second it came out of her mouth. Tonight she had killed, or at least created the conditions for a death. Knowing it was the man's own greed that had killed him didn't make her feel any better about it. Nor was she happy about destroying whatever evidence the cabin might have yielded. But it was done now and as a result the Pascales were alive. Serena had been in law enforcement long enough to know when to count her blessings.

A sweater several sizes two big over rolled-up jeans made Helen Pascale look pale and fragile. Serena would bet that a fisherman's flannel shirt and jeans weren't Dr. Pascale's preferred attire, either, but he wore them with the élan of designer apparel. Her admiration for the couple notched higher.

Brett brought her the coffee, and she smiled her thanks. Reaction would probably catch up with the Pascales later. For now she appreciated their steadfastness as she probed for anything they could tell her about their ordeal. Beyond the name Henri, there wasn't much.

Serena decided not to tell them yet that one of the young

men had died in the burning hut. The memory was likely to trouble her sleep for some time to come. No sense burdening them, as well. They'd been through enough.

"You're sure you don't want me to call a doctor," she asked when she noticed Helen's eyelids start to droop.

"Young lady, I am a doctor," Pascale reminded her tersely. "Under the circumstances we were treated reasonably well. There's nothing physically wrong with us that a good night's sleep and some decent food won't fix. That, and catching the people who think this is any way to treat the court physician and his wife."

"The local law agrees with you, Doctor." She turned to Brett. "Can you find a bed for the Pascales?" She had hoped to fly them all back to Allora tonight but could see that Helen Pascale was at the end of her endurance, despite putting on a brave face. Serena decided to notify the helicopter pilot that they wouldn't be returning to the villa until morning.

Brett reached for his crutches. "No problem. Follow me."

The doctor placed a hand on his wife's shoulder. "You go ahead. I want to have a word with our rescuers."

Helen hesitated as if reluctant to let her husband out of her sight. Not hard to understand, given what she'd endured over the past few days. His smile seemed to reassure her. "I'll say good-night then."

Brett also turned back. "Help yourself to whatever you need. I'll see you in the morning. Gusto, time for bed." The big dog gave Serena's bare legs a last friendly lick and got up, trotting out of the room in Brett's wake.

Doctor Pascale waited until his wife was out of earshot, then leaned toward Serena and Garth. "This has to do with the American president's visit, doesn't it?"

She could see why Prince Lorne regarded the doctor as his confidant. Not much escaped him, she was sure. "It's possible, although we aren't sure of the exact connection yet."

"We think Carramer First wants to destroy any chance of the Americans establishing a base here, although we don't know why," Garth said.

The doctor's eyebrows lifted. "Isn't that outside the scope of their usual activities?"

Garth nodded. "We're fairly sure a Mr. Big, known only as the Hand, is using the members of Carramer First to pursue an agenda of his own. The Hand's followers may not even know what it is."

The doctor's brow wrinkled. "Does this have anything to do with a package the kidnappers kept asking me about?"

Serena traded looks with Garth. "What did they tell you about it?"

"Not much. They seemed to think I already knew where it was and what was in it. It seemed safer to pretend I did."

"Probably the only reason they kept you and Helen alive," Garth surmised.

"I don't think they really wanted to harm us. They weren't much more than kids. Helen got one of them talking and he thought it was all a big adventure."

"An adventure with guns and live ammunition." Serena shuddered at the memory of swimming for her life through a hail of bullets.

Garth was an arm's length away. She wanted to be strong, but she found herself wishing he would move closer. In the warmth of his arms, she might be able to quiet the tremors she couldn't stop.

But he stayed where he was. "Those two sound more like the members of Carramer First I knew."

The air grew thick with the doctor's obvious disapproval. "You belonged to that crazy bunch?"

Garth didn't flinch from the doctor's contempt. "Years ago, until I outgrew them."

She didn't point out that as far as the organization was concerned, Garth was still a high-ranking member. Thinking of the reaction of the crewman aboard the *Cradle Rock* she hoped Garth himself was clear on where his loyalties lay now.

"Looking so much like Lorne, I thought you were a long-lost royal cousin. Now I find you're no different from those juvenile delinquents who kidnapped us."

"Garth may be a lot closer to Prince Lorne than a long-lost cousin," she said quietly. "The contents of the package your captors were so keen to locate may prove he's the prince's older brother."

To his credit the doctor didn't balk, although she saw the quick flare of shock in his pale-blue eyes. *"D'amou,"* he muttered in Carramer. The epithet was short for *mare d'amou,* and literally meant *for the love of the sea,* although there was a much earthier translation that wasn't usually used in polite company.

She wasn't given to swearing, either, but this time she was inclined to agree with the doctor.

He studied Garth intently. "Given the resemblance, it's possible. Not likely, but possible."

"Why not likely?" Garth asked.

Pascale drained his scotch. "Because Lorne's parents lost their first son at birth."

"Prince Lorne already told us about Louis," she said. She went on to detail the investigation so far that suggested the baby may not have been stillborn after all. "After I intercepted the package containing Louis's birth certificate and other identifying material, we expected Carramer First to try to get it back. As the only survivor of the group attending Princess Aimee around the time of Louis's birth, you were probably expected to know more about it than you did."

The doctor cupped his chin between thumb and forefinger. "I always knew Armand Junot was more trouble than he was worth."

She straightened. "Junot was the physician who delivered Prince Louis, wasn't he?"

Pascale nodded. "I hate to admit it, but he and I were colleagues. Or more accurately, rivals for the job of royal physician. He was older than me and he had a big problem." He looked with distaste at the empty glass in his hand. "He liked alcohol more than he liked being a good doctor."

She refrained from pointing out that Pascale had ample justification for drinking tonight. He wouldn't have had such a long, stellar career or be so revered by the royal family if it was a habit. "Our investigation showed he was a problem drinker. Do you mean it affected the performance of his duties the day Louis was born?"

"He used to say alcohol made his hands steadier. I tried to talk to him about it, but he brushed me aside. He left me no choice. I reported his behavior to Prince Eduard." Pascale dragged in a deep breath. "That was the end of Junot's chance of becoming royal physician."

"You got the job instead?" Garth asked.

"I would have preferred to get it without costing another man his career, but there was no alternative. Junot never forgave me for reporting him to the prince."

"He ruined his own career," Garth insisted. She wondered if he was thinking about Junot's role in his own life. If he *was* Prince Louis and Armand Junot had somehow intervened, the course of Garth's future—possibly the future of the entire kingdom—had been irrevocably changed.

She laced her fingers together. "Junot's problem can't have become obvious until after he delivered Princess Aimee's baby, otherwise he would have been relieved of duty."

The doctor put the glass down. His hands were remarkably steady, she noticed, once again impressed by his resilience. "He was about to be relieved the day Princess Aimee was attacked by a former suitor. Keer, I think was his name. I assume you know it was the attack that sent her into labor?" When they nodded, he went on, "Junot had me barred from the delivery room. Since his dismissal wasn't official at that moment, he could get away with it. The princess was already in enough distress without her physicians arguing over who had the right to deliver her child, so I stepped aside."

And he had regretted it ever since; she heard what he didn't say. The self-recrimination was plain on his craggy features. She was amazed at the clarity of the doctor's memories of over thirty years ago. His quick mind was legendary. Now she understood why. "Do you know what happened to Junot after he left the royal household?"

The doctor's mouth tightened. "I wasn't likely to keep in touch, but I heard he gave up medicine in favor of career drinking. His father was one of Prince Guillaume's closest advisors. When he died, he left Armand enough money to indulge his passion without the need to work for a living, not that anybody would employ him after word of his dismissal got around."

She chewed her lower lip thoughtfully. "Police records show that Junot died in a nursing home a few months ago from alcohol-related health problems. Flat broke and alone by then."

Pascale sniffed. "I'm surprised he lasted this long. Didn't he have a wife and son?"

"The son stayed with him at first. Felice Junot left him years before, last heard of in Australia," she supplied, remembering her research.

"From the sound of things, Junot was never in any condition to seek revenge for his dismissal," Garth mused. "Guess that disqualifies him as our Mr. Big."

He stretched an arm along the back of the couch, not touching her, but making unwelcome visions dance in her head. Tonight wasn't her first brush with death, and she was used to the kind of clarity that came with such a near miss. Such experiences had a way of concentrating the mind wonderfully.

Right now hers refused to concentrate on anything except how much she wanted to feel Garth's arm lying across her shoulder, his fingers idly stroking her nape. They were warm, dry and safe for the moment. The pizza and hot coffee was spreading fingers of warmth all through her. She felt herself lean toward him.

With an effort she shook off the vision and straightened. "Junot might not have been capable of plotting revenge on the royal family or against you, Dr. Pascale, but he did have access to the items we found in the package."

Pascale inclined his head in agreement. "He could have taken them after the birth as souvenirs of his glory days, hanging on to them all these years. When he died someone else may have come across them, a staff member from the nursing home, say.''

''It makes sense. If whoever found them belonged to Carramer First, they could have realized the potential of the items and sent word to the Hand. If he's as devious as he's reputed to be, he could have decided to use them and Garth's resemblance to Prince Lorne to further his goals.''

Garth sat up. She tried not to sigh too obviously as he withdrew his arm. ''Shouldn't we check out the people who were around Junot when he died?''

'' 'We' won't do any such thing,'' she denied. ''I'll call in our suspicions and let Matt take care of it.''

The doctor looked interested. ''Matt?''

''My partner when I was a cop, before I joined the R.P.D. He's doing the legwork while I'm taking care of Garth.''

Alongside her she felt Garth's body tense in protest and decided she could have chosen her words with more care. She almost laughed at the demonstration of male ego, until she remembered what he had done for her tonight. ''So far the caretaking is fairly mutual,'' she added. ''But until Prince Lorne gets the results of the DNA test, Garth has to be protected in case he turns out to be the true ruler of Carramer.''

Pascale looked skeptical. ''I agree the resemblance is strong. Do you believe you're Prince Louis?''

''Did you see the baby's body?'' Garth countered.

''Nobody did except Armand Junot and his nurse.''

''Who was conveniently killed in a road accident,'' Serena said.

Shock made the doctor pale. ''So I'm the only one left.''

She nodded. ''This is starting to look more and more like a conspiracy.''

''Stretching over thirty years? It hardly seems possible.''

''It's possible if somebody is working to a time frame of their own choosing,'' she asserted. ''Although it's hard to believe nobody but Junot saw the baby after it was stillborn. What about Princess Aimee herself?''

The doctor folded his arms over his chest in a lecturing pose.

"These days when a baby dies at or soon after birth, it's common to let the mother hold her child and even take photographs to help her through the grieving process, but such things weren't routine thirty years ago. Along with the handpicked staff at the royal retreat, I attended a memorial service, but the child's body had already been taken away for cremation. Princess Aimee was in such a state that her parents decided it would be easier on her if the birth was hushed up and her collapse blamed solely on the shock of being attacked by Keer."

He fixed Garth with a gimlet glare. "Were your parents—I mean the ones who raised you—members of Carramer First?"

"No." Serena answered for him.

"Naturally you checked." Garth's tone was scathing.

"It's my job."

The doctor stifled a yawn. "Do you think you two can continue this discussion without me?"

She jumped to her feet, feeling guilty for not considering the aftereffects of his ordeal. "Of course. If there's anything you need…"

"Only a good night's rest. Helen and I didn't get much sleep at our island retreat."

Garth stepped behind her. "Would you like something to help you rest?"

"If I need chemical help, I'm licensed to prescribe it for myself, thank you. Just direct me to the bedroom."

Garth did so, returning moments later to report that the doctor and his wife were comfortably settled. "I wonder if he speaks so abruptly to Prince Lorne."

"He does," she said. She had begun throwing out the boxes and gathering up glasses and cups. Now she paused with her hands full. "When you've delivered as many royal babies as he's done, including Prince Lorne himself, it probably seems foolish to stand on ceremony."

"Pity he didn't deliver Louis. We might have a few more answers."

She disposed of the remaining pizza and stacked the glasses

on the bar. The rest of the cleanup could wait. "Disappointed?"

"What do you think?"

She touched his arm. "I think you're more disturbed by this situation than you're letting on. There's no shame in admitting it."

"If there's anything to admit, you'll be the first person I'll share it with," he stated.

She masked her disappointment. Still the one-man show. Which reminded her. "Speaking of sharing things, when did you and Brett decide to run your own production tonight without telling me?"

He blew out a breath. "It worked didn't it?"

She ignored this, her anger rising. "You took a hell of a risk. Before you involved Brett, did you tell him who you could be?"

"He's my oldest friend. I'm not about to say, 'Hey buddy, better start bowing to me, because I could be your sovereign ruler.'"

"Even if it turns out that you are?"

His eyes glowed. "What the blazes does it matter?" He stilled suddenly. "That's what this is about, isn't it? You didn't care about me as an ordinary man. Now that there's a chance I could be king of Carramer, you've changed your tune."

"You're crazy. I didn't care about your background when we were at school, and it matters even less to me now."

"Are you sure, Serena? When we were kids, you only kissed me on a bet. Apart from your condolences after my folks died, I never heard from you again until you found out I might have royal blood."

"You didn't hear from me because I didn't think you wanted to."

He didn't believe her, she saw. "If my bloodline is so unimportant, how come you bring it up at every opportunity?"

"If you are the true monarch, it's my job to protect you."

"Ah, yes, my ever-vigilant protector. Refresh my memory. Who saved whose butt tonight?"

She was so angry she had to clench her fists to keep from lashing out at him. "You saved mine. There, I admit it. You saved my life and I'm grateful. In some cultures you would own me, body and soul."

She realized she had said too much when she saw a dangerous glint come into his gaze. He moved closer, sliding both hands over her shoulders to pull her closer. "Now, there's an interesting thought."

In his grasp she felt boneless. She told herself it was reaction to the night's adventures, but knew it had much more to do with finding herself in Garth's embrace. He was wrong. She didn't want him because he might be royal. She wanted him because he was Garth. And never more than right at this moment.

Chapter 10

He slid a finger down to where the robe had gaped open exposing the cleft between her breasts. She felt her breath quicken.

The lights seemed brighter, the sounds sharper, Garth's touch more arousing than she had ever experienced before. She clasped her hands around his neck and pulled his head down until her lips were a breath away from his.

For a heartbeat she thought he was going to resist her kiss. She had started to strain upward, intending to take from him what she needed, when he met her more than halfway, crushing her mouth under his until her mind reeled.

She tried to keep the kiss soft, friendly rather than passionate, but she needed him too much, had waited too long. A faint moan escaped her throat as she took and took the comfort she needed, the affirmation of life she hungered for after all that had gone down tonight.

He trailed kisses along her upper lip and the bridge of her nose. A shudder shook her. His hold tightened. "It's all right, you're safe now."

She stirred in protest. Even now he didn't understand. "It isn't reaction."

"Then what?"

"You."

A teasing glint lit his gaze. "No bet this time?"

"No bet." More like a sure thing. She grazed her hand along the side of his face, feeling the slight rasp of new beard. Not wanting any more misunderstandings, she said quietly but firmly, "Right now I'm where I want to be, doing what I want to do. Got it?"

His eyes danced. "I'm a little slow. You'd better show me."

She didn't need a second invitation. Sliding her hands under his belt, she tugged his shirt free and flattened her palms against his ribs. He was so lean she could practically count them. When she touched them, he squirmed. She laughed. "What's the matter?"

"Ticklish. I think you made your point."

She let her own eyes gleam. "An Achille's heel, Remy? You think I'd give up an advantage like that?"

He dodged her seeking fingers, pulling them out from under his shirt and cuffing them between his own. "You'd better. I'm warning you."

She jerked free and put her hands on her hips. "You and whose army?"

"That does it."

He swung her into his arms. Mindful of the other people in the house, she stifled a cry of mixed pleasure and alarm. "What do you think you're doing?"

"You started this. Now we're going to finish it."

Snapping off lights as he went, he carried her down a hallway, almost tripping over Gusto, who lay on his back with his paws in the air outside one of the doors. Brett's room, she supposed. She crammed a hand over her mouth to stifle her laughter.

The dog opened an eye and regarded them with mild curiosity. "Humans!" its expression seemed to say. Recognizing them, it went back to sleep. With no tug-of-war toys and no food involved, their activities were of little interest, she gathered.

Garth eased a door open with his foot. The room was small and crammed with maritime souvenirs. Brass lanterns, life buoys and flags jostled for space alongside deck chairs, coiled ropes and model sailing ships. A storeroom, she thought at first, then she noticed a bed pushed into one corner amid the chaos. The spread was patterned with anchors and chains.

Still holding her, he pulled the spread back revealing crisp white sheets and a soft almond-colored blanket. He pulled them back, too, then lowered her carefully onto the sheet. "It's a very narrow bed," she whispered.

He went back and closed the door, flicking on a bedside light in the shape of a lighthouse. By its glow, she saw desire darkening his features. Her own powered higher. "We'll work out a way to share it," he said.

His way was to place a knee either side of her hips and as she lay with one arm bent behind her head. As he reared above her she decided she could look at him all night this way, although it would be a terrible waste.

His hands were busy undoing the robe's tie belt. It fell away exposing the navy bathing suit. She saw him frown. "Something wrong?"

He pushed his hair back with one hand. "This has got to be the ultimate challenge."

Like most men his age, Garth could figure out how to undo a wide variety of bras. Panties were a breeze, he thought. How in the devil was he supposed to peel her out of a one-piece bathing suit?

She made it easy for him by shimmying up onto the pillow and sliding the straps off her shoulders. He gulped. In the spill of light from the lamp her skin glowed like opal. He frowned again as he saw the hollow of her throat marred by scratches she'd sustained hurtling through the forest on the island.

He bent to her and touched his tongue to the worst of the scratches, feeling tremors rock her. "You should have Dr. Pascale take a look at these."

Her back arched. "Not right now."

"No." He pushed the stretchy material down to her waist, dragging in a lungful of air at the perfection her breasts revealed. She was as gorgeous as every fantasy he'd ever had. He couldn't help himself. He had to taste.

As he took the first one, then the other into his mouth, his tongue teasing and tasting, he heard a low moan start deep in her throat. Slow and easy, he reminded himself. She'd been through a lot tonight.

Later he'd get her to talk about it. In the meantime, he wanted to give her something else to dream about when she closed her eyes.

They were already closed, he saw when he lifted his head. Her silken lashes lay against her cheeks that were hectic with color. Her head was thrown back and her lips were slightly parted, an invitation he couldn't refuse.

He kissed her slowly, deeply, drawing out the moment. When he stopped, she made a protesting move he interpreted as not wanting him to leave. Fine with him. He wasn't planning on going anywhere for the rest of the night.

He undid the buttons of his shirt and tossed it onto a deck chair inscribed with the name, *Titanic*. Not the real thing, he doubted, although knowing Brett he wouldn't be surprised.

Garth didn't need an iceberg ahead of him to know he was sinking fast. He had promised himself he would stay cool around Serena, not let her get to him this time. Now he accepted she had done that years ago and nothing much had changed.

He was ready for her touch to sweep him to the edge of control, but not for how fast she nearly pushed him over it. As her fingers skimmed down his sides and became busy with the fastening of his jeans, he felt the power of her slam through him, felt himself filling with the need to take what she offered.

She finished undoing the studs and the zipper just as he started to wonder how much longer they could contain him. He stood up long enough to kick his clothes away and heard her pull in a breath he was man enough to read as admiration.

She had scrambled out of the robe and bathing suit. When he pulled her against him he felt fireworks explode in his head. "I want you so much," he said.

"I know. I want you, too." She sounded breathless, but he heard no shadow of doubt in her voice.

He bent his head and skimmed her hairline with his mouth. "You smell of the ocean."

"I didn't get around to showering."

He kissed her parted lips, enjoying the taste of her before he murmured, "I'm a man of the sea, remember? Salt tang turns me on faster than French perfume."

She arched against him. "Show me, now."

It would have been easier to comply. Everything in him wanted to take what he needed without ceremony. But that wasn't how he wanted their first time to be. She deserved more.

"There's no hurry," he soothed. "We have all night."

Gently he pushed her back against the pillow, enjoying the sight of her in the yellow glow of the lighthouse lamp. She was an island of loveliness in a chaotic world. "You're beautiful," he said, unable to tear his eyes away from her.

She reached up and stroked his flanks. "So are you."

"Men aren't beautiful."

"Tonight, when you appeared beside me in the water, you were beautiful."

He grinned. "I thought you were mad at me for coming to your rescue."

"I was mad at you for switching places with Brett and putting yourself in danger."

"And now?"

"I'm still mad, but I don't want you to think I'm not grateful."

He trailed a finger down her stomach, enjoying watching her quiver. "How grateful?"

She pushed his hand away. "This isn't payment for services rendered. I'm here because I want to be. Because I want you."

"I wouldn't have it any other way."

"Just as long as we understand each other."

"I guarantee it." He amazed himself with how well he understood her, perhaps more than she would want him to. He trailed a line of kisses from her throat all the way down between her breasts, lower and lower until he heard her whimper. She didn't need to tell him she wanted him. He could taste and feel her desire every time he touched her.

His own desire threatened to ignite. He fixed his gaze on the *Titanic* deck chair, thinking of icebergs forging through water so chilled it could freeze the soul. It didn't help. She had barely to touch him to turn his blood to steam. She could seduce him just by lying there.

Not that she showed any inclination to be so passive. Holding his gaze with a heavy-lidded look, she caressed him with enchanting care, as if she thought he might break if she was anything but careful. He felt himself slipping. If she kept this up, there was no way he was going to last as long as he wanted to.

He sat up and allowed himself to look at her, giving himself time to regroup. "You're gorgeous," he said. "It's an inadequate word, but there's no other."

"Gorgeous is fine," she said dreamily.

He picked up her hand and pressed a kiss to the inside of her wrist, troubled when he saw her wince as he inadvertently touched the scratches on her arm. "Poor Serena. You're not as tough as you want everyone to think, are you?"

He'd touched a sensitive spot inside her, as well, he understood. She proved it when she said, "Are we going to talk or make love?"

"Why are we here?" he asked on a hunch.

Her eyes flew open. "I would think you could work it out."

"I mean why now? Why not when we were alone at Allora?"

She looked annoyed. "Don't ask difficult questions."

"I am asking. I want you to want *me,* not a remedy for your nightmares."

"What makes you think I'll have nightmares."

"I was keeping a lookout for you from the end of the jetty. I saw what happened at the cabin," he said carefully.

She twisted beneath him, her expression turning bleak. "Then you know a man died because of me tonight."

He shook his head. "He died because of his own greed. It wasn't your fault."

"I know. I was a cop before I joined the R.P.D., remember? You learn to deal with death when it's unavoidable, and you move on."

He stroked the hair away from her brow. "But you never learn to accept being defeated by it."

Seeing her gaze blur, he felt his insides twist. She didn't ask how he knew how she felt. As a Navy DARE, he had undertaken assignments that sometimes involved death and destruction. Like anyone who dealt in the ultimate stakes, he knew how outraged a person felt when death won.

"Nothing you can do now will change what happened," he reminded her.

She sighed. "I know that, too. It's just hard to feel this— this alive, knowing it's at the expense of another life."

"If I learned anything as a DARE it's that love is an affirmation of life," he insisted gently. "Sometimes it's our only way of triumphing over our old enemy."

Some of the distress ebbed out of her expression, replaced by a need he recognized because he shared it. "You're right, and I'm being foolish," she admitted.

He stroked her face, pressing kisses to the inviting hollow of her throat, right above where he felt her pulse throbbing. "It isn't foolish to have regrets. It's what makes you human."

She nodded. "I don't want to become so hardened that events like tonight stop mattering to me."

"There, you see? Asked and answered."

She smiled and he knew she was over the worst of her self-recriminations. They would return in the deep well of night, when she was alone. He knew because they did for him. But for now she was going to be all right.

He had almost decided that she should be left to sleep, alone, when she linked her hands around his neck and pulled his face down to hers. "You sure talk a lot."

Desire surged through him anew, so potent he shook with it. "What would you rather do?"

"You know the answer, and it isn't because I can't bear to be alone," she said. "I mean, I don't want to be alone—but you can be sure it's for all the right reasons."

"*Now* we understand each other."

Begrudging every heartbeat away from her, he reached for his pants and retrieved a condom from his wallet, only enduring the time it took to sheath himself for her protection. Then he stretched out full-length beside her, the narrow bed giving him no choice but to lie half on top of her. Not that he minded. In fact they could make better use of the space if he covered her body with his own, he discovered. When he did, her deep sigh of satisfaction told him she approved.

Judging by the throaty sounds she made when he lifted himself over her and buried himself in her softness, she had no problem with anything he wanted to do. And he was very, very inventive.

Dawn was pushing fingers of iridescent red light into the room as she lay on her side, giving him what room there was and feeling more content than she could ever remember. The sound of Garth's deep breathing mingled with the night sounds outside. She was glad he had made her consider why she wanted him to make love with her.

She hated that he was right. At first she *had* turned to him to banish the nightmare vision of the young kidnapper dashing into the burning cabin seconds before it was engulfed in flames. Falling debris must have knocked the man unconscious with no time even to scream. She welcomed this smallest of mercies.

Asking Garth to make love with her hadn't been a conscious plan. More an act of self-preservation. She simply hadn't wanted to go to bed alone, knowing what awaited her the moment she turned out the light.

She should have known Garth would want more.

He wanted her to want him, only him.

And she did, dear Heaven, how she did.

Sated as she was, and with every part of her singing a sweet song of weariness, she still wanted him at this very moment. She wasn't in love with him, she told herself firmly. What they shared was a bond of wonderful chemistry, nothing more.

There couldn't be anything more. When this was over, he would return to his life—or to the castle, as fate and his DNA decreed—and she would return to her work and her life with memories to last forever.

She liked her life as it was, with no one depending on her to fill their needs. Knowing it was a legacy of her parents' neediness when she was too young to handle it didn't change reality. Love led to a relationship and then to the kind of oppression she'd thrown off so traumatically in her teens.

For the first time she questioned her decision. Then just as firmly rejected the doubts. She'd been there. She knew what would happen. Better to stick to the chemistry.

"Thinking about the island?"

She looked into Garth's open eyes and saw her own contentment reflected there. For a moment guilt gripped her at the self-indulgence of her thoughts. "No," she admitted. "I was thinking about you."

He smiled lazily. "I like the sound of that."

"Egomaniac."

"What man wouldn't? I meant it when I said you're beautiful. Waking up beside you is pretty amazing, without finding I'm dominating your thoughts."

"I didn't say you dominated them. Only that I was thinking about you."

"As in?"

She gave him a shove that almost toppled him off the edge of the bed until he grabbed the first thing handy, which happened to be her. As their bodies connected, fire tore through her and longing so strong it stole her breath. "As in this has to be a one-off experience," she said desperately.

Garth recognized wishful thinking when he heard it. He suspected she knew how close they were to repeating the experience right here and now. *Titanic* he thought. Icebergs. Nothing helped. He sat up and swung his legs to the floor. Maybe if he wasn't touching her.

"I agree next time we should go for a larger bed."

"That isn't the problem."

"Then what is?"

"You. Me. Us. If you turn out to be the ruler of Carramer, you can't have a relationship with your bodyguard."

"I can think of at least one royal who did." He mentioned Mathiaz, Baron Montravel, who had married his former bodyguard, Jacinta Newnham, only a few miles from where they were now. They lived at the royal enclave of Chateau Valmont, a short drive from Brett's house.

"Well you can't have a relationship with me."

"I thought what we shared was pretty spectacular."

She gave vent to a sigh of frustration. Why couldn't he make this easy? "You know it was. Better than spectacular. Extraordinary."

He turned a teasing gaze on her. "You want us to try for whatever comes after extraordinary?"

If it was possible, he would be the man to take her there, and she found herself trembling anew at the prospect. "I'm serious," she insisted. "I don't want to get involved with anyone, extraordinary or not."

He propped himself up on one arm. "Because?"

If she shared her reason with him, he would probably demolish it with logic, the same way her parents used to win every argument with her. "Because I don't want to," she repeated.

He trailed a finger down her backbone, making her shiver. "Have you heard the saying that life is what happens when you're busy making other plans?"

"I thought you didn't want to get involved, either."

She felt his lips glide over the small of her back, and her

bones started to melt. "I've learned never to say never," he told her.

"We should get dressed." What had happened to making this a one-time experience?

"No hurry. Brett hates getting up early, and the Pascales were exhausted enough to sleep well into the morning."

Was it possible that she was saying never because of reasons that were no longer valid? That she was asking herself the question was alarming enough in itself. She knew she should stop this before it went any further. Instead she turned into his arms and let him pull her back down beside him.

"This doesn't mean we're having a relationship," she cautioned, clinging to the last traces of good sense.

"If you say so."

She let her head drop back, panting slightly as he laved openmouthed kisses over her neck. Resistance seemed futile when everything in her ached for him. As he continued his tender explorations, she felt the earth start to tilt on its axis and reached for him as her anchor.

She had never dreamed that not having a relationship could feel so sensational.

Chapter 11

Two days later Serena leaned against the wainscoted wall of the Grand Banquet Hall at Solano Castle, trying not to think about Garth as a lover. It was hard when she had to spend so much time with him. She had told herself she was checking on arrangements for the American president's visit, but the truth was she needed to put some space between herself and Garth.

It wasn't working. He haunted her thoughts as she watched the castle chatelaine, Augustine Beck, plan the welcome reception with the precision of a general martialing her forces for battle.

Augustine, known as August to almost everyone at the castle, could have performed the task on computer, but the sixty-plus martinet was a perfectionist from the top of her iron-gray hair, lacquered so not a wisp was ever out of place, to the toes of her sensible shoes. She notoriously preferred to work in the actual rooms where state occasions were to be held.

The fifty-foot-long table gleamed in the light from a series of crystal chandeliers as footmen, their shoes covered in booties made out of polishing cloths, skated across the surface, chatting as they worked. For the banquet, Serena knew the table would be set with a specially made damask covering, silver, gilt, flowers and china from one of the historic services in the royal collection. Fifty or sixty people would be seated along both sides of the table according to rank, each with their own attendant. August was shuffling place cards now.

The hall was one of the grandest in the castle. Richly painted molded ceilings ingeniously made use of the de Marigny family insignia. The elaborate plaster cove dominating the room had been commissioned by Prince Jacques de Ville de Marigny, to celebrate the unification of Carramer's many islands into one kingdom.

The eighteenth-century French carvings serving as a framework for a collection of Gobelins tapestries that had been a gift from France to mark the centenary of the same event.

It was sobering to think that if Carramer First—or whoever was manipulating them for his own ends—had their way, all the preparation would be for nothing because the banquet would never take place.

She straightened unconsciously. The group had to be stopped before they could disrupt the president's visit and the plans for an American base on Carramer. Not that she'd made a lot of progress so far.

Rescuing the Pascales was progress, she reminded herself. Prince Lorne's reaction had left her in no doubt how worried he had been about his friends. Worried enough to order them all back to the castle at Solano. They had arrived the day before.

There was still no news from the police lab about Garth's DNA test, but the analysis was painstaking and couldn't be hurried. No answer could be expected until almost the eve of the president's arrival. She had no doubt the timing was part of the Hand's plan. Springing a new claimant to the throne on the president would be damaging enough. If her growing suspicion proved correct, the Hand also expected Garth to cham-

pion Carramer First's cause and reject the American involvement.

She didn't want to think he would do such a thing, but how
well did she really know him? Physically was one thing, and
heat flared through her as she remembered how they had made
love well into the morning, before they returned by helicopter
to Allora. Her years on the police force should have made her
a reasonable judge of character, but for once, she was unable
to think beyond how Garth made her feel.

This assignment should have been clear-cut. Instead his involvement had turned her into a seething mass of contradic-
tions. Wanting the job done and the villain vanquished. Wanting to stay with Garth. Just wanting.

She had tried to banish it by thinking about him. According
to his file, he'd made a success of the navy until he was booted
out. She shouldn't be surprised. At school he'd been insub-
ordination on legs. It hadn't stopped him from rising quickly
through naval ranks due to outstanding performance alone. His
superiors might not approve of Garth but they couldn't ignore
his brilliance and dedication.

But not everything was in the file. His missions with the
DAREs were locked away beyond even her level of security
clearance. But she knew enough about the DAREs to be sure
he had risked his life more than once. And his navy buddy,
Brett, hadn't lost his leg on a picnic.

So Garth was brave and clever. Again, no surprise. What
kept catching her unawares was his earthy sensuality. It was
like a currency he minted that only she could spend. And in
this particular currency he was alarmingly wealthy.

"Your office told me I'd find you here." A tall, angular
man with dark curly hair, who could as easily be a basketball
player as the police lieutenant he really was, strode up to her.

Pleasure flooded through her. "Matt, you didn't have to
come in person. You could have telephoned and saved yourself
a trip."

Her former partner shook his head. "I don't get many excuses to visit the castle. This is some dining room, isn't it?"

"I wouldn't like having to do the housework," she said with a laugh.

Matt Hayes watched the footmen skating up and down the table. "I saw that on television once. I didn't think it was for real."

"Can you think of a better way to polish something that size?"

"I have enough trouble scraping crayon off an ordinary table after two children have finished scribbling on it." He looked thoughtful. "Hey, maybe I could borrow the skaters after they're done here?"

"You'll have to take it up with Prince Lorne." She linked her arm through Matt's. "It's good to see you. Apart from the vandalism, how are Melanie and the kids?" She had missed her regular chats with her friend, but time simply hadn't allowed for anything other than duty. Well, almost anything.

"Holding you to your promise to baby-sit on our anniversary," Matt said.

"Yes, well, I may be out of town that night."

"Too late, a promise is a promise." He tapped a file under his arm. "Keep setting me new challenges and you'll be babysitting once a week for the next year."

"In your dreams."

Matt knew her too well to believe she meant it. They had known each other since she graduated from the police academy and he had been her senior on the force by only a couple of months, and by a mere three years in age. He had enjoyed acting as her mentor and friend, and she trusted him, although she would deny needing anyone to her last breath.

In fact she almost had. They had been responding to a radio call when she was shot during a bungled robbery. When he came to her assistance she had tried to push him out of the line of fire. Afterward he had been credited with saving her but he knew it was the other way around. Typical of Serena, she hadn't sought any credit and had been angry when he insisted on setting the record straight.

Now she was godmother to his six-year-old son, Ben, and

honorary aunt to his four-year-old, Carla, who had already made up her mind to join the police force to be like Auntie 'Rena. Not like her dad, he thought with some chagrin, although he knew Carla couldn't have a better role model.

"Is there somewhere we can talk?" he asked.

"Let's go outside."

She indicated a set of paneled double doors leading to a colonnaded terrace overlooking an area known as the green, which provided the setting for many colorful ceremonies. When the American president arrived he would take the salute here at a march with the Royal Guard acting as guard of honor.

Watching over the area was a bronze statue of Amar Mayat, one of the earliest rulers of Carramer, and a renowned leader of the mysterious Mayat people who had reached the islands by sea two thousand years before. Fragments of their jade work were still being unearthed on the outer islands. The statue had been modeled on a stone carving of the king discovered at one of these digs.

Legend credited Amar Mayat with great wisdom. A gleaming patch on his statue revealed where superstitious visitors doing the castle tour, and those merely hedging their bets, had rubbed his ankle for good luck.

As Serena leaned on the balustrade and looked at the statue, she felt tempted to do the same, telling herself she needed all the luck she could get right now. Matt came up beside her. "According to my colleague in Perla, you did a great job getting the Pascales away from their kidnappers."

"There was a price," she said without inflection, knowing it would be in the report.

"It was the kidnapper's choice to go back into the cabin."

"So Garth keeps telling me."

"Ah, Garth Remy, your mystery man."

Only a handful of people knew about Garth's possible connection to the throne. She hated keeping secrets from Matt but this one wasn't hers to share. And he was enough of a professional not to pressure her to reveal more than she could. "He isn't my mystery man," she said in the same level tone.

"Could have fooled me. Whoever he is, he's more than a job to you."

She didn't have to ask how he knew. They'd worked together long enough for him to recognize small signs others would miss. For once the awareness didn't make her feel as comfortable as usual.

What was she afraid of betraying?

"What have you learned about Armand Junot?" she asked.

Matt accepted the change of subject with good grace. "He died at the Theresa Denys Memorial Hospital a year ago, but you already knew that."

"I thought he died in a nursing home?"

"He lived in one until the last few days of his life. He was transferred to the hospital after suffering the stroke that eventually proved fatal."

"Damn, that lengthens the list of who could have had access to his possessions. What about his wife and son?"

"The couple chose to live apart when the boy was about sixteen. He stayed with his father for a time. According to friends who knew both Armand and Felice, they didn't call it a separation because they didn't want to incur the wrath of her family."

With no divorce in Carramer, marriage was considered a lifelong commitment and separation something of a disgrace. "Didn't they approve of her choice of husband?"

"They did when he was in line to become court physician. After his dismissal, Felice evidently wanted to leave him and move back in with her family but they felt she'd made her bed, she should lie in it."

"For sixteen years?"

"You could say for fourteen of them they were already separated. Within two years of marrying the good doctor, she had taken a lover."

She braced herself. "Who was he?"

"You're going to love this. Roy Keer."

Her eyebrows shot up. "The former marine who attacked Princess Aimee?"

Matt consulted his file. "The same. They met while Keer was seeing the princess. He expected to marry her, so I don't know what he thought he was doing carrying on with the doctor's wife. After Aimee ended the relationship with Keer, he found out she was in love with Prince Eduard. Keer went off his head and started making threats. The princess was whisked away to a royal retreat but he tracked her down and tried to intimidate her into coming back to him. During his trial and after he was imprisoned, Felice Junot stuck by him, supposedly out of charity, but it was rumored that her interest in him was a lot more personal."

Evidently Matt hadn't learned that the princess had been pregnant to Prince Eduard when she was sent away. Lorne's family skeleton, and the possible secret of Garth's identity, were still safe. "Where is Felice Junot now?"

"Immigration records show she left Carramer a while back," Matt supplied. "She visited Keer in prison for a few years until they had some kind of falling-out. Could be she got tired of being on her own and took up with another man, and he objected. We know she went to Australia, then she dropped out of sight altogether."

"That leaves only the son. What do we know about him?"

"David Junot hasn't amounted to much, although with a father like his, who can blame him? He lives in Solano and has held a string of short-term jobs, but with no police record, the file's pretty lean. He started attending meetings of Carramer First while he was living with his father and still belongs to the group, but he keeps a low profile."

She felt disappointed. Every instinct told her that David Junot was involved in this somehow, but they would need more evidence than her gut feeling before Matt could obtain so much as a warrant to search the man's home. She hugged Matt, crushing the file in his hands. "Thanks, anyway."

"What were you hoping I'd turn up?"

"A definite suspect at least. David Junot would do nicely,

but having a drunken crackpot for a father doesn't automatically incriminate him. The link between Felice Junot and Roy Keer would be more interesting if Keer hadn't drowned.''

He grinned. ''Yeah, live suspects are always more use to us.''

She liked the way he included her in the ''us.'' Much as she loved the R.P.D., there were times when she missed the close-to-the-bone excitement of police work. Matt knew that, too.

He closed the file. ''I'd better get back. Let me know if there's anything else I can do for you.''

''I'm sorry I can't tell you what this is all about.''

He held up a hand. ''You will when you can.''

''Sure, partner. Let me know when you and Melanie have your anniversary plans set.''

''I will.''

When he'd gone she felt alone suddenly, not only in fact but in spirit. Going to bed with Garth had been a mistake, she knew. Not because it hadn't been wonderful. It had. But because there was no future in it.

She didn't expect that sleeping with a man automatically led to marriage and a baby carriage. But that didn't mean she jumped into bed without a second thought. Sometimes a third. She valued herself too highly to be less than selective. Yet she had made love with Garth, the last man she should have chosen. She still wasn't sure how she felt about that, or what she was going to do about it.

He had hated being summoned back to the castle, but even Garth couldn't argue with the monarch, at least not unless and until he wore the crown himself. Prince Lorne had allocated him an office and a computer, mainly to keep him busy, she suspected. Garth had been playing a computer game when she looked in on him this morning. Recalling the intense way he'd hunched over the screen, dispatching virtual bad guys with single-minded determination, she smiled. For a man of action, being confined to the castle for his own protection had to be torture.

Not sure if her desire to spend more time with him was behind the sudden surge of benevolence, she decided to see if he wanted to join her in the castle gym to work off some energy. She had barely turned from the balustrade when a familiar sight had her whirling back, her eyes crinkling in annoyance.

Beyond the empty expanse of the green, a paved road led away from the castle to the main gate. It was normally only used early in the morning, when deliveries were made to the castle. The only vehicle on it now was a suspiciously familiar-looking pickup.

"Where the devil does he think he's going?" she hissed to herself. Prince Lorne hadn't specifically forbidden Garth from leaving the castle grounds, but he should at least have let her know so she could take proper security precautions. The man was terminally reckless.

She plunged through the doors into the banquet hall and snatched up the nearest house phone. By the time she was put through to the sentry box at the main gate, Garth had already driven through. She cut off the sentry's profuse apologies with a curt word and hung up, furious. Garth might be a spectacular lover, but she hadn't picked him as suicidal. Hadn't he learned anything from what had happened to the Pascales?

There was only one thing she could do. She left word at the R.P.D. command center that she was leaving the castle and asked for her car to be brought around to the Sovereign's Gate. When the duty secretary quite reasonably asked where she could be contacted, Serena came up short, realizing she had no idea where Garth was heading. Then it came to her.

"The fishing port," she said on a sudden certainty.

Garth dragged a plastic chair closer to a table, smiling his thanks as Alice placed a mug of coffee and a heaped platter of freshly caught seafood in front of him. She might not be a palace-trained chef, but he would put her crayfish medallions up against anything that was served to Prince Lorne.

"One day I'll surprise you and order something different for lunch," he joked.

She affected a stern look. "As soon as I saw you drive up, I started cooking your favorites. Like most men, you're a creature of habit."

He feigned hurt feelings. "I'm not sure I like being lumped in with most men."

"Only when it comes to your bad habits. Other than that, you're in a class by yourself."

He started to protest that he had no bad habits, when he saw her head lift and her eyes narrow with recognition. He half turned as a silver-gray Branxton two-door sedan screeched to a halt alongside his pickup. Seeing who was at the wheel, he smiled at Alice. "You'd better bring another cup of coffee. Make it a latte."

"From the look on your friend's face, you'd be safer with a Colt .45."

"I'll settle for the coffee, thanks. I can handle my friend."

Alice went to get the coffee and Garth braced himself. But when Serena steamed to a standstill beside his table, he kept his tone mild. "Glad you decided to join me for lunch. Alice always cooks too much. I've ordered your caffe latte."

"You know where you can put your lunch."

He gave a pained smile. "The crab claws, as well?"

When he saw her mouth twitch he knew he was winning. It was a cliché that women looked good when they were angry. Usually it wasn't even true. Unless the woman was Serena. Temper suffused her delicate features with a becoming rose color and made her eyes shine like stars.

In a pair of white pants and matching jacket over a nautical blue-and-white-striped top, she looked good enough to eat.

Making love with her was probably not the smartest thing he could have done, given her determination to avoid a relationship. But seeing her standing over him like an avenging angel, all he could think about was how soon they could be together again.

He forced the image out of his mind, although banishing it

from the rest of him was more of a challenge. "Join me," he repeated, pushing a plastic chair out with his foot. He knew better than to get up and pull a chair out for any woman who was as angry as Serena looked. He was likely to get it slammed over his head.

She shrugged out of her jacket, revealing that the nautical top had only one sleeve. Her other shoulder was bare, he noticed with interest as she hung the jacket over the back of the chair and sat down. She even smiled and said thank you when Alice put a mug of latte in front of her. Once you'd drunk Alice's superlative coffee, you were hers for life, he knew.

He made a show of cracking a crab claw and digging out the succulent meat. "Sure you won't have some?"

"Is that smoked trout?"

"Mmm-hmm," he said around a mouthful of crab.

Without saying anything, she picked up a fork and broke off a piece of the trout, drizzled juice from a lemon quarter over it and forked the fish into her mouth. Her eyes nearly closed and her head tilted back as she savored the taste.

Alice, your food works better than any psychologist, he thought watching enjoyment overtake anger in Serena's expression.

Unfortunately not for long. She finished the trout and a good portion of the crab, then put the fork down. "You can't tell me you were so starved for seafood you had to sneak out of the castle without telling me?"

"Is it the sneaking or the not telling that bothers you the most?"

"You're impossible."

"So Alice was telling me before you arrived."

Serena looked around, her trained eye assessing the openness of the location and the fact that it was equally accessible by road and sea. "You shouldn't be here. It isn't safe."

"I was going stir-crazy in the castle. How many levels of Hawk Raider can a man master before giving in to the urge to throw the computer off the nearest battlement?"

"You can do other things on a computer besides play games."

"Name one."

His nearness made it hard to think logically. "I just know you can."

His eyes gleamed. "There, tell me you aren't getting stir-crazy yourself?"

She toyed with the handle of her coffee mug. "A little."

"At least while we were at Brett's place at Perla we were doing something."

Thinking of what they had been doing, she almost choked on her latte. "That was different."

The surge of heat staining her cheeks told Garth her thoughts were running along similar lines to his. Not much they could do about it at the castle, surrounded by servants. Another good reason to get away. He hated to think he had chosen the most obvious route out of the castle precisely so she would come after him.

He couldn't stop feeling glad that she had.

She was as transfixed by the moment as he was, remembering all they had shared at Perla and anticipating what might be to come. He heard her breathing quicken and felt his own keeping time. He was so aware of her that the commercial fishing dock faded into a blur of sound and movement.

Everything about her seemed exceptional: from the eager way she angled toward him unconsciously, to the luminous glow in her blue eyes framed by lashes of aspen gold. As he'd come to expect, she wore no makeup except a trace of strawberry-tinted lip gloss, tempting him to sample her mouth to see if taste corresponded to color.

She saw the moment when he wanted to kiss her. Desire whipped through her, as hot and forceful as a desert wind. For long seconds she wanted nothing so much as to yield to it. Having done so once, she knew she couldn't risk it again. Not and walk away from him heart whole when this was over.

"The best thing we can do is wait for the Hand to...er... show his hand," she said haltingly.

He shook his head as if he was also casting off a spell. "Nicely put, but inaccurate. There is something more I can do."

Her heart did a quick skipping beat. "Matt is keeping the investigation on the boil. I'm keeping you out of harm's way, or trying to while we wait for the test results. What else is there?"

"My parents' boat."

She let her narrowed gaze betray her confusion. "What about it?"

"You've convinced me that the explosion wasn't an accident."

She decided to play devil's advocate. "The police investigated the sinking of your parents' boat. There's no suggestion the explosion was caused by anything other than a fuel leak ignited by an electrical fault."

His mouth tightened into a grim line. "I wasn't the only eyewitness. The boat was known to be old and fallible. Nobody suspected foul play, not even me when I dived on the wreck the week after it happened. That doesn't mean we saw everything there was to see."

His expression didn't change, but she saw the quick sweep of pain in his gaze and touched his arm. "Going down there can't have been easy for you."

She felt his muscles jump under her fingers. "I needed to see the boat for myself, convince myself they were really gone."

The rawness in his tone tugged at her, more harrowing than if the experience had been her own. Her relationship with her parents was troubled, but she hadn't yet had to deal with losing them. Suddenly she saw how hard it was going to be. They were still far from seeing things eye-to-eye, but as long as they were alive she could cling to the hope that things would improve between them. Once they were gone, that hope disappeared forever.

"What do you expect to find that you didn't see the first

time?'' she forced herself to ask. She couldn't permit him to do it, but she wanted to know.

He toyed with her fingers, sending shivers arrowing all the way to her heart. "Some evidence to link the sinking with Carramer First and the rest of the conspiracy."

"David Junot," she said, blowing out a breath.

Garth's interest quickened. "What makes you think he's connected to my parents' deaths?"

"I have no proof, but he's connected to something, I'd swear to it," she stated. "This morning Matt Hayes told me that David Junot's mother had a longstanding affair with Roy Keer. Keer's relationship with Princess Aimee, his attack on her triggering the premature birth of her son, and also being involved with Dr. Junot's wife strike me as a few too many coincidences."

"I agree. You don't think David could be the missing heir, do you?"

She realized she had been relying on Garth's resemblance to the royal family, both in appearance and in the genetic trait they shared. "If he is, pity help the kingdom," she said. She stood up. "I'll call Matt and have him send us a recent photograph of David Junot." She cursed herself for not having requested one sooner.

"Do that. In the meantime I'm going diving."

"Not on your own, you're not."

He stopped. "You're welcome to come along."

Her blood chilled. It had been bad enough learning to dive in the sheltered waters off Nuee. She had satisfied herself she could do it, promising herself she would never have to do it again.

He was watching her face, and his own look softened. "Forget I suggested it," he said in a gravel voice. "You can stay in the boat and keep watch from the surface, make sure nothing happens to me. Fair enough?"

She felt her jaw firm. "No, it's not fair enough." If he could face visiting the wreck where his parents had died, she could find the strength to go with him. She had a good idea what it would cost him to go back there. He might not need a body-guard but he was going to need a friend. ''I'm coming with you all the way,'' she said.

''You don't have to.''

''Don't give me all the reasons why not, or you'll talk me out of it.''

''What do you think I'm trying to do?''

He cared, she thought as a glow of triumph stole through her. He might want her to think that all they shared was sexual chemistry, but she read the truth in his gaze. What it meant for them she couldn't consider at this moment.

She stood up. ''Let's go while I still have the nerve.''

Chapter 12

"I thought your boat was laid up for repairs," she said when they reached the end of a sagging dock extending into the harbor.

"When I told the mechanic at the dry dock that I was calling from the castle, and told him to charge the repairs to Prince Lorne, miraculously they discovered they could have the boat ready this afternoon."

She laughed. "I'd like to see the prince's face when he gets the bill."

"I intend to pay it. I couldn't resist flexing a bit of royal muscle."

"This from someone who thinks Carramer should be a republic?"

"Doesn't mean I can't enjoy the power of the castle while it's at my disposal."

He was in danger of falling under Prince Lorne's spell, she realized. It wouldn't be the first time she'd seen a die-hard republican change their opinion after meeting the charismatic monarch. And Garth had done much more than shake hands and exchange a few words of polite conversation. He was facing the possibility that he and Lorne could be brothers.

She began to think the country might be safe in Garth's hands after all, and wondered if Prince Lorne had already reached the same conclusion.

Garth's boat was more like a small barge, broad and flat, scarred at the waterline from encounters with dock pilings, but clean and well maintained. A weathered cabin sat nearly flush with the hull at the sides, with the wheelhouse sitting on top like a miniature second story. Beside the wheelhouse a skiff was neatly stowed upside down. She read the name *Jessica* in fading paint on the side of the boat.

He saw her noticing, correctly interpreting the jealousy she didn't want to feel. "The name came with the boat. Probably the previous owner's wife or daughter. I didn't see any reason to change it."

Able to think of a few, she decided her reaction was quite revealing enough. She feigned nonchalance as she studied the houseboat, as neat as any cottage, complete with chimney pipe from a potbellied stove. "It's charming," she said. Contrarily, for someone who hated being under the water, she liked being out in boats.

He grimaced. "No captain wants to hear his boat described as charming."

"It has little windows, doors, even a little veranda complete with patio furniture."

"You don't have to make it sound like a home for the seven dwarfs."

His growled response didn't fool her. He was pleased that she liked his boat. And she did. She only wished it wasn't quite so—compact. Reminding herself that they were here for a purpose didn't ease the restlessness she felt in his company. Being confined to a limited space together wasn't going to help.

Garth vaulted aboard, then took her hand and helped her to negotiate the narrow plank linking boat to shore. He steadied her with an arm around her waist while she adjusted to the sway. She told herself her heart was racing because of the challenge lying ahead.

The excitement pumping through her couldn't be blamed wholly on the coming dive. Garth held her close. The deck shifted subtly beneath her feet and she knew it would take only a slight move on her part to find herself in his embrace.

It wasn't where she needed to be, she told herself resolutely. Wanted to be, without a doubt. But was that sufficient reason to throw caution to the wind?

Having done so once, she had barely known a moment's peace since. She could practically feel her personal boundaries crumbling and was determined not to let Garth erode any more of her hard-won independence. As a teenager she had almost suffocated under the yoke of being everything to her parents, fighting free only after bitter struggle. Not even a man who left her breathless with wanting him could be allowed to take over where her parents had left off.

He turned away and prepared to cast off, his movements swift and assured.

Left alone, she felt perversely disappointed.

By the time they had cleared the dock, she had used her cell phone to call the castle and let the duty secretary at the R.P.D. command center know where they were.

As luck would have it Jarvis Reid was there and intercepted the call. Their paths hadn't crossed since she and Garth had returned to the castle. "Ah yes, your new assignment. How's it going?" Reid asked.

Like the rest of the division, he had been told only that Garth was Prince Lorne's guest and that she had been seconded to work with him on a special project for the monarch. The kidnapping and rescue of the Pascales couldn't be kept quiet, but Prince Lorne had ensured that the extent of her involvement wouldn't be made public. As far as anyone knew, the kidnapping had been motivated by ransom, and the rescue had been carried out by a team of navy DAREs who couldn't be identified for security reasons. Close enough, she thought, wondering what Reid would say if he knew the truth.

"Well enough," she said, giving nothing away. "Yours?"

"The preparations for the American president's visit are going like clockwork."

"Try not to miss me too much," she said sarcastically.

He chuckled down the line. "No one can take your place, Serena. I hope you'll agree to be my assistant after I'm appointed head of the Solano division."

Anger knifed through her but she refused to give Reid the satisfaction of baiting her. "Unless I get the job. Then you can be my assistant," she rejoined.

"The difference is I'm here, and you're there. Enjoy your harbor cruise with the prince's protégé."

"It's not a cruise, damn it. And Garth isn't…" But he'd already hung up.

Had she expected everything to fall apart because she wasn't in control? Annoyed with herself, she snapped the phone shut. Since returning to the castle she had heard that Jarvis Reid was doing a good job. Her job. If he kept it up he was virtually certain to be offered the promotion.

It could be argued that that was under normal circumstances, and these were anything but normal. Reid didn't know how close to disaster the kingdom hovered. If the DNA test proved conclusively that Garth could not be Lorne's older brother, Reid would never find out. She would have the monarch's gratitude for her help, and the file would be closed on a top-secret episode in Carramer's history.

It wasn't much consolation.

Her mood felt suddenly as choppy as the blue waves surging under the boat as Garth steered them away from the dock. She recognized that part of her discontent arose because she wasn't missing her work as much as she'd expected. After spending the past couple of years working hard for a promotion, this was a heck of a time to start wondering if she really wanted it. If not, then what?

She wasn't going to solve the problem now. Looking up, she saw puffs of white smoke from the diesel engine being shredded by the light breeze. She climbed the steep wooden stairs leading to the wheelhouse. Inside, the boat was more modern than the weathered exterior suggested. "Is that sonar?" she asked in surprise.

His answering look was wry. "What did you expect? A brass sextant and parchment star charts?"

"Of course not, but hardly something so state-of-the-art."

"Think of the side-scan sonar as my designer wardrobe."

She got the message. He preferred to spend his money on items that mattered more to him than appearance. Unlike her, was the irritating implication she couldn't help drawing. Coming on top of Jarvis Reid's taunt, she felt fury roll through her. It was all she could do not to launch herself at Garth and pound the smug expression off his handsome face with her fists. Except she doubted she would win the battle. Her throat dried at the thought of how he would choose to conquer her.

At the helm he looked more in his element than he had at the castle. His strong legs were braced easily against the rolling movement that had her grabbing for handholds every few minutes. His hands lightly caressed the wheel, the movements barely perceptible. *Now* he looked like a king, she thought. Neptune, ruling the waves.

He glanced at the sonar. "The *Onalos* lies in fifty-seven feet of water between Wesley and Rocky Points opposite the entrance to Solander Creek."

"How will you know when you're in the right place?"

"I have a fix on where the boat went down. The sonar reads the bottom of the harbor. When we're in the general vicinity, I keep watch for an image that correlates to the size of the target."

His emotionless tone didn't conceal from her how harrowing the experience was for him. She could see it in the tightness of his mouth and the fine lines radiating from his eyes.

The report of the explosion and the ensuing investigation had been on the news, but the factual details couldn't reveal the anguish he must have felt when his parents' bodies were retrieved from the deep.

"I'm sorry I wasn't there for you," she said, knowing how inadequate it sounded.

His shoulders lifted expressively. "No reason you should have been. You barely knew my parents. They didn't make friends easily. If it hadn't been for the media attention, the funeral would have been a spartan affair."

A chill swept through her as if she was walking across a grave, as in a way she was. She wrapped her arms around herself.

"If you're cold there's wet-weather gear in the cabin," he said.

Out on the open water the breeze was cooler, but she shook her head. "I'm okay."

She remained silent as Garth concentrated on steering and watching the sonar. After what seemed like an age, she felt the boat slow. Looking over his shoulder she saw an image rise on the small screen. "Is that it?"

In answer he throttled the boat back then gestured for her to take the helm. At her look of consternation, a wintry smile lifted the corners of his mouth. "It's only for a second while I lower the anchor and throw out a guideline. Look around, there's nothing for you to hit."

She did and saw he was right. "Just tell me which button controls the brakes."

He went astern without bothering to dignify her feeble attempt at humor with an answer. Now that the moment of truth was here, she wondered if she could go through with this. It was one thing to learn to dive in a hotel swimming pool and gain her certification in the enclosed waters of a lagoon, but quite another to venture into the depths of the harbor among who-knew-what marine horrors.

Her pulse jumped and she breathed deeply to steady it. Garth would be with her. He wouldn't let anything happen to her. Nor she to him.

She felt *Jessica* drift to a stop as the anchor took hold. Garth came back moments later and secured the helm. "Doesn't someone have to stay aboard?'' she asked, knowing she was delaying the evil moment.

"It's wise but not always practical. Are you volunteering?''

Did he know how tempted she was to say yes? "No way. It's a perfect day for a swim.''

However rough and ready the boat appeared from the outside, it was well equipped and the diving gear Garth supplied was faultlessly maintained. When he drilled her on the hand signals they would need to communicate underwater, she was pleased to find she remembered all of them. He got the message when she crooked an arm over her head, the fingertips pointing to her hair in the "I'm OK" signal.

What she had forgotten was how much gear there was. Wet suit, fins, weights, buoyancy control vest, mask and snorkel. The compressed air cylinder felt massive on her back. "Now I know how a turtle feels,'' she said with a shaky laugh as she settled the weight on her shoulders.

He measured her with a look. "A very sexy turtle.''

She busied herself helping him with his gear so he wouldn't see the blush starting. Right now she should be terrified of what they might encounter under the sea. Instead she was worried about what her blush might reveal to Garth.

Then it came to her that his compliment was a deliberate attempt to distract her from her fears. She felt almost good as she fitted her breathing regulator and adjusted the face mask over her eyes. At a signal from Garth she held onto the mask and rolled backward into the harbor.

She had to keep reminding herself of the first rule of diving: keep breathing. The next thing she discovered was how difficult it was to sink at all. While equalizing the pressure in her ears and mask, she had gulped as much air as she could. No wonder she couldn't achieve neutral buoyancy.

Gradually her training came back to her and she was able to follow Garth down the weighted guide rope. As comfortable in the water as the sea lion his wet suit made him resemble, he was remarkably patient with her inexperience, although she knew he would have been on the bottom long before if he hadn't waited for her.

He had told her they would be down for a total of thirty minutes. At first she had worried that it wouldn't give them long enough to reach the wreck of the *Onalos* and search for clues. Now time seemed to stand still as they descended deeper into the silent blue world.

She thought it too much of a coincidence that his parents' boat had blown up leaving no one with firsthand knowledge of his birth. He had been born on the boat when his mother went into early labor, he'd been told. His father had delivered him following radioed instructions from the paramedics. Strange that her investigation had turned up no record of the emergency call, or of the Remys seeking medical help when they returned to port.

Garth's birth hadn't been registered until a few days afterward, not unusual in itself until Serena considered the other circumstances. Still she found it hard to accept him as the lost Prince Louis. Because she didn't want him to be?

Pulling herself carefully down the guide rope, she filled her lungs with compressed air and felt a little light-headed. They weren't going deep enough for nitrogen narcosis—the bends—to be a hazard, so she put the feeling down to confusion. Why couldn't she be clear about what she wanted? She made herself concentrate on the task at hand, and realized in some amazement that she hadn't thought about the possibility of sharks for whole long minutes.

Carramer was well known for its magnificent coral and sponge-encrusted underwater formations. With a current constantly flowing, Serena drifted along almost effortlessly, admiring the kaleidoscope of colors and details.

On the bottom she saw dozens of sea anemones, their crowns of tentacles waving in the current as they held themselves in place by two-foot-long tubes buried in the firm, muddy bottom. Most anemones were light gray, but a few glowed orange or deep purple.

Surrounding her were tropical fish of every shape and hue,

from tiny angel fish to a hundred-pound wrasse colored a vivid turquoise. Her heart thumped wildly and she couldn't stop herself from flinching as a dark, sinuous shape loomed overhead until she realized it was a bottle-nosed dolphin come to check them out. Further away she saw a pod of them playing near the surface.

The *Onalos* had gone down on the sandy mud bottom beyond the coastal patrol breakwater. According to Garth, the explosion had scattered wreckage over a wide area but part of the wheelhouse was intact and accessible.

When she reached the sandy bottom, Garth signaled for her to follow him away from the guide rope. Almost immediately her inexpert finning stirred up a cloud of silt, reducing visibility to zero. For a moment she couldn't see Garth and her sense of panic returned. Then she saw him approach what she'd taken to be a cluster of rocks. As the silt subsided she saw they were the remains of a vessel.

A monster-size lobster scuttled away from her feet as she swam closer. Through the window of Garth's mask his eyes were dark with sadness and anger as he touched what she guessed was the wheel of his parents' boat. Although her wet suit protected her from the cold, she shivered as she reached out and grasped his shoulder.

His nod acknowledged her gesture. Then he began to pick through the wreckage scattered across the sea floor. Serena wondered what they could possibly find that the authorities hadn't already seen.

Taking her cue from him she kicked along above the debris field, not certain what she expected to find. Surely anything of significance would already have been lifted to the surface?

Without warning a rogue current caught her, sweeping her away from Garth. Focusing on the wreckage, he didn't see her futile grab for him as she was dragged along. By the time she managed to halt her progress by wrapping her arms around a coral-studded rock formation, he was lost in the silt cloud kicked up by her helter-skelter passage.

Her breathing sounded as heavy as a crank phone call in her

ears. Keep breathing, she ordered herself. Before the dive, Garth had instructed her to surface and swim for the *Jessica* if they became separated. She could manage that.

Keeping a death grip on the rock, she stilled herself while the silt settled, then looked around. She was in the undersea equivalent of Stonehenge, a roughly circular formation of coral-studded rocks, most about waist high, one or two smaller. From fist-size openings in the rock, the gaping mouths of snowflake eels seemed to grin at her, although she knew they were only waiting to snag a meal as it swam by.

One of the eels protruding from a low opening in the rock looked dead. Its mouth was closed and what she could see of the body was black. Then it shifted slightly with the current and she caught a glint of silver. Not an eel, but what?

Moving slowly to avoid stirring up more silt, she worked her way down the rock. Close up, the object was a black and silver toy submarine. Jammed into the crevice, it resisted her first attempt to remove it. When she freed it, she saw it was about a foot long, the inside crammed with a substance that looked like modeling clay. It was probably nothing more than it seemed, but she decided to show it to Garth anyway.

When she surfaced she was closer to the *Jessica* than she expected. Garth was scanning the water for her. He had pushed his mask up onto his head, and his face was lined with worry. "Where the hell did you go?" he demanded when she reached him.

She grasped the ladder at the back of the boat, unwillingly pleased by his obvious concern. "A current took me away from you. I'm fine."

He levered himself onto the dive platform and offered her his hand. "Next time I won't let you out of my sight."

She let him help her out of the water. "I'm not sure there'll be a next time. It was pretty scary getting swept away."

"Not as scary as finding you gone. What have you got there?"

She had almost forgotten she still clutched her find. "A toy boat I found wedged in an eel hole. It's probably nothing."

He took it from her and studied it for a moment, his expression darkening. "I don't know too many toy boats that come packed with C4 plastic explosive."

Fear jolted through her and she recoiled instinctively from the innocent-looking object. "I thought it was modeling clay, weighting the boat to help it sink."

His hand gripped her shoulder. "It's harmless as it is. You can hit C4 with a hammer and it won't explode until it's triggered by the right detonator."

Despite his assurance, she wanted to put some space between herself and the evil toy, so she accepted Garth's offer to let her go first in the boat's tiny shower. When she came out he was dressed and seated at the table, turning the toy over in his hands. So she wouldn't have to watch, she busied herself making coffee in the compact kitchen, the galley, she reminded herself.

As she waited for the water to boil, she asked, "What is plastic explosive doing inside a toy boat?"

He looked thoughtful. "The day my parents' boat went down, a family regatta was being held at Solander Lagoon, across the bay."

"You think someone used a bomb disguised as a toy to destroy your parents' boat?"

He nodded grimly. "While pretending to take part in the regatta, the saboteur had only to wait until my parents had some obvious engine trouble. Anyone keeping them under observation would have known how unreliable their engine was."

She tensed again as he peered into the sub's tiny conning tower as if seeking answers there. "The saboteur could have aimed one of these at the Onalos, attaching it by remotely activated magnets, then triggered the explosion by remote. To anyone watching, it would look as if the engine had simply blown up."

She thought of the debris she'd seen scattered on the sea

bed. "That toy can't hold more than a handful of explosive, surely not enough to cause so much damage?"

He brushed strands of wet hair away from his eyes, which she saw were cold with anger, making her thankful it wasn't directed at her. "A quarter pound of C4 rolled into a cigar-thick line about eight inches long and placed against a steel beam can cut through it as if you'd used a cutting torch. A pound of it placed at the four corners of a building will take down that building. Water density also increases the concussive effect of the explosion."

She didn't attempt to mask her horror at his matter-of-fact recitation. Nor did she like to think how he had come by his knowledge. "How would the C4 be detonated?"

"From an electrical generator small enough to fit in your hand. It was probably built into a cell phone or even the remote control used to operate the boat."

It was chillingly clever and unbelievably callous. "Why is the toy still in one piece."

"The saboteur probably needed more than one attempt before he got his deadly toy attached to its target."

She handed him a mug of coffee. "Then there may be more of these things out there?"

He wrapped his hands around the mug. "There's no way to tell. On land, C4 can be sniffed out by trained police dogs, but there are no underwater detectors available."

"But now we know your parents' boat *was* sabotaged, the police have something to go on," she said.

His face took on a look of savagery. "Establishing that there was a bomb doesn't tell us a damn thing about who set it."

She added milk to her coffee and slid into the banquette opposite him, wishing he would stop playing with the toy. It may be harmless until detonated but it gave her the creeps. "Carramer First has to be behind this," she said.

"C4 is a military-issue explosive. A group of republican crackpots couldn't get their hands on it easily."

She sipped thoughtfully. "Unless our friend, the Hand, has military connections."

"Or is ex-military himself."

Someone with the kind of training and experience Garth himself possessed, she mused. It reduced the field to—say—a few thousand suspects. Since they still didn't know the Hand's nationality, and were only assuming he was male, the field of candidates was widening instead of narrowing.

He had replaced the toy submarine on the table where it sat between them like a sea snake poised to bite. She touched it gingerly. "I'll ask Matt to see what forensics can make of it."

Garth's hand clamped around her wrist. "Not yet."

She didn't pull away, although her heart began it's now-familiar racing at the touch. "It's evidence in a murder investigation."

"The murder of my parents," he stated coldly. "I still have contacts in the navy. They might know more about this thing's origins. Every demolition expert has his own way of assembling a device. The saboteur may have left clues he was unaware of leaving."

Deliberately she matched his coldness. "While I grieve for your loss, this isn't only about your parents, but about the future of the kingdom. Someone has gone to a lot of trouble—including murder—to put you in line with the throne in time for the arrival of the American president. I can't sit on new evidence while you play secret agent."

In the eyes Garth lifted to her, she saw the blind desire for revenge. Then she saw him master it with a superhuman effort. "Naturally your job must come first."

Her gaze blurred until she shook her head. "Does it have to be a choice?"

"You just made it one. And spelled out which side you're on."

Before she was fully aware of making a decision, the protest screamed from her throat. "No. I'm on your side, Garth, I always have been."

"Then you know why I have to do this my way."

Torn between duty and desire, she knew there was only one answer she could give him. "Damn you, you can have twenty-four hours."

Chapter 13

Garth slammed a brake on the satisfaction bolting through him. He was used to Serena riding her moral high horse. He shouldn't read anything into her decision to climb down off it for twenty-four hours.

She'd agreed for his sake.

And gone diving with him when everything in her had wanted to stay safe and dry aboard the boat. Not only had she kept her head, she'd managed to find the evidence they needed.

Now she was willing to put her career on the line to let him pursue his parents' killers.

She cared.

And now that he knew she did, he didn't want her to. Going to bed with her was one thing. They were both adults and were entitled to take their pleasure where they would. Letting her become emotionally attached to him was something else again.

This morning he hadn't spent all his time playing Hawk Raider. Using a few slightly dubious skills he'd acquired in DARE training, he'd finessed his way into her personnel record, learning that she was on the fast track to the top in her career. He'd found enough good-conduct awards to paper a room, and the details of her earning a commendation for bravery when she'd been shot in the line of duty had made his blood run cold. He'd had to breathe long and deeply to get his temper under control at the thought of anyone harming her.

When had he grown a conscience, he wondered? Some of her lofty principles must be rubbing off. One of them was telling him he couldn't go back to the castle and let her lie to the prince—even by omission—about what they'd learned today.

There was only one solution. He would send her back alone while he learned what he could about the toy submarine. Prince Lorne was fair-minded enough not to hold Serena accountable for Garth slipping his leash, so her record wouldn't be tarnished.

He stood up and pulled a duffel bag out from under the table, beginning to pack it with a few things he would need.

She watched him with interest. "What are you doing?"

"I'm not coming back to the castle with you."

Her expression darkened. "The hell you're not. I'm responsible for your security."

"I'll be secure enough where I'm going."

Her palms flattened against the table's polished wooden surface. "Mind telling me where that is?"

"My parents' house. Now I have proof they were murdered, the house might hold clues I've missed."

"I'm coming with you."

"Prince Lorne expects you back at the castle and that's where you're going to report your findings to him." She reached for the toy submarine but he moved faster. "That stays with me."

"I'll need it as evidence."

"You gave me twenty-four hours to check it out. After that it's yours."

She huffed an impatient breath at him. "You aren't making much sense."

"The only person I have to make sense to is me."

"And you're afraid I'm starting to understand you, is that it?"

He placed the toy boat into the duffel bag and zipped it up. "You don't need to understand me, Serena. I'm not good for you."

Her hand snaked out and caught his wrist. "I'll be the judge of what's good for me."

Her eyes glowed with a warmth he didn't want to see there, but it persisted and a fresh groundswell of desire rolled over him. He could have broken her grip with a move that would have prevented her from using her hand for several weeks. Instead he turned his hand gently but irresistibly and caressed the inside of her wrist, feeling her pulse hammer under his fingers.

Her hair had dried to a soft halo around her head. With the strands backlit by the afternoon sun she looked like a Renaissance angel. He smoothed her hair with his free hand, hearing her make a soft sound he read as encouragement.

He didn't need much. He slid his hand down the side of her face, drawing a strangled breath as she turned her head and kissed his palm. In a minute he would send her on her way, he promised himself.

Like a sleepwalker she stood and linked her arms around his neck, her face upturned, waiting. He lowered his mouth to accept her silent invitation.

The taste of her flowed through him like fine wine. She tasted of coffee and smelled of ocean breezes, seducing his senses until he felt as light-headed as if he'd surfaced too quickly from a technical dive. On a sigh she dropped her head back, and he skimmed his lips over the softness at her throat, aware of an abyss opening at his feet. He wanted to spiral all the way down with her, take her to places she'd only ever dreamed of going.

While he still could, he lifted her hands from his neck, kissing the knuckles of her linked fingers, and lowered them to her sides. "I didn't mean to do that. I was going to tell you how much I admired what you did today."

She wondered if she looked as shell-shocked as she felt. Freeing one hand, she raked it through her hair. "What did I do?"

"The idea of scuba diving scares you half to death. You could have stayed in the boat, yet you came, and you got yourself out of trouble. That took guts."

He couldn't know that he was the wellspring of her courage. Just knowing he was with her empowered her to push herself beyond what she ordinarily thought of as her limits. And not only under the water. She was by no means a passive woman, but neither was she normally as bold as Garth made her feel.

Wanton was an old-fashioned word, but nothing else applied. He made her want to flout every moral rule life had ever drummed into her. She yearned to shed her clothes and make love with him in the most outrageous places—the deck of his boat, the ocean floor, the middle of the castle green. The realization should have shocked her. Instead it excited her.

He'd had the same effect on her when they were teenagers, she remembered. His sporting prowess had inspired her, and in his kiss she'd tasted heaven. She had transmuted her feelings for him into the energy to go out and conquer the world. Not to settle for less than everything she could be.

Now she was fully aware of what he made her feel, and he was stepping back from it. She felt as if he'd thrown seawater into her face. "Thanks for the compliment," she said stiffly.

He seemed to hear what she wasn't saying. "Believe me, it's better this way. You don't need me messing with your future."

Recalling the night they'd already spent together, she laughed hollowly. "Isn't it a bit late to have regrets?"

His gaze darkened. "I don't regret what happened between us for a single minute."

His conviction thrummed through her. "Then what's the problem?"

His hands skimmed her shoulders and settled lightly on her upper arms, allowing her the freedom to shrug him off. When she didn't, he said, "Haven't you worked it out yet? Good sex is all I have to offer you, Serena. This is my life. No home, no kids, and we both know what happened to my career.''

''That was a mistake,'' she said with such conviction that he was shaken.

Having someone believe in him unconditionally was a novelty, even though he didn't want it. ''Unfortunately, the navy doesn't agree with you.''

The glint of battle flashed in her eyes. ''We can make them agree. Prince Lorne has the power.''

''If the truth isn't enough, the hell with it.'' Garth said, bringing her up short. There was only one way to stop her from sacrificing herself for him, although it made him feel like a brute. ''I don't want Prince Lorne's charity, or yours for that matter. My life was fine the way it was until you came into it.''

Anger stemmed any trace of tears in her eyes. ''Then be my guest, go right back to wallowing in your black-sheep status. Too bad if it turns out you're the heir to the throne, because that will really complicate your life.'' She dragged in a breath. ''Oh, I forgot. If that happens, you'll abdicate in favor of Prince Lorne. Shall I tell him the DNA test is a waste of time, because you've already made up your mind to wimp out?''

She had taken two steps when he grabbed her and whirled her to face him. ''What was that about wimping out?''

''What else do you call it?''

''You could try concern for the good of the kingdom.''

His calm assertion defused some of her anger. ''You really believe that, don't you? You're not being cowardly or arrogant.''

He met her gaze levelly. ''I like to think I'm neither. Running a country isn't like running a business. Lorne was born to it. I wasn't.''

''If I believed that, I'd still be modeling,'' she said softly. ''I have you to thank for planting the seed making me aware that I was in control of my life.''

An odd light came into his eyes. ''Maybe I *was* arrogant. You might have become a supermodel earning millions just for getting out of bed in the morning. You're still beautiful enough to grace magazine covers.''

An unwelcome warmth stole over her. ''Thanks, but I'm happy with my choice.'' A sudden realization made her gasp. ''It's not the possibility of the crown. It's the lack of control over your destiny that you object to.''

He smiled mockingly. ''You took your time but you got there. Now in case you haven't noticed, it's getting late.''

While they talked the sun had become a brilliant orange disk low on the horizon. Discussion over, she understood, knowing she was right all the same. She reached a decision. ''I'm not going back to the castle tonight.''

His jaw firmed. ''I hope you'll be comfortable sleeping in your car.''

She kept her expression calm. ''If it comes to that. I'm sure you'll take pity on me and let me use your shower in the morning.''

''Don't count on it.''

''Fine, as long as your conscience won't be bothered by the sight of me camping in your driveway all night.''

''You're assuming I have one.''

''I know you do,'' she said softly and seated herself at the table. ''So—stalemate.''

He ignored her while he snapped off lights and secured the cabin, then he picked up the duffel and walked to the steps. Looking back at her, he said, ''If you're coming, you'd better get a move on.''

The Remy family home was like Garth himself, one of a kind. The first thing she noticed when she pulled up behind Garth's pickup was the long, narrow jetty extending like a crooked finger into Katira Cove. The second thing was the unmistakably nautical style of the building. Crouching on its rocky headland the house looked like a squat white lighthouse.

''Built by my grandfather,'' Garth explained. ''When he was a boy his family were lighthouse keepers on Nuee, and he always wanted to live in one. This was the closest he came."

The glassed-in upper story did look like a lighthouse beacon. It was accessible by a white wrought-iron staircase winding around the lower floors. The view must be spectacular. There couldn't be more than one or two rooms to a floor, she thought. All the windows were round like the portholes of a ship.

There was also no mistaking the general air of neglect as she drove after him into the garage attached to one side of the house. An internal door led directly into the house. Hardly aware of doing so, she automatically assessed the level of security. It was far from ideal but she could do nothing about it other than remain on her guard.

With the key in his hand, Garth hesitated, and she remembered her impression that he'd been living out of his pickup when she tracked him down. "Have you been back here since your parents died?" she asked, gentling her tone.

"Once, to get some things that were needed for the funeral."

She wasn't fooled by his gruff manner. "I went through the same thing after my maternal grandmother died. My mother couldn't bring herself to set foot in grandma's house, so Dad and I sorted through her things. It's hard, isn't it?"

Without answering he turned the key in the lock. The door stuck slightly but yielded to his insistent push. When she went in ahead of him, the hallway glowed in the early-evening light and the air smelled stale.

"Welcome to Chez Remy," he said, closing the front door. "It's a long way from Pearl Point."

She refused to rise to the bait. Although separated from here by only a couple of miles, there was a world of difference between Katira Cove and the affluent suburb of Pearl Point where her parents still lived. The high school they had both attended was located roughly midway between.

"It's different," she said, not sure how to describe the mix of modern furnishings and pieces that looked as if they'd been washed up by the tide. The end result was bizarre but somehow homey.

Thinking of the impersonal apartment she occupied in the staff wing at the castle, she felt wistful. She had thought about making a real home for herself without doing anything about it. Being here made her think it was time she did.

He led the way into a combined kitchen and dining room, dumped his bag on a chair, then went around opening windows. As a fresh sea breeze swirled through the room, she inhaled deeply. "This is a nice place."

"You don't have to be tactful."

"I'm not. The house has warmth and character. It could use a little TLC, but it's a real home." One where you could raise a family, she thought unexpectedly. "You have a problem with it because it isn't moving under your feet."

Touché, she thought when she saw his frown deepen. "So I prefer boats. It isn't a crime."

She touched his hand. "Your parents didn't inherit this house until you were a teenager. It's hardly surprising you feel more at home in the environment you knew best. I like boats myself. I used to envy your living aboard one all the time."

He looked at her in frank surprise, as if he couldn't imagine her envying anything about his life. "You did?"

She dragged a wooden stool nearer to the open window and angled it so she could look at the view while watching him. "I used to think living on a boat was romantic, with the seven seas as your garden."

He opened the duffel and took out a packet of crackers and an assortment of cans, placing them on a counter top. "You always were a dreamer."

"My favorite song says if you never dream, you can't have your dreams come true."

He didn't respond, and she remembered what had happened to his dreams. "How are you at cooking?" he asked, the swift change making it clear the discussion was over. He obviously didn't want her feeling sorry for him.

Like a game-show host, he waved a hand over the line-up

of cans. "They're our ingredients. Unless you have a problem with them."

On the stool she drew herself up, pretending to be offended. "I'll have you know I passed can opening with flying colors."

He tossed her a can. "Prove it."

She fielded it deftly, reading the label on the chicken soup out loud, "Fillet steak with lobster sauce."

He didn't miss a beat. "My mistake, I thought that was the caviar." He scooped up a can of asparagus. "Ah, here it is."

"Did I see pecan pie for dessert."

"Must be in this one." He held up a battered can clearly marked Sliced Peaches.

Enjoying the game, she smiled. "No cream for the pie?"

He rummaged in the hold all and held up two chocolate bars. "Will these do?"

She let her legs swing. "All the comforts of home."

"It's not too late to change your mind and go back to the castle."

If she had any sense she would say yes. This was entirely too cozy. The air felt charged like the atmosphere before a storm, although the evening sky was clear. She opened her mouth to opt for retreat, and instead heard herself say, "I'm staying."

The husky assurance fired Garth's blood and he couldn't resist moving closer. With the endless expanse of sea and sky framed in the window behind her, she looked like a mermaid sitting on her rock, awaiting a lover.

She didn't seem aware that she'd kicked off her shoes. Her toenails were painted an iridescent blue. He liked the frivolity. Liked the suggestion of softness underpinning her tough security-officer persona.

Her eyes were bright with a desire he could feel to the depths of his being. Out on the water the sun had kissed her skin with gold. She had said she wasn't hungry but she looked as if she was. He had enough masculine pride to hope it was for him.

He had never been a fan of fighting temptation as long as

giving in to it hurt no one, although this time he couldn't be sure. And he didn't want to hurt Serena. What he did want to do surprised even him.

Making love to her was only part of it. For the first time he wondered how it would feel to share everything with a woman. Preparing a meal together and eating it by candlelight. Rubbing her feet as she rested them on his lap after a hard day. Holding her hand and lending her his strength as she brought their child into the world.

His thoughts stunned him. No woman had ever made him want those things the way Serena did. Maybe if the DNA test proved he was a prince, he could offer them to her and more. Until then, he had better remember how little he *did* have to offer her: a run-down old house, a boat named after another woman and a promising career in ruins. She deserved better.

She didn't seem to know it as she slid off the stool and came to him, her skin flushed and her eyes bright. Could it really be so simple? Would she be content with what he could give her? Burn for him the way he burned for her?

Even if the answer was yes—hell, *especially* if the answer was yes—he owed it to her not to take advantage until the current crisis was resolved.

It took every bit of self-control he possessed to steer for the window as if admiring the view was what he'd had in mind all along. He could almost feel her puzzlement as he walked past her and stared out to sea. "My grandmother used to say this kitchen has the best view in Solano."

"It's beautiful," she agreed.

The bewilderment he heard in her tone was almost his undoing. One small step, he thought. Then she would be in his arms and he could plunder her mouth with all the abandonment of the pirates that had once roamed this coast. He could sweep her off her feet and carry her upstairs to his old room, to the big sleigh bed his grandfather had made with his own hands. "This is a bed for making babies," his grandfather had said when a young Garth had asked him why he was putting so much care into the construction. Garth had been too young to understand him then, but he did now.

He wanted to make babies with Serena so badly he ached.

Instead he turned slowly, holding his arms rigid at his sides. "We'd better get to work."

Chapter 14

Serena's breath rushed out of her body. She was sure that wasn't what Garth had intended to say. When he came toward her he had looked as if he wanted to kiss her. Annoyed by how much she wanted him too, she contrarily felt disappointed. Never before had she felt so powerfully attracted to a man, and it bothered her. Not so much because it was there, but because it was Garth.

As long as he was convinced he wasn't good enough for her, nothing could come of the pull she felt toward him. The worst of it was, he could be right. She had her life at the castle and a career on the fast track. Involving herself with a known black sheep wouldn't help either one. Too bad her runaway hormones had yet to be convinced.

"You're right," she said, knowing that he was. It was still an effort to sound enthusiastic.

Extending her foot, she felt around under the stool for her shoes. Garth saw the move and picked up one of the pumps that had skidded off as she swung her legs. "Looking for this?"

Dropping to one knee, he took her foot in hand like Cinderella's prince trying the glass slipper on her for size. The touch was so intimate that Serena's resolve trembled on its foundations. As he cupped her instep and slid the shoe slowly over her foot, shivers wound their way up her spine.

She could hardly speak. "I can manage the other one."

But he retrieved it and slid it on to her foot. "You have such neat feet. I like the blue polish."

"It was the beautician's choice. I had a pedicure before all this started." Damn it, why did she have to sound so defensive?

He looked up from his position at her feet. "What else do you do to yourself?"

"Not much. Manicures, a massage now and then. I don't have time for much pampering."

"Remind me to give you a massage sometime. I'm told I have magic fingers."

She hated thinking of the woman—women?—he was quoting. And herself for caring about them. Imagining his strong hands touching, kneading, stroking her, she jellied inside. "Think I'll pass."

"Don't you trust me?"

It was herself she didn't trust in such a situation. "I prefer a woman giving me a massage. They're gentler."

"I can be gentle."

This she already knew from his lovemaking. He could be gentle and caressing, fiercely possessive and everything in between. "What do you want from me?" she asked on a heavy exhalation.

His gaze narrowed and he stood up. "Explain."

"We've already agreed we don't want to get involved. Yet you keep saying things that…offering me massages and…" He also turned her into a blithering fool who couldn't string a complete sentence together, she thought angrily. She took a deep breath. "You confuse me."

"Because you insist on mixing up desire with commitment. We can be good in bed together without getting involved."

"I know men are supposed to be better at separating the two, but I don't know if I want to be."

His mouth curved into a challenging smile. "You did very well at Brett's place."

She took refuge in belligerence. "Are you saying we should have a full-blown affair without expecting anything more from each other?"

His smile widened. "Sounds good to me."

"Well, not to me." At least not that she was prepared to admit. "Are you going to show me around, or am I going to find my own way?"

He watched the mixture of emotions cloud her lovely features. She could still model if she chose. He had never encountered a more ideal blend of bone structure, skin like milk and hair as fine as spun silk. Whether or not they added up to classical beauty, he couldn't say, but they fitted any definition he could imagine.

More than that, she was beautiful inside. He had always known she set high standards for herself, some might say impossibly high. Her personnel record showed she hadn't changed. She still did more than was expected of her, cared more, contributed more. Her actions with him demonstrated it. Not only the diving, but accompanying him here because she thought it was the right thing to do, when she could have earned more brownie points by reporting back to Prince Lorne.

Under his scrutiny, she shifted from one foot to the other. "What?"

"Just looking," he said mildly, enjoying the luxury. He pushed a strand of hair out of her eyes, felt her quiver like a wild deer meeting man for the first time.

"Well, stop," she said, flustered.

"You're asking the impossible."

Twin spots of color bloomed on her cheeks. "You're doing it again."

He didn't have to ask what. The upheaval in her gaze told him. "I enjoy confusing you. When I do, you change from a security officer to a Siren."

"Remember what happened to the men in mythology who let themselves be lured by the Sirens?" she said, sounding shaky.

He nodded. "They met their fate with a huge smile on their faces."

"Greek Mythology 101 never mentioned that part."

"Pity. It was the best part."

Sparring with her was fun, he decided. He meant it when he said he enjoyed confusing her. She had no idea how beautiful she looked in that state. Or how tantalizing. He had never known a woman like her, tough enough to have graduated from the police academy with flying colors. Respected enough to be entrusted with the monarch's personal safety. Yet woman enough to blush scarlet at his innuendos. No wonder he couldn't resist provoking her.

It was far from one-sided, he recognized. He had never felt desire like this in his life. So all consuming that he was hard-pressed to think of anything else when he was with her. And a lot of the time when he wasn't.

He had thought making love to her would satisfy the needs she fired in him. Instead the experience had made him crave more. He was as hooked on her as the most pathetic addict. Nor was he convinced he was as heart whole as he'd assured her. The thought that he might already be in over his head scared the blazes out of him.

So he did what any red-blooded man would do. He turned and ran, figuratively speaking. "As soon as we've locked up down here, we can start in my father's study."

"I also want to see the lighthouse room," she said.

He let out a deep breath. She *would* ask to see that room. It was the one with the sleigh bed.

Serena could swear her feet tingled where Garth had touched them. And did he have to mention how skilled he was at massage? Now her mind insisted on creating fantasies involving her and his magic fingers.

It wasn't going to happen. She was already more attracted

to him than was wise, and she had no intention of indulging *his* fantasy of sex without commitment. She might want to, but she wanted a lot of things that weren't good for her without giving in to them.

His father's study was more of an alcove than a separate room. Garth's parents hadn't been too organized, she saw from the piles of paper almost hiding an old 486 computer on the desk and spilling onto a chair. A quick perusal revealed that most of the files related to normal family affairs, as well as the day-to-day operation of the *Onalos.*

"I went through some of this looking for my parents' wills," Garth said, his voice gruff.

She put a hand on his arm. "I can do the rest myself. It shouldn't take long."

His gaze telegraphed appreciation of the thought, but he shook his head. "We'll work faster together. You're the ex-cop. What should we be looking for?"

She tilted her head to one side, thinking. "Signs of unusual dealings, contact with people your parents wouldn't ordinarily associate with."

"Criminals, you mean?" His tone hardened in denial.

It had to be said. "Someone wanted them dead. We need to find out who and why."

He closed his eyes then opened them again. "Let's get on with it."

By unspoken agreement he tackled the computer. She found herself admiring the way his fingers skimmed across the keyboard as he coaxed information out of the old machine. Admiring him.

Watching him wouldn't get the job done, she reminded herself crossly, and picked up an armful of papers. Sitting cross-legged on the floor, she began to read. As she'd expected there was nothing untoward. All the same she set them aside for Matt Hayes and his team to sift through later in case anything had been missed.

After an hour she stretched her arms over her head.

"There's nothing here to find. Either your folks kept another set of records or they had no connection with their killer."

"There's nothing useful on the hard drive or any of the disks I looked at."

"But you did find something?"

"I accessed a few Internet sites related to plastic explosives."

Looking for information on the deadly toy, she assumed. "And?"

"Nothing. I've e-mailed a couple of friends who may be more helpful, but I don't expect them to get back to me until the morning."

She didn't ask what kind of friends would have those answers? "Did your parents keep a file of family stuff, marriage certificates, birth certificates, that kind of thing?" she asked.

He handed her a plastic binder. "They're in here."

He would have needed the documents for the funeral. She took the file, careful to avoid any contact with him. The heightened emotions involved in what they were doing meant her control was at a premium right now. She suspected his wasn't much better.

Returning to her spot on the floor she opened the file. Minutes later she closed it, giving vent to a sigh of frustration. "No sign of your birth certificate."

"If you're hoping it lists Prince Eduard and Princess Aimee under mother and father, sorry to disappoint you. The details match the public record." He pulled a faded piece of paper out of his wallet and handed it to her.

She read the birth certificate and gave it back to him. "I didn't think it would be that easy."

"Few things ever are."

She stood up, pressing both hands against the small of her back. "We have to be missing something." The instincts honed during her years on the police force were fairly screaming at her. All she had to do was pay attention.

"Unless there's nothing to miss. Maybe I'm exactly who I'm supposed to be. No mystery, no drama."

"Except for the items we found in the package meant for the Hand."

"Unless…"

When he didn't continue she frowned. "Unless what?"

"The Hand could have concocted this scheme to get you away from handling security for the presidential visit."

"How could he be sure I'd be assigned to you?"

Garth hooked his thumbs into the pockets of his jeans. "By his choice of candidate for monarch."

"How would he know there was a connection between us?"

"I told him."

A chill feathered down her spine. Her earlier doubts about what side Garth was on came rushing back until she squashed them. "To do that you'd have to know his identity."

He shoved aside a pile of papers and settled his hip on a corner of the desk, folding his arms. "I haven't had the pleasure yet. It's more likely that I tipped him off indirectly. When I joined Carramer First I had to list people I was close to who might be useful to the organization. I gave them your name as coming from a well-to-do family."

"So the Hand only had to check the group's membership files to learn that you and I go back a long way?"

"I may have created the impression that we were…more than friends."

She felt her face heat and willed the color away. "You told the group we were lovers?"

"It was wishful thinking, damn it. After we kissed, you stayed in my thoughts for a long time."

So it hadn't been entirely one-sided. She dragged her thoughts onto a more productive track. "What would the Hand gain from having me replaced?"

"Maybe he's hoping Jarvis Reid can be bought."

Flattered that Garth was so sure Serena couldn't, she said, "I hope you're wrong. I don't like Reid, but it doesn't make him a traitor to the crown."

"But you will check to make sure he hasn't come into any sudden fortunes?"

She reached for her cell phone. "I'll contact Matt."

* * *

Watching her talk to her former partner, Garth's mind was busy. He knew why he had bragged about her to Carramer First, and it hadn't been to give him status within the group, although he'd let her think so. He had lied about being her lover because he'd wanted it to be true.

He still wanted it. Making love to her was supposed to get her out of his system once and for all. Instead it had only banked the flames higher. Knowing how perfectly they fitted together, he wanted more. He wanted her to belong to him in mind, body and spirit.

The longer this went on, the more convinced he became that he wasn't a lost prince of Carramer, so there was no point in waiting until he had a crown to offer her. If he wanted her— hell, there was no "if" about it—he would have to make sure he was worthy of her.

That meant going back to the navy and hounding them until he convinced them to investigate the defective equipment that had led to his dishonorable discharge. Enough of this lone-wolf stuff. He would even use Prince Lorne's influence to get a new hearing, if that's what it took. Garth knew that Serena meant more to him than his stubborn pride.

He didn't like admitting how much power she held over him, even to himself. But the truth was there in the way he reacted simply to watching her make a phone call. She sat cross-legged on the floor, the off-the-shoulder top revealing an expanse of creamy skin that made him want to press his lips to it.

When she stretched her legs out, her scent drifted up to him, sinful and sexy and uniquely hers. She must have reapplied it after the dive. It deserved to be named Aphrodisiac.

She pushed a hand through her hair, tousling it. Then she looked up and caught him watching her, and he was amused to hear a stammer come into her voice. He enjoyed seeing his effect on her. For his own amusement he dropped his hands to her shoulders and began to knead.

"Oh, God." She collected herself hastily. "Sorry, Matt, I was distracted."

Her back arched and her eyes starred with pleasure as his thumbs found the sensitive points on her shoulders. A shuddering breath forced its way past her lips. With her free hand she batted at Garth's. "Matt, I have to go. Something just came up."

Garth almost choked. It was true that touching her had had a startlingly physical outcome, but he didn't think she'd noticed yet. "How did you guess?" he asked when she snapped the phone closed.

"Merely a figure of speech." Her voice shook.

"A graphic one, considering your effect on me."

He could have toasted marshmallows on the fire in her cheeks. "Your own fault. You shouldn't have started massaging me while I was on the phone."

"Couldn't resist."

"Next time, try harder." Garth was pleased to hear her sounding more baffled than angry.

"What did Matt say?"

"He's going to look into Jarvis Reid's finances." She took a breath. "There's also no evidence that your folks were involved in anything underhanded, at least not recently."

Desire fled, replaced by rising anger. "Explain that."

She scrambled to her feet. "It seems your mother had an unorthodox pregnancy. No recorded visits to her doctor, no attendance at prenatal classes and no postnatal follow-ups."

He felt his gut clench. "So she was healthy and independent."

"Or else she was never pregnant."

"So where the hell did I come from?" He spread his hands. "And don't give me that 'lost prince' malarkey."

"All right, I won't. But you must agree there's something unusual about your arrival into the world."

"Of course there is. My father delivered me himself out at sea. The ambulance people talked him through it by radio telephone."

"He could have staged the emergency to cover up an illegal adoption."

Slowly he unclenched his fists. None of this was Serena's fault. If anything, his parents were to blame for withholding the truth—whatever it was—from him. "If it's true," his icy tone emphasized the *if*, "I'll find out one way or another."

She matched him for coldness. "The police will find out. They don't need a vigilante getting in their way."

"You expect me to sit and wait to find out who the hell I am?"

"That's exactly what I expect. Or you could give me the guided tour you promised."

Serena couldn't care less about seeing the rest of the house, but she had to do something to head off the rage she saw building in Garth. Not that she could blame him. She would be furious too if everything she'd ever been told about her life had turned out to be a lie.

She saw the moment he won the battle with himself, for now at least. "There isn't much. You saw most of it on the way in." His flat tone belied the tension in every line of his body. "But I'll show you what there is if it's what you want."

What she wanted was to soothe him with her touch, but she forced herself to stillness, trying to calm the hammering of her heart. Who he was mattered to her far less than what he was— a man she cared about more than she wanted to admit. It was crazy. They had nothing in common except sizzling passion, and that wasn't enough to build a future together.

He was a rebel. She was a conformist. He was a drifter. She was a homebody. He took life as it came. She had plans for hers. Oil and water would blend more successfully than the two of them. She had to make herself remember it.

Her resolve held until she saw the bed.

It was the centerpiece of what she thought of as the light-house room. It was reached by a spiral staircase from the inside, as well as the wrought-iron one she'd seen from the outside on arrival. The outside stairs opened onto a narrow widow's walk all the way around. Inside, the walls of the ten-foot-square room were almost entirely uncurtained glass, set so high above the surroundings that privacy wasn't an issue.

By night the room seemed to float on a sea of stars. She couldn't see the breakers far below, only hear them rolling endlessly onto the rocks. Flashes of phosphorescence out to sea made it look as if wraiths with lanterns patrolled the bay.

The floor rugs looked to be handmade, the quilt as if it was an heirloom. It was spread over the most impressive piece of furniture she'd ever seen. "The timber looks ancient. Where did it come from?" she asked, instinctively lowering her voice.

"Salvaged from an eighteenth-century sailing ship that was wrecked off Nuee. When my grandparents built this house, they brought the timber with them. Grandpa said he was waiting for it to tell him exactly what he should make with it."

She stroked the curved teak bed end, imagining Garth's grandfather sitting beside the timber, waiting for inspiration. It hadn't failed him. The massive bedhead swept back in imitation of an ocean wave, with a slightly lower foot to match. The mattress, as wide as it was long, came up to her thigh, making her think of Goldilocks confronted by the largest of the three bears' beds.

"How on earth did he move it up here?" she asked.

"By making it in sections, then assembling it in this room. It was never intended to leave."

"He did good work."

"My parents didn't agree. That's how I got to have this room for my own. They never slept here. Said it would be like sleeping in a fishbowl."

"A fishbowl filled with stars."

"Grandpa would have approved of you." He touched her cheek. "He said this bed was meant for making babies."

She managed a shaky smile. "He must have been some man."

"He was, but he was thinking of the future generations he hoped would sleep in the bed."

Her legs felt unable to hold her suddenly, and she sat on the only available support, the bed itself. Bad idea she thought as Garth leaned over her. She was still thinking "bad idea" when his mouth found hers, and suddenly it seemed like the best idea in the world.

She wasn't sure how she ended up stretched out full length, but somehow she was lying in his arms. There was plenty of room, but she didn't feel inclined to use any more of it for the moment.

He tugged a pillow under her head, then propped himself up on one elbow beside her. His finger traced a line from her forehead down her nose until she captured the tip in her mouth and suckled, hearing his breath catch.

Her own throat felt tight. This wasn't supposed to happen, and yet she didn't want it to stop. He slid his hand around the curve of her jaw and tilted her face up. She closed her eyes as he found her mouth again, and sensation speared all the way to her core.

"Open your eyes," he urged softly. "I want you to look at me when we make love."

She did and almost closed them again as the heat from his gaze ignited her internal temperature nearly to flashpoint. "We aren't going to make love," she said without any real conviction.

His mouth moved over hers, robbing her of breath. "Of course not. What we're going to do will be so astonishing we'll have to find a new way to describe it."

Chapter 15

The blood roared in her head. "This is a mistake," she said but couldn't make herself roll away from him.

He nibbled her earlobe. "Everybody's entitled to one."

"Then we've had our quota."

He twined a lock of her hair around his finger. "That wasn't a mistake. That was an experiment. Any scientist knows your results aren't valid unless you can repeat them."

"We aren't scientists."

"Speak for yourself." He began to kiss her bare shoulder, anointing each spot with his tongue. "Right now I'm collecting data on the taste of the human female."

Each time his tongue made contact, fire tore through her. Her voice came out as a strangled whisper. "Isn't this experiment a bit one-sided."

He continued licking and kissing a trail along her collarbone until he encountered the sleeve of her top. He tugged at the garment. "You'll get your turn. Does this thing have any fastenings."

"It pulls on," she said tremulously, wondering why she was

helping him instead of fighting him. The drumming of her pulse made it hard to think straight.

"What pulls on can pull off, right?" He was already easing the stretchy fabric down over her shoulder, lifting her unresisting arm and peeling the single sleeve off until the top fell to her waist, exposing her lacy strapless bra. He pushed that down as well and began to kiss her breasts in turn. Sheet lightning speared through her.

She threw her head back, panting for air. "This experiment of yours is killing me. I can't…"

"Tell me you want me," he said.

His teeth nipped and teased. Drawing a whole breath became a memory. "You know I do."

"I want to hear you say it."

"Yes, yes." If he left her now she didn't know what she would do. Still, sanity struggled to surface. "We shouldn't. shouldn't…"

His fingers skimmed heated flesh, shaping her to his desire "Shouldn't stop?" he asked, faking innocence.

She rolled her head from side to side, her fingers digging into the mattress, "Yes, no. Don't ask trick questions."

He lifted her across his lap. "Then I'll make it simple. want to make love to you. Right here, right now. If you want me to stop, you'd better tell me while it's still an option. Because it won't be for very much longer."

She slid her arms around his neck and pressed her throbbing body against him. Everything ached. Everything tingled. There was only one possible answer. "This is crazy. I don't want you to stop." Not ever, she suspected, her mind spinning.

His breath blasted out. He'd actually feared she would end this, she realized. How could she when every touch of his mouth was the most exquisite torment?

She slid her hands down and worried at his shirt buttons tremors making her fingers clumsy. Getting it undone at last she splayed her fingers over his chest. Wonderful, rock-hard body. Sensuous rasp of fine hairs scraping nerve endings raw Fast beating heart keeping time with her own.

He caught her shoulders and pressed her to him, his teeth teasing the side of her neck as he brought them both to their feet. Unsure that her legs would support her, she clung to him, meeting fire with fire. If he doubted what she wanted, needed, craved, she would show him.

Wantonly, recklessly, she did.

"Do you know what you're doing to me?" he rasped, sounding tortured.

"Yes." Because his effect on her was just as all-consuming. "I haven't been able to stop thinking about you. About us."

"Thinking isn't what I have in mind right now."

Just as well because she was barely capable of rational thought any longer. He released her, and she swayed as he unzipped his jeans and kicked them off. Shrugging out of his shirt he balled it and tossed it aside, then hooked his thumbs into narrow black briefs, sliding them off.

Drugged by passion, she didn't even try to look away, devouring his incredible male beauty with heavy-lidded eyes. He was everything she had dreamed of in a man, and more. And he wanted her.

When he stepped back and ran his hands down her arms, she shuddered with pleasure.

Then urgency gripped her and she pulled the top over her head, dropping it on the floor. The rest of her clothes followed, her fingers tangling with his as he tried to help. And they were falling, falling back onto the vast bed with nothing between them but the scorching, slick, passionate collision of skin to skin.

Whoever he might be, he was hers, she recognized. As she was his. Right now nothing else was allowed to matter.

She whimpered when he pulled away, but it was only to delve into a drawer beside the bed. "Sorry, Grandpa," he said, using his teeth to open the small packet.

His grandfather had intended the bed to be used by future generations to make babies, she remembered. A pang shot through her. Garth was only considering her, but as he covered himself, she felt a tearing ache deep in her womb. It dragged at her, catching her unawares. She didn't want Garth's child, did she?

The answer crashed over her like a tidal wave. Yes.

This bed must be making her crazy, she thought. After being used by her parents for so much of her youth, the need for a child of her own had never been on Serena's radar screen. Now it was abruptly there, clamoring for attention as if the alarm on her biological clock had suddenly gone off.

What was the matter with her?

He was the matter. Garth had believed in her before she had the confidence to believe in herself. He had wanted the best for her. He still did, warning her against getting involved with him because he wouldn't be good for her.

Just how good he was sent her senses reeling. His touch, his murmured words, the very scent of him made her wild. She wound herself around him, touching, tasting, insatiable.

"Serena," he said warningly, bucking underneath her, beneath the frantic demands of her hands and mouth.

"You said I'd get my turn."

His fingers tangled in her hair, lifting her head. "Have you ever heard a grown man beg?"

She smiled. "Might be exciting."

"No, *this* is exciting."

And he rolled her onto her back, lifting himself over her, making her mindless with anticipation. She kept her eyes open, feasting on the tempestuous look in his, glorying in her power to drive him to the edge of control and beyond.

In the end it was she whose control snapped. Unable to bear the suspense and the wanting a moment longer, she wound her legs and arms around him, pulling him down and into her until he was part of her.

It was more mutual giving than surrender, the miracle of shared joy surging through her as great tremors of emotion carried her on a cresting wave of fulfillment beyond words. Then he was with her, shuddering with the power of his release, crying her name, tumbling with her over a cliff edge of sensation, falling, falling, until at last there was only serenity and the jagged sound of breath mingling.

The stars were out, millions of them, as dazzling as diamonds in the velvet blackness. Garth crooked a hand behind his head and looked at them, then at Serena curled against his chest, his other arm around her. In sleep she looked so vulnerable that his heart constricted.

After the night at Brett's place, Garth had promised himself this wouldn't happen again. That no matter what it cost him, he would keep his distance unless and until he had something more to offer her. He had truly meant to keep the promise—until tonight. Learning that he was unlikely to be his parents' biological son had shaken something loose, stirring elemental needs that only Serena had been able to assuage.

As well as wanting her, he had needed her.

His behavior was inexcusably selfish. Hadn't he condemned her parents for using her to fulfill their needs? He was no better. That she had wanted him, too, was also no excuse. Then she opened her eyes and smiled at him, and he knew he would do it again in a heartbeat.

So much for honor and virtue.

There was no condemnation in her look. Just sleepy satisfaction and something else he was almost afraid to interpret. "Is it morning yet?" she asked, stifling a delicate yawn.

He activated the liquid-crystal display on his diver's watch. "Just after midnight."

Absently she stroked a hand down his chest and would have continued lower but he caught her hand and held it, giving honor a fighting chance, however belatedly.

"What are you doing awake?" she asked.

He could ask her the same thing. "I didn't mean to disturb you."

"You didn't. I just realized I'm hungry."

"There's a good reason for that. We never got around to dinner."

She tried to tug her hand free. "I'll go down and make us some supper."

He kissed her fingertips. "I'll do it. I know my way around this place. I'll bring a tray up here."

She gave a sigh of contentment and lay back against the pillow. "Room service? I like the sound of that."

He didn't tell her that unless he got out of the bed, there would be no room service anytime soon. Her touch had triggered a fresh battle with himself and this time he was determined to win. He stood up and tugged on his jeans, leaving his feet bare. Then he leaned over and kissed her lightly. "I won't be long."

Her arms wound around his neck and her lips parted. "You taste much better than canned chicken soup."

Cursing honor and virtue, he uncoiled her arms. "But chicken soup is what's on the menu."

"Pity," he heard her murmur as he slipped away.

By the time he returned with the tray, she was asleep again. He placed the tray on the bedside, switched on the lamp and stood beside the bed, drinking in the sight of her. Her hair spilled across the pillow like moonbeams. She had rolled the blanket around herself so she looked like a beautiful butterfly emerging from a cocoon. Her blue-painted toes peeped from beneath the bedroll.

He tickled her toes gently, amused when she withdrew them into the cocoon. He followed, tickling again, and she withdrew farther. Gradually he became aware he was playing with fire, and straightened. "Serena?"

The sharpness in his tone penetrated her torpor. She pushed the hair out of her eyes and stretched her legs out. "What's wrong?"

"Room service."

"Oh."

Rubbing her eyes, she sat up, dragging the blanket with her. He placed the tray between them, as much a barrier as a source of nourishment. On it were two mugs of chicken soup he'd mixed with the canned asparagus and heated in the microwave, as well as a bowl of crackers. "No lobster, it's the chef's night off," he said.

She curled her fingers around a mug of soup and sipped it. "I'll eat anything someone else cooks. It's delicious."

He crumbled crackers into his soup. "Serena, about what I did tonight."

Reaching across the tray, she touched a finger to his lips. "You didn't do anything. We did. And it was very, very mutual."

He should be grateful for her assurance. Instead he felt angrier with himself. "I don't even know who the hell I am."

"Does it matter?"

"It should."

"Not to me. Disappointed because I've broken through your tough-guy facade?"

"There's an even tougher guy underneath."

Serena didn't smile as she sipped her soup thoughtfully, her whole body vibrating with achy pleasure. Whoever he turned out to be, he was still the one man who could set her on fire. She finished the soup and crackers and put the mug on the tray. "Thanks for the porridge."

His brows made a vee of confusion. "What?"

"In this bed I feel like Goldilocks in Papa Bear's too-big bed."

He put his mug down and lifted the tray onto the bedside. Two heartbeats were all it took for honor and virtue to shatter into bits. He snapped off the light and reached for her. "Want to know how that story ends?"

She had a fair idea how this version would. Suddenly she tensed, her security-honed senses jumping to alert. "Hear that? Someone's downstairs."

"I'll check. It's probably only the house settling."

They both knew it wasn't. She hooked a hand around his wrist. "I'll go, it's my job."

He lifted her hand, kissing her knuckles, and desire shot through her as potent as it was inopportune. "We'll both go."

There was no time to argue with him. Her clothes were a

twisted mess, and dressing took seconds longer than she liked, but she didn't want to switch on the lamp. Whoever was downstairs was an amateur, stumbling and knocking into furniture. A herd of sun deer would have moved more stealthily.

She groped for her bag and cursed colorfully. Her phone was still on the desk in Garth's study and her bag was in the kitchen with her wallet-size P32 revolver in the specially made pocket of her jacket. She had stupidly let passion overwhelm years of training. What was that going to cost them?

Signaling to Garth that she was going outside, she gestured to him, then the staircase, her meaning clear. He nodded and started down, silent as a shadow. The sea breeze tore at her as she stepped onto the widow's walk. She hoped the name wouldn't turn out to be too literal.

There was no point crouching. The wrought-iron railing left her completely exposed, so she hurried to the staircase and took the steps two at a time. On the ground she scouted around, satisfying herself the intruder had left no backup outside.

Courtesy of their guest, the kitchen door she'd heard being jimmied stood ajar. Keeping to one side, she eased it open. No one inside. Her jacket was draped over her bag beside the stool and she padded to it, feeling better as soon as she had the weapon in hand and a spare magazine in her pocket. At only a third the weight of the R.P.D.-issue .38 revolver, the P32 took up less space than a spare magazine for a 9mm pistol. The plastic frame might feel less solid than steel but the stopping power was respectable, the intimidation effect every bit as good.

Flattening herself against the wall, she held the gun against her shoulder and pulled the door open with her free hand. The hall was empty. Faint movements from her left had her swinging the barrel around. Seeing Garth come into the hall, she lowered the gun and cocked her head toward the study alcove. He nodded. Someone was definitely in there.

The intruder was dressed in black jeans and a black shirt and had his back to them as he riffled through files. She saw

Garth's hand snake around the arched entrance, then a light snapped on. "Looking for something?" he asked.

The man went for his pocket and she stepped out, leveling the gun. "Stop right there." Seeing the black circle aimed at his heart, the man lifted his hands away from his body. Serena patted his pockets, retrieving a bone-handled hunting knife that she passed hilt first to Garth. "Who are you?" she demanded.

The man had recognized Garth, she saw from his reaction. Even more interesting, Garth had evidently recognized him. "You're David Lebrun, the attendant from the gym."

The man straightened. "What of it?"

"What are you doing in my house?"

"I thought you were away. I needed cash, so I decided to rob the place."

A lie if ever she heard one. "You bypassed my purse, didn't even check the money in it. Nobody would blame me for shooting an intruder in self-defense." She aimed at his knees and saw him blanch.

"Don't, please."

"Give me a good reason not to, starting with your real name."

She was too focused to look at Garth, but she heard his breath tighten. The intruder seemed to collapse in on himself. "It's David Junot, but you already know, don't you?"

She nodded. "Other than Dr. Pascale, you're the only one left with connections to Prince Louis's birth. I suppose you're looking for the package of souvenirs your father left?"

His gaze flared. "You have it?" He looked at Garth, "I thought you…"

"Do you think I'd be stupid enough to keep it here?" Garth played with the knife and she saw the intruder swallow hard. "Who sent you?"

The man's eyes never left the blade as Garth turned it to catch the light. "Nobody, I swear. The stuff belonged to my father. I wanted it back, that's all."

"A sentimental family treasure, is that it?"

"Yes."

Garth stepped closer, touching the tip of the blade to the man's chest. With a careless flick, he sliced off a shirt button. David Junot looked as if his knees would crumble. "It's so precious that you'd let the Hand use it to keep the Americans out of Carramer," Garth said.

"I didn't know that's what he planned to do with it." Realizing he'd betrayed himself, David Junot slumped against the desk.

Garth's mouth curled into a sneer. "What did you think he'd do, frame it?"

"He only wants to make the royals look foolish."

"By using me."

She put a hand on Garth's shoulder. "Don't let him get to you, he isn't worth it." To David Junot, she said, "Since you're the Hand's buddy, you must know his identity."

Junot shot Garth a nervous look, not trusting him with the knife. She thought the fear was probably justified. "I was told what to do by phone. I've never met him. None of us has," he squeaked as the blade neared his throat.

Garth lowered the tip fractionally. "Why pick on me for your dirty scheme?"

"My father told me the royal kid he delivered had two webbed toes. When I saw your feet in the gym, and how much you looked like Lorne de Marigny, I got this crazy idea—what if you were the real prince, alive after all this time? I took a photo of you and showed it at a Carramer First meeting, thinking it would get a laugh."

Serena nodded. "Instead they took you seriously. When did the Hand approach you?"

"He called me as soon as I got home, wanting to know more about Garth. I don't know how, but the Hand already knew about the baby souvenirs. He said I was to give them and the photos to another member who'd be told where to deliver them."

The member being the undercover agent they'd spirited to safety after the R.P.D. intercepted the delivery, Serena surmised. How had the Hand known that David Junot's father had kept items from the baby's birth? Was he a palace insider after all? A member of the royal family?

"The Hand must be thrilled that you lost the package," she drawled.

Terror clouded Junot's gaze. "He's going to hurt me unless I get it back."

Garth ostentatiously cleaned his fingernails with the tip of the blade. "Seems nobody values your safety too highly right now."

Junot looked wildly at Serena. "You can't let him knife me."

"What makes you think I'd stop him?"

"You're the law. I have rights."

"I used to be the law. Now I'm R.P.D. We play by our own rules. What was the Hand going to do with the package?"

"I'm not saying any more without guarantees. How do I know you won't kill me as soon as I've told you all I know?"

Garth's eyes narrowed. "You don't. But if you don't start talking, it won't even be in question."

He pushed the blade against Junot's throat. The slightest additional pressure would draw blood. She thought the man was going to faint. Not confident that Garth wouldn't carry out his threat, she moved the knife aside with her hand. "I'm prepared to guarantee your safety provided you tell us everything you know about the Hand and his plans."

"You can't mean to make a deal with this lowlife? He killed my parents."

She flinched inwardly from the fury in Garth's tone, but kept her expression impassive. "Somehow I don't think David had anything to do with the sinking of the boat, did you?"

She used the man's first name deliberately, instinctively falling into the good-cop, bad-cop routine she'd become skilled at while in uniform. Garth wasn't aware of how naturally he played bad cop, if he was playing at all.

Now Junot's head shook furiously. "I'm not a murderer. I only found out about the sinking afterward. The idea was to make the monarchy look foolish in front of the Americans. Nobody was supposed to get hurt.''

''Not by you, anyway,'' Serena said. ''Do we have a deal?''

''How are you going to guarantee my safety?''

Aware of Garth's restlessness beside her, Serena said, ''We'll get you out of Carramer to a neighboring island.''

''That won't do any good. The Hand lives outside territorial waters.''

Garth looked interested. ''Where exactly?''

Junot looked miserable. ''I don't know. He comes here when he has business, then goes again. That's all I know. Some say he lives on his own artificial island, out of reach of any law.''

''That would take a lot of money,'' Serena said. She recalled her theory that the Hand lived aboard a boat. If she was right, the island story could have grown up around his anonymity and elusiveness.

''He has money,'' Junot stated. ''I think he's some kind of big-time criminal using Carramer First for his own benefit.''

''That's the first logical thing you've said so far,'' Garth growled. He stuck the knife into his belt. ''Much as I hate to deal with the likes of you, you're all we've got.'' His shoulders sagged as he turned to Serena. ''Call your police friends and tell them to get this scum out of here.''

Her restrained sigh was echoed by Junot. ''Don't think you're getting off lightly,'' she warned. ''If it turns out you had anything to do with the Remy murders, you'll live to regret it.''

''I swear I didn't.''

She retrieved her cell phone from the desk and punched in Matt's number. He was going to love being disturbed in the middle of the night, but this was in a good cause.

While she spoke, Garth turned to Junot. ''If you had found the package, how did the Hand plan to take delivery?''

Junot's anxious gaze flicked to Serena and back to Garth, fixing on the knife at his belt. Without taking his eyes off it, he mumbled, ''I was to take it to the fishing port and leave it under pier nine, where it would be picked up by a yacht that sounded like some place on Nuee.''

''*Cradle Rock?*''

''That's it. The skipper must be a friend of the Hand's because he sometimes delivers instructions for our meetings.''

''Could the skipper himself be the Hand?''

''I don't think so. He has an accent. The man on the phone sounded like he comes from Solano. When he called me, his voice sounded familiar, but I couldn't place the reason.''

''I suggest you keep trying,'' Serena said, finished with her call. ''Matt is on his way. He'll arrange for you to be taken to a safe house.'' To Garth she said, ''He also told me due to a situation at home, the U.S. president has moved his visit up by three days. He'll be here in less than a week.''

Chapter 16

When Matt Hayes arrived he looked as rumpled and irritable as she'd expected. With him was a thin, freckled, redheaded officer who looked as if he was fresh out of the academy. Serena waited until the young officer had escorted Junot out to the police car, then she filled Matt in on what Garth had dubbed Operation Monarch.

Matt raked a hand through his already-spiky hair. "Quite a situation. I'm glad you finally told me."

"This is need-to-know information. You need to know. Besides, you've earned the right after all you've done to help."

"Not to mention getting up at dawn to take care of David Junot." Matt glanced at Garth, who was working at the computer. "Can he really be Prince Lorne's older brother?"

She steered Matt into the kitchen, out of earshot of Garth. "I don't know, but I'm going to find out."

He didn't like this, she saw when he frowned. "I hope you're not planning anything reckless or illegal."

She feigned innocence. "Who, me?"

"Yes you, who thinks laws are flexible and her body is bulletproof."

She pulled a face. "I've never broken a law in my life. Bent a few when lives were at stake, but never broken any." She didn't touch the bulletproof part.

Matt nodded. "That's what I'm talking about. If the Hand shows up in Solano, I want you to promise me you'll let the law handle him."

"What can you charge him with? David Junot is the only one with any connection to him, and he never saw him face-to-face."

His expression said he noticed she hadn't given any promises. "What makes you think you can do better?"

"Because I have to."

Matt had known her for a long time, through good times and bad. He saw now what she wasn't saying and lowered his voice. "You really care about Garth, don't you?"

She answered in the same low tone, "What does that have to do with anything?"

Her brittle denial told him more than she wanted it to. "Worse than I thought, this time it's love."

She felt her face heating and said grimly, "Refer to my previous response."

Matt held up his hands. "Okay, as long as Melanie and I get an invitation to the wedding. And you don't let your feelings cloud your professional judgment."

"I won't," she said, answering only the part that suited her. *If* she loved Garth, and she wasn't sure that the intimacy between them was the same as love, it was nobody's business but hers.

"I have another question," Matt said, letting her off the hook. "With Junot in protective custody and the evidence of Garth's possible heritage safely at the castle, what can Carramer First do to damage the kingdom's relations with the U.S.?"

Garth appeared in the doorway in time to catch the question. "I was wondering the same thing."

How much of the exchange between her and Matt had Garth heard? Had any of her answers incriminated her? She didn't think so. Damn Matt for mentioning weddings. She was sure they weren't on Garth's agenda right now, if ever. Nor on hers, right? The heated look he gave her only added to her confusion.

Garth went to the coffeemaker and flicked it on. Matt met his raised-eyebrow query with a shudder. "I'd still like to sleep through what's left of the night."

"Serena?" At her nod, Garth passed her a mug, then poured one for himself. "The Carramer First members I knew wouldn't resort to murder just to disrupt a presidential visit."

"They kidnapped the Pascales to get information. And they probably also killed your parents. That's a lot more than disruption," Matt said.

She took a sip of coffee, wincing at its strength. "Maybe disruption is only the beginning."

Garth nodded. "If the Hand wants to keep America out of this region, the more mayhem he creates, the better."

Matt looked thoughtful. "It sounds as if you don't expect this to stop once your claim to the throne is settled."

"Not if the Hand intended it as a diversion," Garth said.

She tightened her grip on the mug. "Then he would need something bigger to convince the Americans to stay out."

Garth read her thoughts. "Such as an assassination attempt on the president's life."

Matt paled visibly. "Security's as tight as my people and yours can make it."

"Nobody saw anything the day my parents' boat was sunk," Garth reminded them. "Last night while Serena was going through the files, I e-mailed Brett Curtin details of the toy submarine we found near the wreck. According to him the delivery method is used by the marines in training simulations. We'll have to get the C4 analyzed for chemical identifiers, but I'll bet it turns out to be military issue as well. We're dealing with someone who can stay a step ahead of any security measures."

Someone with training as specialized as Garth's, she interpreted. "So the Hand not only has a military background, but the skills to try out the simulation in real life."

Matt nodded agreement. "As soon as we've stowed David Junot away, I'll sift through the Carramer First files for disenchanted marines with republican tendencies and explosives know-how."

Garth's look reminded her that the description could also fit him. Except that she didn't believe he had murdered his parents. He hadn't always seen eye-to-eye with them, but he wasn't a cold-blooded killer.

She hoped what was between them wasn't blinding her to possibilities, and she saw him recognize that, too. Heat rushed through her. In all her years with the police, she'd never understood how any woman could love a convicted killer, although she'd encountered some who did, even one who'd married a prisoner serving time.

Now Serena knew the truth. Feelings didn't change to fit social demands. No matter who or what Garth turned out to be, she would still feel the magnetic pull of attraction piercing her to her core. Her whole being sang with it. She wanted this over so they could go up to his grandfather's amazing bed in the lighthouse room and not come down until they were both quivering wrecks.

She chased the thought away with difficulty. "While you're working from your end, we'll keep trying to identify the Hand from ours," she told Matt.

Matt shook his head. "We agreed this is a job for the police."

"You agreed," she denied. "It's still my area of responsibility."

"And mine," Garth added savagely. "When the Hand started meddling in my life, he made it personal."

She had no counter to that and didn't blame him for wanting to get to the Hand before the law did. But she couldn't allow it. "The Hand won't want to miss seeing his scheme bear fruit.

He's probably on his way to Solano now. As soon as we pin down his whereabouts, we'll let your people take over, Matt.''

Her proposal was as popular with Garth as an attack of the bends, she saw. Braced for an argument, she saw him set his jaw instead. She was going to have to keep him on a tight leash if their quarry was to be brought to trial, she decided, wondering how she was going to manage that feat.

Matt slanted a doubtful look at them both. "I've a good mind to assign a couple of my men to you to make sure you stick by that.''

She smiled sweetly at him. "But you won't.''

"Unfortunately, I don't have anyone to spare. They're all occupied with the presidential visit. I want you to check in with me every two hours from now until you call for backup. Understood?''

"Understood,'' she said. Garth said nothing.

After Matt and his partner left with David Junot, Serena found it impossible to get back to sleep, mainly because Garth thought of more inventive ways for them to spend the time in bed. She had never known a lover like him, and the aftermath left her sated but somehow energized.

"We really should make some plans,'' she said, barely able to breathe because of what Garth was doing to her.

He lifted his head, his eyes flashing. "I couldn't agree more. How does that feel?''

She squirmed, sighed, arched her back in ecstasy. "You're amazing. And a worry, too. How do you know all this stuff? On second thought, don't answer that.''

He grinned. "My team used to say that DAREs stood for Devilishly Adventurous Resourceful Sex.''

"I believe it.''

Rolling him over she managed to plant herself on top of him. Not smart, she learned when he lifted her so he was inside her again. He moved boldly beneath her until all her internal fuses blew at once. Her last coherent thought was that until the Hand found out about Junot's arrest, he wasn't likely to try anything new.

* * *

Serena eyed the rusting fourteen-foot aluminum runabout dubiously. "Are you sure this thing's seaworthy?" Unlike Brett's boat, the rust on this one was real. She'd checked after Garth arranged to borrow it from Alice, who kept it tied up alongside her kiosk.

He cast off from the jetty and joined her onboard. "The flimsy look will add weight to your story."

As the boat rocked, she grabbed the railing. "It won't help me if I drown on the way."

When they finally got around to making plans early that morning, they had agreed the *Cradle Rock* was their only link with the Hand. They knew the yacht would be in the vicinity of the fishing port, waiting for David Junot to deliver the package. "So we find them first," Garth had said.

It took him three tries to start the aging outboard motor. "From the sound of that, I won't have to pretend to break down," she said.

"So much the better."

"Easy for you to say. You like being up to your neck in water."

He steered expertly between the commercial fishing vessels where the morning's catch was being cleaned. Seagulls wheeled noisily overhead, and the sun was already hot, making her appreciate the shelter provided by the boat's cuddy cabin.

The yellow bikini she'd purchased that morning felt uncomfortably revealing, although Garth had seen much, much more of her during the long night. Somehow the scraps of polka-dot fabric made her feel more exposed, not less.

She recognized the problem. Matt was right, she was more involved with Garth than she wanted to be. Not only because they made sublime love together, but because he was everything she had ever dreamed of in a man. Strong, intelligent, resourceful and caring enough to prepare a meal and bring it to her in bed.

He'd be horrified if he knew how close she was to falling in love with him. The uncertainty about his background had only fueled his reluctance to get involved. And maybe he was right. As long as he preferred being footloose and unencumbered, and she wanted a stable future, what hope was there for them?

She wasn't going to settle it now, she told herself. They had a job to do. Although solving the mystery of his past might be her best chance of settling it at all.

"Yacht at ten o'clock," Garth said, lowering the binoculars.

She peered over the top of the cuddy cabin, locating a distant vessel, a yacht all right, although the sails were furled. "Is it the *Cradle Rock?*"

He checked through the binoculars, "The configuration looks right. Yes, it's her."

Her heart picked up speed. "Time for us to change places."

He moved toward the cuddy cabin while she came cautiously forward and replaced him at the tiller. As they passed, he clasped her shoulders and lowered his mouth to hers in a hard, possessive kiss.

"For luck," he said before she could gather enough breath to react.

The impact punched through her. The desire in his eyes burned as hot as the sun overhead. Despite her apprehension at being miles out to sea in a rusty boat, at that moment she wouldn't exchange it for a luxury liner as long as she could be this close to him. He even made her forget the hazards lurking in the depths underneath them.

He made her forget everything.

As perhaps he'd intended, the kiss distracted her as she inexpertly steered for the yacht. Then, apparently alone on the runabout, she waited until she could read the name on the yacht's side before turning the outboard motor on and off several times to simulate a breakdown, as Garth had shown her.

There was a shout of annoyance as she deliberately rammed the port side of the yacht. A man leaned over the side, gesturing furiously, and she recognized the hulking islander they'd dubbed Tiny Tim. "What the hell are you doing?" he demanded. He hadn't seen her the last time, and his anger was aimed at the damage she'd done to the yacht, she guessed.

She puffed out her chest, helped by the padding on the barely there bra, and adopted her best "maiden in distress" expression. "I couldn't stop. My motor thingy is acting up. Can you help me?"

"What are you doing out in a boat if you can't handle it?"

"I was tied up at the dock at Solano and dozed off. My mooring rope must have come undone and I woke up way out here. Every time I get the motor started it cuts out on me."

She stood up, balancing haphazardly for effect, and saw Garth wince as she almost toppled into the sea. Tiny Tim was convinced. "Throw me the rope and I'll take you in tow back to the dock."

"Can I please come aboard? I feel so alone out here."

The man withdrew his head. Moments later he returned and tossed a rope ladder over the side. "Try not to fall in."

She was sufficiently inept at scaling the ladder to give Garth heart failure. He wished he knew if she was acting. He breathed a sigh of relief as the seaman helped her aboard, although the glimpse he caught of the man's hand splayed across her back was enough to make Garth feel murderous.

Later for that, he thought, but wondered at the strength of the feeling. He had never felt this way about a woman before, and he knew it had little to do with the breathtaking sex they had enjoyed for most of the night. Not that he objected to great sex, but instinctively he sensed that she meant a lot more to him than a warm body in his bed.

When he'd brought their supper and found her sleeping, something had cracked open inside him, some well of tenderness he hadn't known he could feel. He didn't like feeling it now. He was used to being in control. She made him feel as if he was sinking fast with no land in sight.

With nothing to do except lie low until she managed to lure the crew to starboard so he could sneak aboard, he was forced to face the unthinkable—he was falling in love with her. Falling or had fallen? Now was the wrong time to ask the question, but it persisted, almost paralyzing him until he reminded himself that she didn't know how he felt. And she wouldn't if he had anything to do with it. His life was complicated enough without love.

What was taking so long? The plan was to distract the crew while Garth sneaked aboard and searched the yacht. He heard her peal of laughter, the breathy sound intended to reinforce her pose of a ditzy female lost at sea, but it grabbed at his gut. She was literally laughing in the face of danger. But he couldn't deny her assertion that she had to be the one to try this. He would have been recognized instantly. Besides, she looked a hell of a lot more fetching in a yellow polka-dot bikini.

He schooled himself to patience.

The sailor's hand on Serena's back felt obscenely warm, although he had almost wrenched her arm out of its socket dragging her aboard. She pasted a toothy smile on her face. "Thanks. I was scared to death out there."

The man took his time releasing her. "Always happy to help a lady."

She restrained a shudder. "This is some ship, mister."

"Nick," he said. "And it's a boat. Yachts are called boats."

She tried to look impressed, and ran a hand over his hairy forearm. "You must be rich to own a boat like this, Nick."

The man grew six inches taller and patted her hand. "Are you vacationing in Solano?"

"Call me Tina," she said, returning the favor. "I'm traveling with my girlfriend, Suzy. We're both nurses. She was supposed to meet me at the dock, but she was late and I dozed off."

"Your runabout doesn't look too seaworthy. Maybe you and Suzy should come cruising with me instead."

She widened her eyes and fluttered her lashes. "Can we? That'd be cool."

Nick's tongue slid over his lips in obvious anticipation. "I have to drop some people off at the dock first, then we can go out for a couple of hours, just the three of us. Do you like champagne?"

"My favorite. Suzy's, too. Only she…'' She hesitated, then added in a low voice, "She overdoes it a bit, gets giggly and loses her inhibitions, you know?'' Nick looked as if he did know and it was fine by him.

Suddenly Serena rushed to the starboard side, leaning out and pointing. "Oh my God, is that a shark fin?''

As she'd hoped, Nick followed her. "They're harmless white-tipped reef sharks. Those big guys, the gray whalers are the real villains.''

She had no trouble injecting a tremor into her voice. "They're following the boat.''

He put a reassuring arm around her shoulders and pointed out a bloodstained shelf near the stern. She didn't have to pretend to shudder at the litter of knives and gore. "I was cleaning a catch of tuna when you rammed…when you arrived. The sharks are scavenging the scraps.''

"Thank God you were out here fishing. I'm so grateful.'' He almost salivated as she traced a figure eight across his broad chest with an extended finger.

A noise on the port side caught both their attention. Nick looked back but Serena fisted the collar of his shirt and turned him away from the noise. "I'll make you glad you saved my life.''

He had lowered his head, and she was bracing herself for the contact when a thickly accented voice demanded, "What the hell is she doing here?''

Nick jerked away from her as if stung. "Sorry, Skipper. The lady's runabout broke down, and I offered her a tow back to Solano.''

She pretended confusion. "Aren't you the skipper, Nick?''

"I will be this afternoon.'' He lowered his voice, trying to salvage the situation.

"When the boss sees her you'll be fish bait,'' the skipper growled, looming over them. "This is no pleasure cruise.''

"Especially for Miss Cordeaux. Serena, isn't it?'' a voice asked.

Her act vanished in her shock at seeing the man who followed the skipper out of the saloon. He was in his late fifties or early sixties, hard as nails, with skin the color of mahogany as if from spending too many hours in the glare of the sun. A five-inch scar gleamed whitely along his jaw. He was dressed in charcoal Levi's and a black T-shirt emblazoned with the name of a heavy metal band and in his hand was a .38 Special revolver.

"Roy Keer," she said flatly. He was older than the last police photo she'd seen of him, but he looked surprisingly fit for a man who had drowned at sea ten years before.

His gaze was so lethal that she felt ill. She could well believe he was a murderer. He looked as if killing her would be an absolute pleasure.

He lifted the gun. "Where's Garth Remy?"

She met him glare for glare, while praying that Garth wouldn't give his presence away. The element of surprise was all they had right now. "I have no idea. As I told Nick, I drifted out to sea and couldn't get the motor started."

Keer slammed the back of his free hand across her mouth so hard that she staggered. "You and Remy have been joined at the hip since you got your hands on a package meant for me. So where is he?"

She stood her ground, but touched a finger to the corner of her mouth. It came away red. "I should have known you're the Hand. It adds up. Military background, knowledge of explosives, long prison record, no scruples whatsoever."

Keer moved toward her, and she couldn't help flinching. But he didn't strike her again. "Yes, I'm the Hand. For all the good knowing it will do you."

Because she wouldn't live to tell anyone, she assumed. Keep him talking, give Garth the chance to act. "I thought you were dead," she said.

"You were meant to think so. Who blames a dead man when a crime is committed?"

"It is quite an alibi. Is it true you live on your own artificial island, by your own laws?"

"Part of it is true. You decide which part," he said conversationally. "Not that you'll have long to wonder. As soon as I get hold of Remy, your life is over."

More afraid than she wanted him to see, she said, "Not exactly an incentive. If you agree to let me live, I'll tell you what you want to know."

"You want my word?" He laughed, an ugly sound that sent shivers down her spine. "You've obviously never been in prison."

"Not on the same side of the bars as you, anyway."

He grabbed a handful of her hair and pulled her head back painfully. "Being an ex-cop gives me another reason to kill you."

"Tell me one thing before you do. How did you know about Armand Junot's souvenirs of the royal baby?"

"His wife was my lover. When she visited me in prison, she told me what the drunken fool had kept. I had plenty of time to plan how they might help me to destroy the useless parasites you call the royal family."

"Because you weren't allowed to be one of them," she gasped. Her scalp was on fire, but she was buying time until Garth could find a way aboard and back her up.

Keer released her so abruptly her neck cracked. "There's more at stake here than revenge, satisfying as it is. Using the fools in Carramer First, I was building a profitable international organization until your royals invited the Americans to put a base in Carramer. I can't let it happen. Some of my best clients are very anti-American." •

"So you hatched this scheme to scare them away," she said. "It isn't going to work."

"You won't be around to know," he snapped. To Nick, he said, "Search her runabout. If Remy's onboard, bring him here. Either he rediscovers his loyalty to Carramer First or he watches her die slowly and painfully in front of him."

Garth was about to board the yacht when Keer's arrival drove him back. Only years of DARE training kept him from storming to Serena's aid, but he knew she would be dead be-

fore he reached her. So he slipped quietly back into the runabout. Within three minutes he had disabled the outboard motor and dropped the oars overboard. He put ready a few other
items he'd secreted in the cabin before they left the dock.

Then he waited and listened.

As soon as the sailor called Nick set foot on board, he acted.
The man had no idea what hit him. One moment he was stepping cautiously onto the runabout, the next he had a length of
mooring rope coiled around his neck. His eyes bulged and he
scrabbled at the noose but Garth kept up the pressure until the
man lost consciousness. Dropping his burden to the deck,
Garth felt for a pulse. Still alive. He must be losing his touch,
he thought, or Serena was making him sentimental.

Having evened the odds a bit more, he turned his attention
to the yacht but pulled up short when he saw Roy Keer bending Serena backward over the railing. "I thought this might
get your attention," Keer said when he saw Garth freeze.

"Let her go."

"When you agree to play your part."

"What part?"

"Crown prince of Carramer."

"You know that's a bloody lie."

"Is it?" Keer exerted more pressure on Serena's spine. "By
now you've learned that you're not the Remys' son. Why not
the real monarch?"

"Let her go and we'll talk about it."

A waterspout erupted beside the runabout as a bloody chunk
of tuna landed in the sea. Within seconds, two dorsal fins broke
the surface. Three more converged on the party. Garth saw the
skipper lob more fish carcasses overboard, and the ocean became a boiling mass of shark activity.

Keeping the gun at her head, Keer flipped Serena over, forc-
ing her to lean over the railing and look in horror at the frenzy
below. "You have ten seconds to surrender or the next bait
going in there is Miss Cordeaux."

Chapter 17

"No, Garth." Serena cried, ignoring the pain in her abused spine. "If you surrender he'll kill me anyway."

Dragging her gaze away from the feeding sharks, she was confronted by a worse nightmare. Garth was pulling the runabout hand over hand along the mooring line toward the rope ladder. Despair swamped her. He was going to give himself up for her sake, and it would all be over for both of them.

She could almost smell Keer's anticipation as Garth brought the small boat steadily closer until he was right in the middle of the feeding frenzy, the runabout rocked repeatedly by torpedo-shaped bodies ramming it in their haste to reach the food.

Garth was looking right at her. Suddenly she caught a movement of his right arm, a pushing gesture with fingers extended. The diving signal for "Go under" done so quickly she almost missed it. In another lightning gesture, he pointed with both hands, index fingers extended in the same direction. "You lead, I'll follow," she translated. Surely he didn't mean what she thought he meant? She made herself remember his assurance that sharks almost never attacked scuba divers. If she understood what he wanted from her, he'd better be right or so help her, she'd never stop haunting him.

Time was running out. She had to trust him.

With a savage cry she raised her bent right arm and drove it backward into Keer's chest near his heart. He reeled away, cursing. That he still had the breath to swear showed she hadn't struck nearly hard enough. She saw him lift the gun over her head, butt first.

She didn't give herself time for second thoughts, but threw herself over the railing into the sea. As soon as she surfaced, threshing sandpaper-textured bodies brushed her on all sides and she glimpsed double rows of backward-facing rapier teeth. Her vision turned red with blood from the fish being ripped apart in the frenzy. She had never been so terrified in her life.

At least Keer wasn't wasting bullets on her, she thought, although it wasn't much consolation. This was probably his idea of entertainment. But where the hell was Garth?

Her heart almost stopped as a gray whaler collided with her arm, but it was aiming for a chunk of tailfin floating beside her. She pushed the meat into the shark's jaws and saw them snap closed with the force of a steel trap. In a moment of surreal timelessness, she was aware of the strange sight of each fish arching its back and pulling its pectoral fins in close to its body. Around her the sea boiled. If Garth planned on saving her, he'd better make it soon before she died of fright.

Maybe she should just give up and sink beneath the churning water. Drowning had to be easier than being eaten. But she had been a fighter for as long as she could remember. What was modeling if not another kind of feeding frenzy? She hadn't given up then, nor during the toughest challenges the police force had thrown at her. She wasn't about to give up now. Garth would come.

A shark as long as her body surged through the water toward her. Something hard bumped against her and her heart leaped to her mouth until she saw it was a floating oar. Treading water she grabbed the oar and lifted it out of the water one-handed, bringing it down on the nose of the shark with all the force she could muster.

The oar splintered but the shark veered away, its jaws closing on a floating chunk of meat. Safe for the moment she looked around for the runabout.

It had disappeared. The mooring rope slapped uselessly against the side of the yacht. Surely she hadn't misunderstood Garth's hand signals? If she had, she was dead meat.

Her vision blurred. Damned seawater getting in her eyes. She swabbed at them angrily. Hell of a time to realize you loved a man, two seconds before you breathed your last breath.

Because she *did* love him. No matter that she might never have the chance to tell him. At least she had known a love few people ever experienced.

Damn it, she wasn't going to die if she could help it, she told herself. She would live and she would tell him, even if he didn't want to hear it. "I love you, Garth," she shouted to the churning waves mere seconds before a massive pointed head filled her field of vision.

This time there was to be no reprieve. The nightmare teeth were bared at her, just another chunk of meat as far as the shark was concerned. She closed her eyes, then opened them resolutely and rammed the remaining length of oar into the gaping jaws, wedging them open. As the great head threshed, trying to free the oar, she dived under the water.

Garth was ready. His heart drummed and the blood pounded in his head but he forced himself into the icy calm that had kept him and others alive through countless DARE missions. He had to trust it would help him to save Serena now.

Seconds before she threw herself into the water, he'd untied the mooring rope at the runabout end, keeping his foot on it as he negotiated with Keer. Now it snapped back toward the yacht as Garth went over the side, at the same time strapping on an oxygen cylinder and backpack. His dive mask was already on his head and he pulled it over his face. He'd hidden the gear in the cabin after borrowing the runabout. Keer's attention was so transfixed by the sight of Serena fighting off the sharks that he didn't see Garth go into the water.

He was a dozen feet from the small boat and pulling the regulator into his mouth before Keer realized what was going on. Shouts of rage reached Garth but he dived and was breathing underwater by the time shots peppered the waves above.

The contrast was astonishing. Above him the water churned with the activity of the gray whalers, their feeding frenzy provoked by the slabs of meat thrown from the yacht. Below, he was in a world of silence except for the hiss of his breathing. The sharks' activity had greatly reduced the visibility but would also disguise his trail of bubbles from Keer and the captain on the yacht.

He was beginning to think he wasn't going to find Serena in the seething water. What had he done? Then he spotted her spiraling downward, her eyes wide with terror. Above her a threshing shape the size of a small car told its own story.

He kicked for her and wrapped his arms around her to halt her tumble to the sandy floor. Locked in her nightmare she struck at him with clenched fists until he saw recognition penetrate the fear. He felt her go limp in his arms and he feared he was too late, but it was with relief, he saw. And something else. Reviving, she clawed at his hair and shoulders as if she needed to touch him to assure herself they were both alive.

He gave her the regulator and she took deep breaths, her thumbs-up signaling when it was okay for him to take it back. He continued to buddy-breathe with her as he kicked down to a pair of rocky outcrops forming a natural arch on the sea floor a few feet from the feeding site. From this shelter, they watched the sharks ripping into the tuna. Shreds of meat drifted down, to be snapped up by smaller fish and a leopard-spotted eel they'd displaced from the arch.

At one point a white-tipped reef shark became entangled in one of the fish heads. It fought dramatically to shake off the burden then suddenly went still and floated to the top of the arch where it flopped lifelessly.

Serena shot Garth a questioning look. It was her turn at the regulator and he smiled. He prodded the limp body on the rock above them but the shark didn't move. He prodded it again, still with no result. She gave him the regulator and mouthed, "Heart attack?"

Garth shook his head, waiting. As he knew it would, the shark suddenly flicked its tail and shot away. He had seen sharks playing dead before, but never this close up.

He was starting to worry about their air supply when the feeding frenzy began to dissipate. One by one the satiated fish swam away to digest their meal until the sea was calm again, the fragments of tuna being worried by smaller fish the only sign that the frenzy had ever happened.

When he signaled to Serena that they should surface, she nodded understanding. He allowed himself the luxury of appreciating how beautiful she looked in his element with her hair floating in a golden halo around her and her movements as graceful as a ballet dancer.

He would bring her back here, he promised himself as he passed the regulator to her and buddy-breathed with her in a controlled ascent. Not in fear but in the exhilaration of exploring the last frontier on the planet.

It wouldn't matter if she refused. After this experience he wouldn't blame her. As long as she agreed to marry him somewhere, sometime. When she'd thrown herself in among the sharks at his behest, he'd known the worst terror of his life. He wouldn't rest until she was his to love, honor and protect for a lifetime.

As he'd planned, they surfaced under the stern of the yacht and Garth braced himself to feel shots tearing through him, shielding Serena with his body. But none came and he heard laughter from the deck above as they trod water. Keer and his skipper had decided that the sharks had done their work for them. He pushed his mask back and grasped the dangling rope he'd cut free from the runabout.

Exhausted, half-drowned, her eyes shone as she also took

hold of the rope and kissed him hard and fast. "That's for saving my life."

"It's becoming a habit."

"Practically a full-time job."

"Exactly my thought. Will you marry me?"

She didn't hesitate. "Yes."

"Not the ideal setting for a proposal."

"Consider it a rehearsal. Keer is our problem right now."

He nodded. "Give me a minute, then follow me up." He swarmed hand over hand up the rope. Keeping his head below the level of the deck, he used the regulator to tap against the hull.

She recognized the Morse code message and smiled. He was tapping out the word *hand*.

Moments later the skipper leaned over the edge. He had a gun but Garth was faster, yanking his feet out from under him. The man hit the water with a mighty splash.

Serena followed Garth up the rope, pleasure sweeping through her at finding a solid surface under her feet again. She didn't waste time indulging it. Roy Keer was still onboard and armed. Her gaze raked the deck, and Garth checked the flying bridge. Both were deserted.

A glance at the sea showed the skipper swimming for the runabout drifting a hundred feet away from the yacht.

Garth's gaze followed hers and they saw the man reach the runabout. "He'll be company for Tiny Tim."

"As long as they don't get away."

He began to unstrap his diving gear. "They won't get far. I cut the fuel line."

A shot whistled between them. Keer was standing on a spar in the rigging above their heads. Keeping the gun on them, he jumped to the deck. "I'd offer to be your best man but you're too much trouble."

Why hadn't she looked upward? Fuming because Keer must have overheard Garth's proposal, she could do nothing but raise her hands in the air. Garth hooked his around the straps of the air tank he'd been about to remove, but retained enough defiance to say, "Go to hell."

"I've spent most of my life there, thanks to the royal family. Now they're going to pay."

"How, Keer?" she demanded. "You're alone out here. You could contact someone in Carramer First, but a police helicopter will be overhead before anyone else can get here."

The gun didn't waver. "You're bluffing but it doesn't matter. I don't even have to kill you anymore. I'll simply lock you up onboard until it's too late for Prince Lorne and the American president."

She thought furiously. "Security is too tight for you to do anything inside the castle."

"Unless he has a contact on the inside," Garth pointed out.

Keer nodded. "As it happens, I do. This is where I'm supposed to tell you who it is then you overpower me and storm the battlements, saving the day."

"It would save a lot of time," Garth said easily.

What was he up to? He sounded too relaxed not to have something in mind. She decided to give him the chance to make his move. With a theatrical groan she began to sway and then crumple.

All Garth needed was the split second when Keer's attention shifted to her. In one smooth movement he swung his air tank over his head and hurled it at Keer, catching the man full in the chest. The gun flew overboard, and Keer went down as if poleaxed. "Dead?" she asked as Garth bent over the unconscious Keer.

"No, but he has a few crushed ribs. He's going to feel them when he eventually comes around."

She didn't waste time worrying about it. "By then I hope he'll be under guard in Solano hospital. You deal with our friend. I'll go downstairs and radio Matt."

"Below," Garth amended, casting around for some rope to tie up Keer. "On a yacht, you go below."

"Wherever. I hope you don't want us to buy one after we're married."

"Wouldn't think of it." There went his dream of an underwater wedding, he thought. Suddenly he studied Serena. "Why are you standing at that angle?"

"I have trouble with a floor that won't stay still. Why?"

"Because I think we're sinking."

She rushed to the port side, looking in horror at a jagged pattern of cracks in the side where the sea was already pouring in, further widening the breach. "When I rammed the yacht, I must have done more damage than I realized. Do we have lifeboats?"

He was already taking stock. "Inflatables."

The deck's list had already increased sharply. "We don't have time to blow up a rubber boat."

"They're self-inflating." He nudged a bulky container to the railing and pushed it over the side where it blossomed into a life raft. He looped its mooring rope loosely over a railing. Then he got his arms under Keer.

She saw what he was doing. They were going to need Keer to lead them to the castle insider before the American president arrived. She grabbed the unconscious man's feet. "How will we get him into the raft?"

"The short way. On three."

Keer dropped like a stone into the raft, leaving them to clamber down the runabout's dangling rope after him. "I'm getting mighty tired of doing this," she said.

Garth yanked on the raft's mooring, freeing it from the yacht. He snapped together two pieces of plastic that turned out to be a paddle, assembling another one for her. "We'd better get away from the yacht."

If Serena was tired of being in the water, being under it again had even less appeal. She began to paddle.

From a safe distance she saw the *Cradle Rock* appear to lie down on its side until only the hull was visible. Debris floated around the semisubmerged hull. She looked around but could see only a dot on the horizon that was probably the drifting runabout. "I don't suppose this thing has a radio," she asked, trying to sound less hopeless than she felt.

He rummaged near his feet. "Locator beacon. We should be found before nightfall."

As he activated it she shoved wet hair out of her face and began to shiver, wishing she had more covering than a sodden bikini. "We'd better."

"What kind of honeymoon do you want?" he asked, completing his task.

She knew he was trying to distract her from the discomfort and the dorsal fins cutting through the water a dozen feet from the raft. "When we get out of this I'm going to put this paddle on my shoulder and walk inland until somebody asks me what I'm carrying. I'm spending my honeymoon right there."

"I guess a water bed is out then?"

"Unless you want to sleep in it alone."

His heated look dismissed any such notion. Shards of sensation speared through her. "In case we don't get out of this, I love you," she said fiercely.

He frowned. "Even without knowing who I am?"

"It won't change my feelings."

His look was transparent enough not to require words, but she treasured them anyway. "I love you, Serena. And we are going to get out of this. We have to put an end to Keer's killing spree."

A spree that had included his parents and may yet include Prince Lorne and the American president, she thought, then said, "David Junot was right about Keer using Carramer First for his own ends."

"He's afraid the Americans will get in the way of his plans. He did say his best clients are anti-American."

"We can't let him use Carramer as a base for international crime."

Garth looked at the unconscious man on the raft floor between them. "Some snakes go on living even after you cut the head off. His organization isn't going to be one of them."

A steady sound began to beat at her ears and the waves were chopped by an updraft. "Looks like the beacon worked," she called over the increasing clamor of the approaching helicopter.

Exhaustion was etched on his face as he tilted his head back. "God, I hope they're on our side."

Chapter 18

"From the look of you two, I wouldn't want to see the loser," Prince Lorne said as they met with him in his office. The monarch was behind his vast mahogany desk while she and Garth were seated on a leather couch. Princess Alison had given them a curious look as they passed her on the way, but hadn't asked questions. Not that their battered condition could be easily explained in a few words.

After they had failed to report in every two hours as agreed, Matt had sent a chopper looking for them, homing in on Garth's beacon. With the unconscious Keer, they'd been winched out of the ocean. Keer and his men were taken into custody while she and Garth were flown to the castle by the police helicopter. They'd spent a taxing forty minutes being checked over in the castle infirmary by Alain Pascale, who had fussed over their cuts and bruises, then prescribed rest for them both.

It was a seductive idea and her body ached for it, although she wasn't sure how much actual rest would be possible if Garth was in the bed beside her. Finding out would have to remain a luxury until Prince Lorne and the American president were safe.

They had spared a few minutes to change into dry clothes before answering the monarch's summons but they still looked a sad and sorry pair, she knew. "Matt arrested Roy Keer, along with the skipper of the yacht and the crewman Garth set adrift in his friend's runabout," she told the prince. "None of them looks particularly pretty, but they're all in condition to talk, although with Keer's years of experience in prison, I doubt the police will get much out of him."

Prince Lorne looked thoughtful. "Keer was the one man I never considered as the Hand."

Serena felt her features tighten. "If I'd had any sense I would have, Your Highness."

The prince gave her a sharp look. "Explain."

"The name of the yacht he used to commute between his hideout and Carramer was called *Cradle Rock*. We convinced ourselves it was the name of a landmark on Nuee, when all along it was a colossal clue. You must have heard the old saying, 'The hand that rocks the cradle, rules the world'?"

The monarch looked bleak. "From what I've heard of Keer, he'd take delight in dangling such a clue under our noses. Horrible to think that if my mother had married him instead of Prince Eduard, he could have been my father."

She didn't have to remind the prince that it was Princess Aimee's rejection of Keer that had set the wheels in motion for everything that followed. Aimee had ended the relationship because she had feared his temper and cruel nature, and time had proved her judgment correct.

"We didn't suspect him because he went to a lot of trouble to make everyone think he'd drowned at sea soon after getting out of prison," Garth observed.

Lorne nodded. "It's a tragedy that the yacht sank. We could have learned more from it about Keer's operations."

On this, at least, she had good news to report. "It only capsized, sir. The police are pumping it out so it can be towed to the dock and searched."

Garth massaged his chin where a two-day growth of beard made him look more the bad boy than usual. In Prince Lorne's elegant quarters she had more difficulty than ever imagining Garth as the country's ruler.

"Not that I expect it will reveal much that we don't already know," he said. "If the police learn the location of Keer's hideout and it is offshore as we suspect, they won't have jurisdiction."

Lorne stood up. "Then we must trust it's located somewhere friendly to Carramer, not that finding it will help the present situation."

"Have you considered postponing the president's visit?" she asked, aware that this wasn't her jurisdiction, either, but the question had to be asked.

The monarch's tight-lipped expression confirmed it. "I've discussed the threat directly with the president, but he feels the negotiations for the base are too important to postpone. He's relying on us to guarantee his safety."

"Until we know who Keer's contact in the castle is and what they're planning, we can't give any guarantees, Your Highness," she said worriedly.

The prince paced to the window, then turned back, his hands clasped behind his back in a pose she'd seen captured in photographs many times. "Could Keer be lying about having an operative inside the castle?"

"We can't rely on that," she said.

The prince came closer. "I want the investigation stepped up till we get some answers."

Garth stood to meet the prince eye-to-eye. "With the president due in Solano tomorrow, there isn't much time, sir."

"Do what you can." Lorne's aristocratic features softened. "And don't think I'm not grateful for all you've gone through to get this far. Having the Hand in custody is a big step. Your country is in your debt."

She stood beside Garth, in some inexplicable way feeling as if she was drawing strength from him. "We appreciate that,

Your Highness, but I'll feel a lot happier when we have Keer's contact in custody as well."

"As would we all. Do you have any leads?"

Garth was aware of her reluctance to admit her suspicions in case she was being less than objective. He had no such compunction. "Jarvis Reid is the most likely suspect, sir," he stated.

Lorne's eyebrows lifted. "Before being employed, he would have gone through a series of stringent security checks."

"As would everyone working at the castle," she pointed out.

Lorne sighed. "Indeed."

"But what about after they're employed?" Garth persisted. "Chatting casually to a couple of his co-workers, I learned that he's become a regular at the casino. He could be in need of extra money."

Serena frowned. "I'll have Matt investigate that possibility right away." One more thing needed to be said. "Your Highness, with respect, I'd like to recommend that you evacuate Princess Alison and Crown Prince Nori from the castle, perhaps to Allora, until the crisis is over."

Conflicted emotions chased across the prince's handsome features until they settled into an expression of iron resolve. "I assume you're sufficiently well acquainted with my wife to know how she would regard your recommendation, and what she would suggest I do with it?"

Her faint smile recognized the truth of this. "Then perhaps the crown prince…?"

"He will continue his normal routine, except where State needs conflict with his schedule."

She understood the monarch's decision, although she could hardly agree with it. Not that Prince Lorne needed her agreement. At the dismissal she heard in his tone, she turned to leave but Garth stood his ground. "Any word yet on the results of the DNA test, sir?"

"I'm told we'll have the results by tonight. Believe me, I'm as anxious as you are."

Because his throne was also at stake, she understood. She inclined her head respectfully, aware of Garth doing the same. As she started to lead the way out of the prince's presence, he motioned for her to remain. "I'll only keep her a moment," he assured Garth, making it clear that he wanted to see Serena alone.

When she joined him in the anteroom a few minutes later, she felt as if she was walking on air. Garth took a look at her shining eyes. "The prince made you chief of the R.P.D."

She shook her head, not having given the promotion a thought. "The decision hasn't been made yet. He wanted to give me an update on an investigation that should be finalized soon."

"As long as it was good news. We could both use some right now." He touched her shoulder. "Like to check out the banquet hall?"

"A hunch?"

"An act of desperation."

Following him, she knew how he felt because the same sense of helplessness was close to paralyzing her. Well, to perdition with that. Until they solved this, not only was the country not safe, but she couldn't do what she was aching to do—make love with him from now until forever.

Keer had said his plans involved Prince Lorne and the president. Garth had reached the same conclusion she had, that Keer had arranged for something to happen during the welcoming banquet.

At the entrance to the great hall, a security guard barred their way. Flashing her R.P.D. credentials had no effect. "What the blazes is this?" she demanded. "I'm cleared at the highest possible level. Check with Prince Lorne if you doubt me."

The guard shook his head. "Clearance isn't the problem, Ms. Cordeaux. The banquet hall has been declared clean by Mr. Reid. Only the housekeeper and her senior staff are allowed in until the banquet starts."

She shot Garth a furious look. "When did this rule come in?"

"You'll have to ask Mr. Reid."

"You bet I will."

Fuming, she resisted when Garth steered her into an alcove out of sight of the entrance. "I can't simply accept this."

"I strongly suggest you do."

Suspicion coiled through her. "What are you planning?"

"You might not be able to get in there, but I can."

"I'm coming with you."

He shook his head. "They can't fire me. You'd be risking your career."

"They might just shoot you instead. You mean more to me than my career."

Heat flamed in his gaze and he crushed her against him. "It means a lot to hear you say so."

"Did you doubt it?"

"Not anymore." His lips found hers and he kissed her hard. "A down payment for when this is over."

"I'll hold you to it. And to your marriage proposal."

He hesitated. "We need to talk about that, too."

Apprehension gripped her. "I haven't changed my mind." Had he?

He kissed her again. "I'll be back as soon as I can. Where will I find you?"

"In my office. Before we left Matt, I asked him to dig out some of the castle's old personnel records. I'm hoping he can help us to identify the traitor inside the castle."

"A hunch?" Garth echoed her words.

She smiled narrowly. "An act of desperation."

They were down to that, she thought as she settled at her desk, nerves strumming. She had given Matt a password that would let him access the archived records of castle staff who'd been with the royal household at the time of Prince Louis's birth. He had told her he would send anything promising to the Criminal Identification Squad who could run them through a facial composition and editing program. He must have called in every favor he had, she thought, because according to her computer, the results were waiting.

Her hands shook as she punched in her password and opened the documents. What if nothing helpful showed up? There was the chance Garth might spot something untoward in the banquet hall, but an equal chance of him being arrested as the spy himself. She should never have allowed him to try it.

Her own hubris forced a smile. As if she had any control over him except in the bedroom. Had she been kidding herself about that, too? Was his marriage proposal no more than a heat-of-the-moment response to their brush with death? The possibility made her want to wrap her arms around herself and rock with pain. But she wouldn't. Long ago he had inspired her to fight for what she wanted. If she had to she would fight Garth himself. He was going to learn that marrying her was a lot less trouble than backing out.

First she had work to do.

The first photos Matt had e-mailed to her revealed nothing helpful. The computer program was called Cranio Graphic Enhancement and was designed to update old photographs, usually of people who'd been missing for a considerable time, to show how they would have aged or changed with time.

Comparing thirty-year-old photos with how the subjects would look now was fascinating. She was tempted to send Matt one of her own photos to see how she was going to turn out, but knew she wouldn't. There were some things she felt better off not knowing.

Suddenly a chill prickled along her spine as she studied one of the graphically enhanced photos. There was no mistaking the likeness of a woman Serena had known since she joined the R.P.D.

With a trembling hand, she hit the print button, barely waiting until the result emerged from the printer to tear the page out and head for the door. If she was right, Garth was walking into terrible danger. She had to find him before it was too late.

* * *

Garth located the right cellar without too much difficulty. It was only logical that a laundry chute should lead to a laundry, and it did. Fortunately the vast commercial setup was deserted for the moment, enabling him to look around without having to come up with a plausible excuse.

When he'd been at loose ends at the castle previously, he'd taken himself on a tour of exploration and had noticed the laundry chute connecting the banquet hall with this area only because he'd been curious about the purpose of a small, almost hidden door in the wainscoting.

A helpful footman had explained that the playing-field-size tablecloths and mountain of napkins used on state occasions could hardly be carried through the castle. Instead they were dropped down the chute directly to the laundry in the cellar.

A massive receptacle revealed where they normally landed, and he flicked a glance around before going to it and peering up. Between the cellar and the banquet hall was a distance of about seventy feet, he estimated. The chute was a little over a foot square, lined with metal ducting, the entrance presently criss-crossed by plastic tape bearing the R.P.D. seal and dire warnings against its removal.

He intended to ignore the warnings, but fitting into the chute was another matter. Nothing for it. He stripped off everything but his black briefs, dropping the clothes into the nearest filled basket. Telling himself it was no different from the chimney climbing he'd done as part of DARE training, he snapped the tape and angled his body inside.

The so-called chimneys in most mountain climbs were narrow vertical openings climbed by pushing against the opposing walls and shimmying upward. Wider chimneys were ascended with your back to one wall and feet and knees to the other, but the chute was the much more difficult squeeze climb, involving a reptilian squirm that was slow, strenuous and graceless.

With no face holds on the sides of the chute, he had to resort to jamming himself upward using shoulders, elbows and knees. When it became seemingly impossible, he held fast to an image of Serena, so beautiful, so desirable. For her and the future he wanted with her, he pushed himself on.

By the time he saw the small door indicating he was nearing the banquet hall, he could barely grip the chute for the perspiration streaming off him. When the door refused to yield to pressure he had the panicky thought that it was locked from the inside. He heaved a sigh of relief when he managed to crack it open.

Peering through the gap, he made sure the hall was empty before squirming out through the narrow opening, destroying more security seals as he did so. His arms ached and his elbow, hip and shoulder bones felt crushed. The bruises he'd have tomorrow should really be something.

Dismissing the discomfort, he padded to the long table that was already set for the president's welcome banquet. Low centerpieces of Carramer's famous wild orchids interspersed with candles trailed over the pristine white linen. He poked among them, finding nothing suspicious.

Next he checked the bases, simple bowls made of gold and engraved with the royal crest. Underneath the center one he hit the jackpot. Mixed in with the florists' foam holding the flowers in place, he found a yielding plastic substance colored the same innocuous green. Every one of the floral displays held at least some plastic explosive blended in with the foam. His flesh crawled. There was enough C4 on the table to destroy this entire wing of the castle.

How in the devil had the would-be assassin managed to get them past security? There was only one possible answer.

A cool breeze feathered his skin and he looked up to see the main doors opening. He dropped and rolled beneath the table letting the cloth conceal him, hoping he hadn't moved anything out of alignment. On his self-guided tour he'd seen the staff measuring distances between everything on the table and guessed that their experienced eye would spot the slightest thing out of place.

The arrival was female, he saw. The shoes were the sensible, low-heeled kind nurses usually wore and the stockings were flesh-colored. Not many women wore stockings in Carramer's tropical climate. He tried to remember who he'd seen wearing them, but drew a blank.

As she moved along the table, closer to his hiding place, he made his breathing slow and shallow. He needn't have bothered.

"You can come out of there, or I can summon the guard to shoot you through the cloth."

He rolled out from under the table and uncoiled slowly. His state of undress showed he wasn't armed but he held his hands up and away from his body, not wanting to give the woman any excuse to call the guard.

She looked more than capable. She had the kind of hard face he associated with female prison wardens in gangster movies, and her iron-gray hair was lacquered to within an inch of its life, not a curl out of place.

Her blue uniform with the royal coat of arms embroidered on the left breast came down to her calves, above the flesh-colored hosiery. For such a formidable-looking woman, she had a figure that women half her years would envy. "August Beck," he said, finally able to place her.

"Her real name is Felice Junot," Serena said, moving into the room, amazed to see Garth standing there clad only in his briefs. Some men would have been embarrassed. He made it look like the uniform of the day.

Determined to match his composure, although her heart was racing, she showed him the printout. "This was done by a computer program that forecasts how Felice would look in her sixties. Amazingly accurate, isn't it?"

August—Felice—barely glanced at the printout. "How did you get in here?"

"I had Prince Lorne personally direct the guard to let me through," she said. "He could hardly argue with the monarch."

Felice Junot's face screwed up in pure hatred. "Lorne's kind destroyed my life. They hunted my poor husband to his grave."

Serena brushed away an imaginary tear. "Touching, except that you were cheating on your husband with Roy Keer long before Armand's dismissal from the royal household."

Obviously shocked by the reference to Keer, Felice tried to bluff it out. "You can't prove it. Roy drowned years ago."

"Don't worry, you'll see him again. He's already in police custody in Solano."

Felice's legs gave and she grabbed the banquet table for support. "How? When?"

"More importantly, how did you fool castle security and obtain the position of chatelaine?"

"Easy. I was working at the castle until I married Armand. When I went to Australia, my references from the royal family gained me a position in Government House. The real Augustine Beck was my boss until she died of pneumonia. When Roy left prison and wanted me to live with him, I decided to borrow Beck's identity to help Roy get even with the royals. Augustine Beck's references checked out, and nobody remembered Felice Junot after thirty years." She almost spat the words out. "None of the royals see us as people, only as servants. They saw what they expected to see."

Serena had been no better, she thought, furious with herself for the oversight. The lacquered hair that the rest of the staff joked about was undoubtedly a wig, and the changes in Felice in three decades had done the rest. Still, hiring an imposter was a serious breach of security and although it had happened before her time, Serena intended to make it her business to ensure such a thing couldn't happen again.

"Where does Jarvis Reid come in?" Garth asked.

"Why don't you ask him? He's behind you."

Serena wasn't about fall for the old trick until Jarvis himself spoke. "I didn't believe August when she said you were a traitor, Serena."

She did turn then, to find Jarvis holding a gun on them. "Her real name is Felice Junot and she's the traitor."

"She's rigged the centerpieces with explosives," Garth contributed.

Jarvis looked taken aback. "August doesn't want to hurt anybody, only to show the royals up. If there are explosives, you planted them after I sealed this hall."

She shook her head. "No, Jarvis. Felice and her lover, Roy Keer, also known as the Hand, are using you. They're going to kill Prince Lorne and the president."

"That's not true. I wouldn't…"

"Prove it. Put the gun down," Garth urged.

August shifted in alarm. "Don't do it, Jarvis. I told you they'd say anything to put Garth Remy on the throne. They're in this together."

Jarvis's gun wavered slightly then firmed on Garth. "Is it true you're claiming the crown?"

"Not until DNA testing reveals who I really am."

"What will you do when you find out you're my son by Roy Keer?" Felice demanded.

Serena's gasp of shock was drowned out by Garth's roar of denial. As he moved toward Felice, evidently goaded beyond reason by her statement, Reid's gun swung wildly to keep up with him. Serena braced herself to see the man she loved go down in a burst of gunfire.

Before Reid could open fire, Garth changed direction in a heartbeat and launched himself in a flat dive across the room. He slammed into Reid, knocking the gun out of his hand. The momentum carried them across the vast hall, ending in a sickening crack as Reid's head connected with a paneled wall.

Seizing her chance, Serena threw herself at Felice. The older woman exploded like dynamite, raging almost incoherently against the unraveling of her carefully laid plan. Holding her was like holding a tiger, but Serena hung on grimly, ducking to avoid fingernails like talons raking the air near her face.

"I've had about enough of you," Serena snapped after the nails came within an inch of her eye. She backhanded the woman across the face. Not exactly a textbook defense, but immensely satisfying. Felice's raving cut off abruptly, although her eyes blazed hatred at Serena. Well, that made them even, she thought, twisting Felice's arms behind her.

Garth was climbing to his feet beside Reid who lay like a broken doll, his head twisted at an unnatural angle against the wall. Intercepting Serena's questioning look, Garth shook his head.

Serena's stomach roiled but she fought it. "We'd better contact the R.P.D. command center direct. I don't trust the guard on the door. He might be working with these two."

"He isn't," Felice said in a hollow voice. "Jarvis wasn't involved with us until I promised him a substantial payment. He thought he'd get to 'discover' the plot and be a hero, gaining the promotion meant for you. He had no idea what we really planned." Her shoulders slumped and she said in a beaten voice, "There's no point going on with this now."

"There's still the question of my real parents." Garth's voice rang with command.

"The truth died with Armand," Felice said. "I disowned David after he sided with his father against me, and I desperately wanted Roy's child, but he couldn't make me pregnant. It was wishful thinking, telling you you're our son."

Tears began to seep from under her lashes and she blinked hard. "Roy had big plans for the organization and clients willing to pay well to keep the Americans out. Now it's all been for nothing." She jerked her head to indicate the walkie-talkie clipped to her belt. "You may as well call your people."

Cuffing Felice's hands in one of hers, Serena reached for the walkie-talkie with her free hand. Before she could activate it, Garth said urgently, "Don't touch it. The C4 in the flowers is probably triggered by a signal from that walkie-talkie."

In seconds Felice's pose changed from defeat to sly amusement. "You can't blame me for trying."

Chilled by how close she had come to being the instrument of so much destruction, Serena let her hand drop. "I'll call the command center from a house phone."

Chapter 19

The grandeur of the monarch's private audience chamber made quite a contrast with the five-year-old child galloping around it on a hobby horse, Serena thought as she and Garth were shown into Prince Lorne's presence later that evening.

He stood with an arm around Princess Alison's shoulders, the couple smiling at the antics of their son. They made such a warm, loving picture that Serena's heart squeezed with longing. Would she and Garth look at their child that way one day?

For the audience she had changed into an etched floral tie-neck dress with a short crocheted cardigan, and Garth's look of sensual appreciation brought a flush to her cheeks. He looked disturbingly handsome in a navy golf shirt with white-trimmed collar, and tailored navy pants, although she couldn't help thinking of how magnificent he'd looked storming the banquet hall wearingly only black briefs.

That he was clean-shaven testified to the importance he accorded this meeting. Serena missed the designer stubble but it was hardly appropriate for a monarch, if that's what he turned out to be. The truth wouldn't change her love for him. But what about Garth's feelings for her?

Princess Alison greeted them warmly before speaking gently to Prince Nori. The child dropped the hobby horse and flung his arms around his father's knees, looking up at him winningly. "Will you tell me a bedtime story?"

"Don't I every night I possibly can, *coquine?*" Lorne asked. He ruffled the child's dark hair. "I'll join you as soon as you're in bed."

Bidding them a pleasant good-night, Princess Alison took Nori through a door leading to the family's private apartments. When the door closed, Lorne gestured for them to join him at a group of chairs arranged around a low table. As soon as they were seated, he pulled a leather-bound folder bearing the royal seal toward him. Serena's hand found Garth's. His fingers felt cold in hers but his grip was firm. She held on tight, not sure who was supporting whom.

Lorne got straight to the point. "According to the results of the DNA tests, you are not my older brother, Prince Louis. Sadly, it seems that he truly did die at birth."

She heard Garth's breath rush out, but in unmistakable relief. "Do we have any idea of my real parentage, sir?"

Lorne nodded. "As you know I arranged to have as many members of my immediate family tested as possible. You are the son of my late uncle, Prince Leon de Marigny, and half-brother to his son, Josquin, the Prince Regent of Valmont Province until the heir, Cristophe, comes of age."

"Half brother? Not the son of Leon's widow, Princess Fleur?"

Lorne inclined his head in negation. "I believe that your biological mother will turn out to be Lady Paulette Georges, a former member of Prince Leon's staff, now serving at our embassy in Paris. Of course she would need to be tested as well, for absolute certainty."

Lorne took a breath. "Leon and Fleur had considerable financial difficulties that undermined their relationship for a time. I know because my father helped them out of trouble on more than one occasion. He was aware that Leon was seeing Lady Paulette and counseled him about it, but it wasn't his place to intervene in their private affairs as long as he didn't cause a scandal.'' He gave a wry smile. ''They were exceedingly discreet.''

''So it would seem,'' Garth agreed.

Serena thought he was taking the news of his royal birth amazingly well. ''How did their child come to be raised by the Remys?'' she asked.

''Strange as it seems, Leon loved his wife and son and didn't want them to know about his indiscretion. In any case I suspect Paulette was the driving force behind the relationship. She was ambitious and talented, and a child may have impeded her career. I do know she was a tireless worker for many causes including the Marine Benevolent Society.''

''My mother—adoptive mother—used to go there once a week to visit the old sailors,'' Garth recalled, his voice tightening.

''If Paulette learned that your mother was desperate to have a child, that may have seemed like the answer to everyone's prayers,'' Serena suggested.

Lorne closed the leather folder. ''I can recall Paulette to Carramer, or place my private jet at your disposal so you can meet her in Paris as you prefer.''

Serena was sure she looked as stunned as Prince Lorne when Garth said, ''No, thank you, Your Highness.''

The monarch gave a slight smile. ''We are cousins, Prince Garth de Marigny, so you may as well get used to calling me Lorne. Which option displeases you?''

''Both of them…Lorne. Lady Paulette—if she is my biological mother—obviously didn't want a child, and Leon's widow may know nothing about her husband's affair. There's nothing to be gained by dragging it out into the open now. I've been happy thus far as Garth Remy, and I see no reason to change.''

Her heart swelled for Garth.

''Your readiness to put the good of others before yourself

marks you as a true de Marigny,'' Lorne said. "I am proud to acknowledge you—even if only privately—as a member of my family."

"But not as Prince Garth, please?"

"It is your choice. As I mentioned, Leon's financial affairs were troubled, so there is no inheritance of any consequence. However he held a number of secondary titles, one of which would normally pass to a younger son."

She could feel Garth's resistance in every muscle as he cautioned, "Don't do it, Lorne."

The monarch shook his head. "In this, my will must prevail. I now create you Garth, Earl of Marin. Publicly, the title will be your reward for services to the crown. Privately, it allows me to welcome you into the family on equal terms. You should be proud to bear such an old and honorable title, Lord Marin."

Lorne shifted uncomfortably under the weight of the new role, but said decisively, "In that case, I accept."

Lorne looked bemused. "I'm glad I have your approval. Having you in the family will be refreshing."

"Better than having me on the throne?"

"Infinitely," the monarch said dryly. "I shall explain the situation to Josquin myself. He has frequently expressed a wish for a brother, and we can rely on him to be discreet in sharing the news." Lorne stood up. "Please excuse me. I have a presidential visit to prepare for. Thanks to you both, it should be a memorable occasion—for all the right reasons."

She knew her expression of relief mirrored the monarch's. "We're glad to have been of service, sir."

When she started to rise, Lorne motioned her to remain where she was. "Stay here as long as you like. You have much to discuss. I'm assuming congratulations are in order?"

How did he know? Unless the radiant love she'd seen between Lorne and his wife could be observed between her and Garth. It thrilled her to think so.

"I'm new at this protocol business, Lorne. Are we supposed to ask for your blessing?" Garth queried.

The prince smiled. "I would never stand in the way of true

love. After what you two have done for the country, you deserve every happiness.''

Serena felt her eyes mist. ''Thank you, Your Highness.''

''Lorne…since it appears you will soon be my cousin by marriage. As well as the new chief of the Solano R.P.D. from this moment.''

It was said so casually that the impact took whole seconds to be felt. Garth's arm came around her. ''Congratulations, darling.''

''Well deserved,'' Lorne agreed. He gestured to another folder on the table. ''There's also the matter we discussed earlier. You'll find the written resolution in there, Serena.''

Her heart felt overfull and she could only nod her thanks. The prince looked satisfied as he left them alone.

''This is a lot to get used to,'' she said.

''The promotion or the marriage part, Lady Marin?'' Garth teased.

She knew which meant the most to her. ''What do you think?''

His expression sobered. ''Are you sure I didn't pressure you into saying yes? We were in mortal danger when I proposed.''

Anxiety stabbed through her. ''Do *you* feel pressured?''

''God, no. My only worry was who you would be marrying.''

Her certainty projected into her voice. ''I didn't care. I said yes to a man, not a title.''

''No second thoughts?''

For herself, she had none. Her fears about Garth eroding her carefully built independence seemed foolish when compared with the heaven she had found in his arms. During the crisis, she had seen enough to know that he would never seek to control her life the way her parents had done. She could still be her own person, but with the man she loved at her side. It was enough to give her the courage to say firmly, ''Not a one. Unless you have doubts?''

He pulled her into his arms. ''How can I when I love you more than life itself? When you threw yourself into the sea, trusting me to be there for you, I knew I couldn't live without you." His hand cupped her nape. "Although, if you put yourself at such risk again, I may have to wring your beautiful neck."

"I love it when you're so romantic," she murmured.

He grinned. "Then try this. I want to wake up beside you every morning, make a life with you, father your children."

"Whoa, I didn't think you wanted children."

"I didn't think I wanted a lot of things, until you showed me what I was missing. At least now I have something to offer our sons or daughters."

She tensed. "You always had a lot to offer."

"Perhaps as Lord Marin. Not as the navy's black sheep."

She reached for the second folder, her smile widening as she perused the contents. "This morning Lorne told me he hoped to have some good news about that tonight. When this began, I asked him to reopen the investigation into your discharge. According to these documents, the defective equipment was supplied by the brother-in-law of the admiral who brought the charges against you."

Garth nodded. "By the time I found out the truth, I was already out of the service. The admiral didn't want the truth coming out."

She handed him the folder. "In here is a full apology from the navy, as well as restoration of your rank and record. You can return to active service whenever you want." She didn't let her tone betray how hard it would be to deal with being apart from him when his duty required, but she suspected he knew. They both had adjustments to make, but a love as strong as theirs was a powerful incentive. "So you have no more excuses," she added.

He looked puzzled. "Excuses for what?"

"For not shaping up, my Lord Marin."

His hand grazed the side of her face. "I guess this means we can't live out of the pickup or aboard my boat?"

Nuzzling his palm, she affected a sigh. "It's tough, but I

don't think Carramer is ready to have an earl living aboard a dive boat."

He laughed, the warm sound making her tingle from head to toe. "I can't blame you if you never want to set foot on a boat again."

In this she could surprise him, too. "A lot depends on my diving buddy. When I wasn't being besieged by sharks or dodging bullets, I found the experience more agreeable than I expected to. Breathing the same air is wonderfully intimate."

His breathing quickened and she saw his eyes darken at the memory. "You mean like this?"

As his mouth closed over hers, the room rocked. "Mmm-hmm," she said around the delicious pressure of his lips.

"I knew there was something special about you the first time I kissed you," Garth murmured.

She lifted her head, remembering not only the kiss but the strength of the youthful feelings for him that had led to it. She was filled with wonder to think those first tender yearnings had flowered into the all-consuming love engulfing her now. "When we first kissed, you laughed at me," she reminded him.

"I was terrified of you—so beautiful, so capable, so far beyond my wildest dreams."

"And now?"

"You're still the most beautiful, capable woman in the world, and now you're mine."

She fanned herself theatrically. "I need oxygen."

"Delighted to assist."

Sharing air was definitely an intimate experience, she thought as she gave herself up to the heady pleasure of his kisses.

Garth could hardly believe his good fortune. Discovering he was of royal blood and part of the country's first family was astonishing enough. He would have to take some time to deal with his feelings about that. More amazing still was the woman in his arms. "You actually went to bat for me with the Royal Carramer Navy?" he murmured.

Her eyes shone. "I'd take on the world for the man I love."

He rained kisses over her eyes and nose. "I knew there was something I loved about you."

She kissed him back. "Nothing else?"

"Why don't we go back to my suite and I'll show you."

She pretended affront but her pulse throbbed. "Think of my reputation!"

"I am thinking about it. You've been way too good for too long."

"Why do I think that's about to change?"

"Because it is. As Carramer's first bad-boy royal, I warn you I'm going to be a thoroughly disturbing influence on you."

He'd already started and she had no complaints. "Until we have children, then we have to set a good example."

"True."

A thrill of anticipation coursed through her. "But not just yet."

His mouth crushed hers. "Definitely not tonight."

As he swung her into his arms and she linked her hands around the strong column of his neck, she felt duty bound to agree with him in this, at least.

In matters of the heart, she knew they would always be in complete accord.

* * * * *

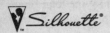

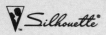

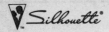

If you enjoyed what you just read,
then we've got an offer you can't resist!

Take 2 bestselling love stories FREE!

Plus get a FREE surprise gift!

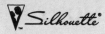

COMING NEXT MONTH

SIMCNM0104